PRICE'S PRICE

'The exploits of an expat, expertly told. Authentic and revealing, an enjoyable romp (or series of romps!) through colonial Hong Kong. Maden tells it like it was . . . with barely a nod to modern sensitivities.'
– Stephen Griffiths, author of *Kowloon English Club* (Blacksmith Books)

'A frank, funny and painfully sharp examination of expat mores and entrepreneurial excesses in late colonial Hong Kong. The narrator's youthful plans for grand expeditions turn inward when he finds himself in Hong Kong, sending him down a rabbit hole of lust and deception from which there may be no escape.'
– Peter Humphreys, author of *Hong Kong Rocks* (Proverse)

'Chris Maden stylishly evokes the clipped argot of the ex-serviceman bewildered by Chinese business practice, thieving partners, and dodgy investment brokers. He wastes no time in irrelevancies and gets us right into the heart of the matter. . . . And every word rings true!'
– Lawrence Gray, Founder of Hong Kong Writers' Circle, screenwriter, director, novelist, and now online game-show host.

PRICE'S PRICE

Chris Maden

PRICE'S PRICE
Published by
Mung Cha Cha Press
www.mungchachapress.com
Hong Kong

© 2021 Chris Maden

Book Design by Alan Sargent
Cover by Spiffing Covers (*www.spiffingcovers.com*)

ISBN 978-988-75659-1-8 (paperback)
ISBN 978-988-75659-4-9 (hardback)
ISBN 978-988-75659-2-5 (ebook)
ISBN 978-988-75659-3-2 (print on demand)

Printed in Hong Kong by Regal Printing

To the People of Hong Kong

Chapter 1

'SOD HIM. SOD HIM IN SPADES, sod him in trumps. And the rest of 'em, too.' From under my eyes, the bugger had taken her, Venus, she of the gossamer hair and laughter like chimes, she of the hazelnut eyes and lustrous skin, she who offered the lifeline, she—

She who was late. But that would be Eric, sod him.

I look down the bar, a foreign intrusion on what to this day remains Mao's 'pimple on the arsehole of China.' The room is long and narrow, there's an oak-and-livery-greenness to the decor and a large mirror behind the bar that reflects halogen spotlights through bottles of spirits. The bass line of a pop song thumps in the background; a whiff of stale beer fights a residue of cigarette smoke. The night is early and the bar all but deserted. Two young men sit in a booth, suited, their ties undone and their hair cut short and gelled up in the current fashion. How things have changed. It was innocent then, when I was their age, and the two Chinese ladies at the bar counter – the only stools occupied – with their whispered words and gentle gestures, curvaceous figures and almond eyes, would not have gone unapproached; no, I would have moved in: the bespoke suit and military bearing, five foot ten, a full head of brown hair; a rakish smile, a nod and a wink and a visage unmarred by a conscience; the poise, the confidence and a gracious acceptance of 'no' before moving swiftly on. It was easy back then for Stanley Featherstonehaugh Price. When did it change?

I'd never intended to come to Hong Kong, yet the Fates catapulted me into the maelstrom – and I was a willing submissive. She was a town on the make, tempestuous, brash and, if she were a person, wanton in bed. Fuelled by the hordes escaping from communist China, she went from backwater to byword, beguiling magnates and gangsters, harlots and heroes, moguls and mobsters; and I – I surfed the tsunami. I'd put my trust in the Fates, the Daughters of Night and they did not disappoint. Ah, the lies that I told, the trusts I betrayed and the ripping good times that I had. Then Venus appeared and, to this day, I don't understand why it worked out as it did. And so I sit here this evening, thirty years on. Think not of closure – such psychobabble is not of my generation – it's more of a mental pinch on the arm: did I do what I did?

But I get far, far ahead of myself. It was the Fates who launched me at Hong Kong but, as is the wont of Greek deities, they presented themselves in disguise, in my case divine: Emma's spectacular cleavage.

The Fates were spinning their thread, however, well before my encounter with Emma's adequate charms.

I was born in a well-endowed land, in what is now Harare in Zimbabwe. Godwin Edgar Price had been despatched from England to manage a plantation or, as he put it, to watch the grass grow. He was a jolly old chap who walked with a cane because of his gout. He'd married well: my mother, who shall remain nameless as she's alive to this day, was the daughter of some minor baron in France who had renounced his title but not his land. My third language, French, after Swahili and English, is but one of her gifts.

Only fragments remain of those childhood days: the red earth and cerulean skies, the echoing rhythm of song from the workers' church, a half-deflated football I kicked around with my playmates. And – one of those childhood memories that I'm not sure is my own or implanted in the retelling – a Sunday-morning panic when nobody could find me to take me to church. It turned out that I'd gone all by myself, but to *their* church, the church of my playmates, where all was joy and good cheer, unlike the grim aspect of 'ours'.

But what set my course was a safari.

A Land Rover spun its tyres in a quagmire, projecting a spout of mud as the engine screeched. There was a rich, sickly-sweet smell overlaying a whiff of ordure; a fan of palm fronds in front of a towering tree with leaves the size of a dinner plate; a raucous chorus of insects and cooing of birds over splashes of water from a fast-flowing, brown river. Whorls and eddies swept by on the surface. A pair of eyes emerged and a grinning, wobbly set of teeth. Curious, I approached. There was a scream and a commotion; a sudden arm around my tummy scooped me away. I was planted on the back seat of the car as my mother told me – tears of anguish and relief streaming down her cheeks – never, ever to leave the car without asking permission. I'd almost become a crocodile's hors d'oeuvre.

Later, on the grasslands, the distant cone of Kilimanjaro dominating the background, she gasped a sudden, 'Stop, Godwin,' and pointed at a pride of lions lounging in the sun not thirty yards from the car, their amber eyes a dare to step closer. And yet later, my delighted giggles at a hippopotamus marking its patch. They use their tail as a propeller blade to scatter their dung in a wide arc as they gallop.

My astonishment at the turquoise waves lapping at a beach of blazing white sand in what must have been

Mombasa: my first sight ever of the sea. A girl on the steamer to a country called 'home'. Her red curls with which I was endlessly fascinated; she once insisted on a game of doctors and nurses, which involved an inspection that turned out to be both painful and enjoyable.

And thus I decided: I was to be an explorer.

My parent's car disappeared out of sight down the driveway of my preparatory school in that alien land, 'home'. The barren hills on either side of the driveway were the walls of a gaol, the leaden sky pressed down as scattered gusts of rain drove into my face, concealing my tears.

I spent my first few weeks gazing out of the window, the meaningless blather of the teachers ignored as I wondered if that episode by the river was the reason for this cruel exile.

'Price, what is it this time?' the headmaster would ask.

'He called my friend Jemima a bad word.'

The headmaster looked at a photo sent to me from Africa. 'What bad word?'

'A d-da-dark—'

He looked at the photo again. A frown formed. 'That's what they are. Now, no more fights or else it'll be ten of the best.'

Even in those distant days of corporal punishment, he was reputed for his ten of the best.

The people at school were as cold as the weather; summers became what I lived for. All children do, but mine were to skies the proper colour and rain that, when it came, was no half-hearted drizzle. I was back with friends with whom I could play without being mocked as the 'White Savage from Darkest Africa', in a country so open-hearted that didn't know locks on doors.

Towards the end of one such holiday, unable to sleep, I

crept downstairs to the dining room. My father was hosting a dinner party: the servants, that evening in uniform, stood like waxworks. The women having retired, cigar smoke surrounded the men like a shroud. My father was holding forth: '. . . Masai are the most beautiful of the native women. I had once one with knockers this—' He came to an abrupt halt as his gaze came to rest on me. A panicked, startled expression flitted across his face; he lowered his hands from an imaginary pair of melons and, in the silence that followed, a voice came: 'He'll know them soon enough, Godwin.' There was a wink: 'I gather he's taken a shine to Jemima.'

My father's eyes dilated in shock. The following day, the house of Jemima's family was empty. It stayed that way to the summer's end and I was shushed when I asked where she'd gone. But I'd taught her doctors and nurses, and there remained a warm glow from our medical investigations.

Three months after that holiday, I was rushed from school to a church. Mutters of 'how unexpected' and 'cerebral malaria' rang in the air. Everyone talked of my father – 'We are gathered today to celebrate the life of Godwin Edgar Price' – as though he was there. Daddy loved celebrations, but he wasn't at this one.

It was to be a long time before I worked out that I would not be seeing my father again.

Subsequent summers passed in a blur of dreary manors in France; prep school became transitory became secondary. The generous smiles of my former playmates on the plantation, the amber evil in the lions' eyes and the whirling blade of the hippo's tail had left their mark. The teachers went unheard: already primed by the strange lands and exotic habits recounted in Herodotus – Classics and geography were the only subjects with any appeal – I lapped up accounts of Burton, Speke, Livingstone and, of course, Stanley. Contemporary achievements only aggravated the itch: Wilfred Thesiger, aka Mubarak bin London, had crossed Arabia's Empty Quarter on camel at the time I'd first been banished to school; Hillary and Tenzing had summited Everest the very same day Her Majesty ascended the throne. There wasn't just a world waiting to be explored; exploration was still possible in my very lifetime.

I missed my father and resented his demise, but it did mean that a juicy inheritance awaited me on my coming of age. Everest may have been taken, but the centre of Africa, although not a blank on the map, was less than *terra cognita*. And, reading every book I could on the subject and pausing over the photographs therein – and this at an age at which doctors and nurses were at the forefront of my mind – it struck me that, while women in that part of the world put their beauty on proud display, those in Blighty hid theirs from view. I wondered what made ours ashamed.

It turned out they kept the best parts hidden from view. Enter Emma.

The summer of my seventeenth birthday, instead of some dusty manor or château, my mother chose to holiday in a resort. It had a tennis court and, one day, amongst the octogenarian gargoyles who were in the majority, there stood a girl my age. It was almost as if she had a personal glow, a halo that set her apart. Her complexion was a line out of Rabbie Burns, her hair an explosion of blonde and her figure – to the Stanley just turned a peak testosterone age – a revelation. I offered her the tramlines to even the match but, apart from being an excellent player in her own right, she wasn't wearing a bra: the bounces I followed were not those of the tennis ball.

Emma's mother and mine, delighted to have us off their hands, settled down to a summer of gin rummy and gin of the alcoholic variety. Left to our own devices, braless tennis aside, Emma and I discovered a beach in an intimate cove and 'Yes, there Stanley' guided my curious hands with the suntan lotion. On rainy days, poker, gin rummy and canasta became the strip versions and 'Stanley, we shouldn't' became 'Yes, Stanley, let's'. My elder by a year, I wasn't her first: the beach, the back seat of the car and, once, in the local cinema. How she didn't become pregnant, I'll never know.

The holiday over, Emma and I promised to write. There was one last interminable year at school: at nights, while my classmates shared puerile pornography and wondered what 'it' would be like, Stanley Featherstonehaugh Price lay awake remembering what it had been like or, now understanding those imaginary melons in my father's hands, planned his exploration of the world, of the most beautiful women and—

With Emma in Swiss finishing school for the year, including holidays, I had to make my own entertainment. Distant continents and unexplored jungles were out of my reach but London was not. One evening, my school chum, Brian, and I noticed a plentitude of tall blondes in short skirts with much leg and cleavage on show, loitering on street corners in Covent Garden and Piccadilly.

One stopped me and asked for a light. She had green eyes and flaming red hair in a pageboy cut; a waft of rose perfume caught me. My eyes wandered south to her low-cut T-shirt. I stuttered something about not smoking; she said 'Dun't matter. Fancy a quickie?'

I nodded, uncertain.

'Sharon,' she introduced herself.

I blurted out my own name.

'All those letters for "Fenshaw" – gosh, you're dead posh

you are,' she said. 'I'll call you Fenny, darling.'

An hour later, in her room, as I lay with an idiotic grin on my face and Sharon clambered back into suspenders and lacy underwear, she said 'That'll be a fiver, then, Fenny, darling.'

I responded with a slack-jawed gawp.

'You didn't know?' she asked, gave me a glance of genuine astonishment and released a series of chuckles.

'She . . . she . . . she asked to be paid,' I stuttered to Brian, the next time I saw him.

'You didn't know?' he asked, gave me a glance of genuine astonishment and released a sneer of disdain.

I returned for the final term at school, endured it and passed out with equal relief on the school's part and mine. Back in London, when not cavorting with Sharon, I buried myself in the British Library reading up on the Central Highlands of Africa, planning my first expedition. Had Godwin Edgar Price still been alive, I needn't have waited, but with my eighteenth birthday around the corner, my inheritance was imminent: I'd need transport to my jumping-off point, all sorts of equipment, plus people to carry it. I made my plans, deaf to the laughter of the Fates.

As to Emma, our correspondence had fizzled out.

Until the 13th of June 1965 arrived and I found out that I would not inherit, and not be exploring anywhere, until I was twenty-five years of age—

'Never mind, Fenny darling.'

—or married.

The previous summer, sixteen going on seventeen, with the energy of our tender years entirely consumed by the physical, Emma and I had been too fagged out to bother with anything beyond post-coital murmurs of affection. The only time we'd come close to actual conversation had been when our mothers insisted we join them for dinner, and the only way to keep our lusty giggles under control had been to consume copious quantities of whatever alcohol was put on the table. And, of course, we'd been of an age when we slept like the just – or the truly damned. As a result, I knew almost nothing about her.

'Mr Price, do come in,' said an aged man in a bow tie at the front door of their terraced house in Belgravia.

I'd gleaned that her family was well-to-do; I hadn't expected this minor palace. The hallway was dominated by a humongous staircase with marble balustrades but, before I could take it in, I was conducted to the drawing room. It was large enough to house an Olympic-sized pool, light streamed in through windows twice the height of a man, Turners and Constables hung from the walls. The antique on which I was seated was probably worth enough to fund my first expedition.

I was about to congratulate myself on my choice of bride, when 'Stanley' was hissed into my ear.

After an involuntary jump, I turned to see a blue rinse that was immobile, yellow-tinted spectacles perched on the tip of a nose and, at half-past ten in the morning, she was sipping what seemed to be her fourth sherry.

I'd quite forgotten about Emma's mother: 'Emma will be down shortly,' she said. 'I don't think you've met Howard?'

My eyes came to rest on a shadow of a man, short, skinny, a few strands of hair swept over a gleaming scalp, the package encased in a suit that had already given up on life and hung in loose folds from his frame. Emma's father hadn't joined us in France; I'd assumed that all teenagers were orphans.

The whiff of something long dead assaulted my olfactory senses as he extended his hand. Shaking his hand was like gripping a dead fish: 'Awfully pleas—'

'My,' said mother, cutting him off and turning to me:

'quite the dashing young man about town. One sees so few young men these days who take trouble over their appearance, don't you think, father?'

'Well, quite, just as—'

'And where did you get that tie, Stanley? And the cut of the jacket. Lovely material, don't-you-think-father?'

'Well quite, yes, marvell—'

Her head swivelled towards me. 'I suppose you've decided whether it's to be Oxford or Cambridge?'

The question came as a rude affront: what need had an explorer of yet more of the sorry twaddle that is education? The only future I'd ever envisaged was an unending reliving of that childhood safari, albeit augmented by ever more beautiful women.

Anyone who lived in this palace could find the money to sponsor an expedition or two.

Emma arrived, radiant. I drank in her sapphire eyes, her ruby lips and her creamy English complexion ... that magnificent wobble beneath her blouse ... my inheritance ... the way her pinkie stayed in the air when lifting her cup to her mouth. ...

'*Ou peut-être La Sorbonne?*' I attempted.

... her mother's agate eyes, malachite lips, grey complexion ... the sagging dowager's bosom ... the inheritance ... the way she kept her pinkie aloft. ...

'Whisky,' I nodded to the aged retainer.

'And such a lovely French accent, don't-you-think-father?'

Well quite—

It's lovely, isn't it? The way that even the stupidest people – Emma, for example – can wreck everything with just three words:

'You've changed.'

We were alone. Her parents had wandered off in pursuit

of some other distraction. I had been vetted, it had been so nice for Howard to meet me at last, hope to see me on the links soon. I was home and dry, inheritance soon to be bagged and I would be off and away—

There was a glare in her eye. 'You were never like that with my parents before. Never so—' Emma grappled the English language into submission '—obsequious.'

'I – um, we, scarcely saw them last summer.'

'You have changed.'

'So have you—' The glare. 'We all have—' Like a scimitar wielded. The awful truth dawned. 'I didn't think—' the words caught in my throat. Sharon sold only her body; my very soul hung in the balance '—of them as in-laws back then.'

'Oh, Stanley.'

I took her to a club for lunch. A bottle of claret later, things were back on track. She laughed, our knees bumped under the table and, as the claret went down, stayed touching for longer. By the time dessert arrived – trifle – the funniest things stick in one's mind – our fingers were entwined, one foot was out of her shoe and caressing the inside of my thigh.

'It's so good to see you again, Stan,' she purred.

I was so distracted that I didn't even object to the diminutive form of my name, which I abhor. 'Perhaps,' I gasped, 'we could find somewhere a little more intimate?'

A world explorer could hardly be seen checking into a hotel at three in the afternoon, and a repeat of the feral experiences we'd enjoyed in an exclusive French resort were out of the question in central London, so we caught the matinée performance of a musical that was all the rage. I took a box: the box came alive . . . with the sounds of bonking . . . that kept going on . . . as the cast muddled through.

As we lurched out of theatre I heard: 'Fenny, darling?'

It couldn't be.

'New 'bout here?' Sharon enquired of Emma.

'Emma,' I improvised: 'This is Brian's sister.'

News to Brian, indeed.

The Greeks deem no man fortunate until he be dead. With the voracity and frequency of Emma's and my love-making, not to mention Sharon's and her peers' boisterous professionalism, my survival that summer was a close-run thing. Nevertheless, had I expired, I would have been in the running. I had love (well, sex), money, a roof over my head; the promise of a lucrative marriage and the happy illusion that all would work out.

I hadn't counted on Howard.

'Shall we?' he asked one morning.

'Um, yes,' I replied, mystified. But it turned out that he was making good on his promise to golf with me. A little father-in-law–son-in-law time together.

'So,' I summarised, as we approached the eighteenth green, Howard having left the previous seventeen scarred with divots like pot bunkers, 'Central Africa is unexplored territory. I plan to start at the southern end of Lake Tanganyika and work downstream and northwards to Lake Edward, with an ascent of Mount Stanley to finish things off.'

I missed a perfectly easy putt and tch-tched. The difficult part of losing to players who are worse than oneself is to make it look honest.

'Africa?'

'I've been in touch with an agency in Kampala, and they reckon transport, equipment and sundries could be funded for a few thousand pounds.'

He missed a perfectly easy putt. All arms and no swing: he wasn't pretending. We holed out, shook hands and he regarded me for a moment.

'Hrmph,' he hrmphed.

We threw the bags in the back of his Silver Shadow – spanking new – and he drove into the City. We rolled to a halt outside an imposing facade with Ionic columns and a massive brass door.

'You're not the studying type,' he opined. It would be a decade before I met another man who opined.

His opinion, though, was on the money. The British public school system of which I was a product, knocks out three kinds of finished goods: first, the majority, administrators of Empire and captains of industry. Second, eccentrics. Third, soldiers. My attention span was too short and my marks too poor to administer Empire, let alone captain industry; the eccentrics were those who survived the system unscathed, which I had not, and that left the army.

'Can't have the husband of my daughter running around being shot at by fuzzy-wuzzies,' he opined, oblivious to my instinctive clench of the fists – what were 'fuzzy-wuzzies' to him had been best friends to me.

He parked the car in a reserved parking slot, which struck me as cheeky, and marched me into a cavernous hall, with a marble floor and tellers.

'Good morning, Mr Humphreys,' said one of the tellers as he strolled past her.

Still fuming, I trailed in his wake. The banking hall – it dawned on me that this was a bank – was the size of a cathedral. Row after row of tellers sat in drab uniformity, peeping out from over stacks of ledgers and paper, which they passed from one desk to another. This was the sixties and the girls outside were burning their bras but here, even though many were young, each found a different way to look old: a blue-rinse here, a brooch of semi-precious stone there, a frock patterned with vines over there. I recoiled in terror.

'Good morning, Mr Humphreys,' said the lift-boy, sliding the grate shut behind us.

A vague sense of curiosity surfaced. Howard hadn't stopped off to cash a cheque or to attend to some other minor transaction. It seemed that more was afoot. I'd been nagging him for some time on the expedition: had it paid off?

The lift stopped, the lift-boy opened the grate. A man stood waiting, a stack of files clasped to his chest, his face as grey as the stone of the walls, his eyes lifeless and dull. The smell of dusty paper permeated the air. Behind him a hall full of typists sat in uniform rows, the clattering din echoing through the Victorian hall. The man's eyes widened: 'Sorry, Mr Humphreys,' he said, and shook his head at the lift boy. The door was shut, the lift jerked once more into ascent.

Howard, I thought, with his Belgravian mansion and Rolls-Royce, must be a privileged customer. All the better for me.

The dial stopped when it indicated the top floor. More like it, I thought to myself. Howard was rich, after all. Of course he wouldn't dally with *hoi polloi* below, but rather would deal direct with some senior functionary. He was going to set me up with an account, an allowance, the better to fill those gaps on the map. Oh yes, and care for his daughter.

'Good morning, Mr Humphreys,' chorused a row of secretaries as we walked down a wide corridor. We came to a set of imposing oak doors. A senior secretary bustled her way forwards and threw them open with a flourish, while a phalanx followed in tow.

The room occupied half the floor, had a drinks cabinet

set into a wall and a couple of leather sofas. There was a massive desk at the end, set in front of a circular window that looked out over the Strand. There was no one at the chair behind the desk, which I found odd.

'He wants me to work at his bank,' I told Brian over brandy and cigars (his – I could never abide tobacco). 'As in the bank that he owns. Said he could "fit me in".'

Just for a split-second, a flicker of avarice crossed Brian's face. Surely not? Brian, after all, came from a family that owned half a county; he drove an Aston Martin DB2. 'Ooo' he said. He drawled his speech, which had a Lancashire twang. 'Is the castration before or after you start?'

The ash fell off his cigar, trickled down his red-chequered jacket and came to rest by a large gravy stain which he regarded with a momentary benevolence.

'Your choice, Stanley. Banking, marriage, the inevitable sprogs. Next thing you know, you'll be fat, fifty and fossilised. Is she worth it? She'll turn out like her mother.'

'Don't be absurd.'

'Temper. They all do.'

'I'm not angry,' I spat, unclenching my fists and taking a few deep breaths. 'You couldn't know. You've never met her. Or her mother.'

'As best man, don't you think we should fix that?'

I didn't. But he did have a point.

'Do tell me about him,' Emma said with a pout while we waited for Brian. He is one Nature's belateds. Emma's fingers were entwined with mine: I had a sudden almost irresistible urge to skip lunch and catch *The Sound of Music*. By then – from the floor of our box when taking a breather – we'd glanced several fragments, and I was curious as to the plot.

'Fenny darling.'

My neck went rigid. I must be hearing things, this was far from her patch.

In slow-motion, I wheeled. Her red hair caught in the sun, her green eyes, the cleavage under her frock. I blinked.

'Stanley, I didn't realise you'd met Sharon,' came Brian's voice.

'Brian,' I stammered. 'Of course I've met your . . . your *sister*.'

Brian's thick, ruby lips turned up at the corners in a grin of pure malice. A breeze caught his long, flyaway hair. Behind him, the Georgian terrace outside the club was caught in a beam of sunlight, the white walls sharp against cotton-wool clouds suspended in a pale blue sky. He looked at me. 'Sister?' He nodded at Sharon. She giggled and pecked him on the cheek. 'Where on earth did you get that impression?'

Emma's face was caught in the moment, her mouth widening into an 'O', her eyebrows moulding themselves into squiggles of consternation. Her ears reddened.

Did I hear Sharon say, 'Sister? You don't fuck your sister and wouldn't pay if you did.'

Words drifted by from another group going past on the steps to the club – 'Mexico in the World Cup next year, we'll be fine' – and the sound of raucous laughter snapped me out of it.

'The expression on your face,' Emma managed through her guffaws.

It was three in the morning. I sat, my bow tie hanging loose, as the party roared on around me. Dinner had started at seven. 'Price?' the host had asked. His brow had wrinkled, he'd shaken his head as if water were stuck in his ear and he'd said: 'Of. . . ?'

I wheeled out, as I did at every one of these tiresome affairs, my mother's family name and that of her father's château (an over-grand term for what was in fact a minor and crumbling manor).

'They renounced their title, didn't they?'

Put in my place, I'd suffered through yet another dinner of name- and title-dropping, made polite conversation about people of whom I knew little and cared less, and subjects – politics, current affairs, pop music – of which I was willfully ignorant. I'd suggested to Emma three hours previously that we leave so that I could be at Lords with the sparrows.

'Don't be such a bore.'

'Cricket's such a beautiful game,' I'd protested. 'The strategy, aggression and skill—'

'Is that Mick Jagger?' her voice tailed off as someone, probably famous, went past. I'd knuckled down. I needed her to talk sense into her parents about my future career; we'd waltzed, guzzled champagne and – this was the sixties – been offered a cornucopia of drugs.

'Why don't you bunk off?' Brian came to my rescue. 'I'll see Emma home.'

She gave me a glower, but the next day was the third and decisive test against South Africa and the Pollock brothers were on fire. It wasn't quite hacking through the jungles of Africa, but it was more interesting than this.

'Thank you,' I said.

'I really wish you'd make more effort,' said Emma. 'They are my friends after all.'

'What should I do?' I sought Sharon's wise counsel.

'It'll work out, Fenny darlin.'

Greek deities sometimes embody themselves in a person. I wouldn't have pegged Sharon as one such.

'Miss Emma is at the country estate,' said Howard's aged retainer.

'I was to take her to a show,' I blustered, brandishing the flowers I'd bought. The cricket had been magnificent, but Emma hadn't returned my calls so I'd taken the hint and had come to patch things up. Grovel, if you will. 'You wouldn't have its address?'

It took some wheedling, but he took pity on me.

Brian's DB2 was at my disposal in his pad in the Mews. It so happened it wasn't there – glorious weather, why would it be? – so I packed a bag and took the train. At the station in Surrey I was all set to walk, but popped in for a fortifying pint and a pie only to be told that the driveway to their estate was an expedition unto itself.

I hired a driver who told me that, when Howard's ancestors had started the meat trade with South America, they'd made so much money that they only thing they could think to do with it was to start their own bank. With a background rooted in distant parts of the world, I thought, Howard could surely be talked out of death-by-banking and into funding his future son-in-law's expeditions. His daughter's happiness was at stake, after all. Emma wouldn't be happily married if it was to a man who moped away his days doing a job for which he was manifestly unsuited.

We came to a gatehouse. Behind it, between a row of oaks, stretched a driveway. Those were the days before CCTV and razor-wire everywhere; there was nothing to stop us.

As we started that final leg, a smile grew on my face. I would follow in my father's footsteps and marry well. Once I'd put the ring on Emma's finger, Howard would have no choice but to come around to my way of thinking.

We rounded the final corner. A stately home swung into view, two dozen windows wide and three floors high. At the bottom of the front staircase stood Howard's Rolls-

Royce and, as we rounded the turning circle, another car swung into view.

A DB2.

Many years later, when Emma – by then quite like her mother – divorced Brian – a fat, fifty and fossilised banker – he looked me up and confessed, 'It was her tits; I fell for her on the spot. And after that prank I pulled with Sharon, I wanted to make a clean break. I wanted my relationship with Emma to be honest. I thought if you found out, you'd bring it up, all the carousing we did that summer. And I knew you didn't care for her, not the way I did.'

Brian had assumed that I would be raging with jealousy, so cut himself out of my life. To the contrary, at first a sense of relief, then of freedom, and finally of intense gratitude formed. Towards Brian. Towards Emma – well, her cleavage – for seducing him. Towards the Pollock brothers and cricket. And towards the Fates. Had Sharon been thirty seconds sooner or later, her encounter with Emma would never have happened and I'd have been condemned to the fate that Brian embraced.

Thus, I formed my creed. What the Fates have in store is beyond the ken of any mortal, but the point is to face their whims with a sense of adventure and fun. Not fatalism, which is an abnegation of life, but rather a vicarious acceptance of all that they threw in my path.

Nevertheless, I still hadn't the means to mount an expedition. The army in those days could still be persuaded to fund one and, if that fell through, the inheritance would be there at the end of a seven-year contract. I spent a year at Sandhurst, where I learnt a great deal more about the etiquette of formal dinners than anything as inconsequential as military strategy, and a second year becoming uncon-scionably fit in the mountains of Nepal with the Brigade of Gurkhas, to which I was assigned.

'Where,' they asked me at the end of it all, 'do you want to be stationed?'

I'd have to put in a tour of duty before the army would equip an expedition, but there were plenty of places where I could make my mark. I scanned the list of postings: Kenya, Kilimanjaro and the vast plains of the Serengeti – not to mention the handsome women of the Masai; a communist insurgency in the jungles of Malaya – surrounded by the dusky beauty of the Malays; a revolution in the no-longer-quite-so-Dutch East Indies in the company of – whichever women were there. I wasn't quite sure. But I was sure of one thing.

'Anywhere but Hong Kong,' I replied.

That barren rock.

Chapter 2

I STOOD IN A DINNER JACKET and bow tie. Tree branches arched over the swimming pool of the officers' mess; beyond them, rounded brown hills shimmered in the heat mirages of the day's lingering shadows. A shrill drone of mosquitoes accompanied the dull murmur of polite conversation; there was a smell like old socks of some rotting tropical fruit.

I suppressed a sigh. I'd arrived three months previously after a dizzying blur of military transports that saw me arrive on the Forces' own airstrip in the middle of the night to be bundled into a lorry to the officers' quarters. After three hours' sleep, at reveille the next morning, I'd been given a perfunctory introduction to my troops, who marched me off to a range of grassy but unremarkable hills that overlooked China. So much for the Serengeti and those most handsome of women, or bashing through the tiger-infested jungles of Malaya: to my south from the hills, peasants toiled away as they had for millennia in the rice paddies of Hong Kong; to the north, peasants toiled away in the rice paddies of the People's Republic of China. My job – assisted by a fence – was to keep those two groups of peasants apart.

'We saw some weal action in Malaya,' said Wogeh, the co.

There was no shortage of weal action in Hong Kong: the Cultural Revolution had spilt over into the colony, causing riots and chaos. But the army's part in combatting those disturbances was supportive rather than primary: two months before my arrival a rabble of Red Guards had shown up and killed a few police officers only to do an abrupt about-face when our Gurkhas showed up. That aside, the police did the work – and were later rewarded with a royal charter for their bravery.

'One chap, wather amusing—'

Four years and nine months to go. In the heat and humidity of Hong Kong's summer, the gin and tonics were tepid on arrival, redolent with the sweat that dripped off the orderlies' hands when they poured them. The cucumber sandwiches were a soggy mess of white pulp and green limpness. Everything sagged. The trees sagged. We sagged. The women, mostly wives or fiancées of officers – the women sagged worst.

They stood in clusters, gossiping – 'new posting here' and 'passed over for promotion, again, what a pity' said with a malicious grin – glasses held with little fingers aloft in the air. Not so different from the parties Emma had so liked, but with the glamour, sex and drugs stripped out. I took a deep breath and suppressed a sigh. At some future point, the inheritance would be mine and I could buy myself out. But five more years? Of trudging through snake-infested, sodden grass, apprehending dumpy peasant girls?

There was a sudden commotion. A man on the opposite side of the pool downed a glass of champagne, threw it over his shoulder and, as a flock of white hands like fluttering doves leapt into the air to catch it, there was a flash of black and white like a penguin in flight, and a splash as he dived into the pool.

Fully dressed, he emerged.

'Forsythe?' said Wogeh. 'I didn't wealise you were back fwom leave.'

Forsythe, dripping wet, walked past Wogeh as if he were a lamp post, though not without lifting the glass from his hand. He patted his pockets, extracted from one a pair of spectacles twice as wide as his face, extended a still-dripping hand and said, 'Boring here, isn't it?' and emitted a series of asthmatic hoots which I realised were laughter. 'Let's go and explore.'

I'd already tried. Disappointed but undaunted by the unexotic surroundings and unchallenging nature of the posting, on my first weekend of leave, having been told that Hong Kong was quite the thing, I'd set off. The only town within reach of the base was Fanling. It had taken an hour to walk there and turned out to consist of a cluster of hovels which took me half an hour to traverse from one end to the other. Its residents directed hostile stares at me or scurried out of my path; my attempt to buy a beer met with a blank stare, a refusal to even make the effort to understand a simple request: they didn't speak English, I didn't speak Cantonese, and that was the end of it. And, as to the most handsome of women. . . .

The explorer within me was quashed. I'd hoard my leave for something worthwhile.

'You didn't know where to go,' said Forsythe.

He marched me out of the mess and, the next thing I knew, we were at one of a dingy line of sheds I'd passed on the way to Fanling.

'Mee-see-da Foh-see,' he was greeted by a grinning old crone with a toothless but broad smile.

'My name in Cantonese,' he said. 'It's the nearest they can get to it. "Foh" means fire and "see" means shit. Wonderful, isn't it?' He released another series of asthmatic hoots.

We entered. Barely the size of a garden shed, it contained a bar counter with half-a-dozen rickety high chairs. The rest was in shadows. We got chatting: 'Same as me,' he said. 'Hopeless at school. Only good at the subjects that nobody wants any more. History mostly.'

More beer came, we went to another bar and one more. My first noodles required my first attempt at chopsticks: a hand on mine, confident, sensuous and strong, taught me how to manipulate them. The memories start to get hazy: a squalid room of benches, more beer; a shadier room of dark figures and a girl first at my side then holding my hand. She smiled and said something in pidgin English as her hand came to rest on my thigh; more beer and a twinge of curiosity mingled with terror – I mustn't sleep with the enemy? – rushed through my mind as she led me to a small room containing a bed. Her smile. The pleasure.

Outside, afterwards: 'We all do it,' said Fireshit.

The flame was rekindled. With Forsythe, fearless in his boundless curiosity, I went on random explorations that ended at fishing villages where life was unmarked by the passage of centuries, the houses on stilts and boats powered with the gentle splashing of oars rather than the staccato putt-putt of outboard engines; to Buddhist and other temples rancid with the smell of joss sticks, noisy with the clangs of bells and rumbles of gongs, guarded by figurines of grotesque gods; to paddies where peasants in black pyjamas and wide-brimmed, conical bamboo hats stood knee-deep between lime-green stalks of sprouting rice, farming by hand. Or we would stop at random in quiet pathways lined by ancient houses, and sit and watch the world go by as the waves lapped at the piers, the stench of drying fish permeating the air and, as summer gave way to a brief autumn and then the cool, crisp winter, we would drink on credit a succession of idle beers.

As to the hostile stares and scurrying away, 'Just smile,' said Forsythe. The response was not universal, but more smiles than scowls were returned.

At one village market – Tai Po would be my guess – Forsythe spotted a wizened old man holding a brush and some paper. Where I held back because of the lingo, Forsythe was free of such inhibitions: 'Painter?' he asked.

'Letter-writer,' the ancient replied in accentless English. He took the brush, dipped it in ink, and magicked up a trail of delicate, neat Chinese characters. It turned out that he was a schoolteacher who wrote letters in his spare time for a little extra cash: many of the newcomers from China were illiterate. 'It's not really the money,' he said. 'News from afar lifts the heart.'

It was a slap in the face. Whilst Africans and Indians had their places in the pantheon of imperial stereotypes that were my upbringing, the Chinese were a race apart; mysterious, inscrutable and in some undefinable way, almost not human. Yet, here was this not-quite-human saying the most humane of things.

Forsythe commissioned a love letter and, never one to pause before turning plans into action, put it to the test that very night with the whores near the base. To much merriment, he was led away to a discreet curtained area.

'Thirty?' I asked, slack-jawed, when I'd acquitted myself. 'You're thirty years old?'

My young belle's eyes stared up at me from the body of a woman a decade younger. When one has just turned twenty, a thirty-year-old is a granny.

I fled.

'Chinese women,' said Forsythe, a quick finisher and

already waiting outside. 'Don't know how they stay so young-looking. But most around here are of that vintage.'

'Thirty?'

'You're repeating yourself.'

I glugged a bottle of beer to wash the horror away.

'Try Wanchai,' said Forsythe. 'Expensive though.'

Damn the expense.

Hong Kong was annexed in 1842, Kowloon in 1861 and the New Territories, where I was billeted, were tacked on 1898. The NT formed three quarters of Hong Kong's land mass and were separated from the older parts by a range of hills. Forsythe drove through the Lion Rock Tunnel and came out on the Kowloon side of that range.

'Stop the car,' I said. 'Now.'

There she was, splayed before me in all her succulent glory. Beneath us lay the Kowloon peninsula, green in those days. Nearest to us and beneath us lay fields and large houses. Carpeting the hills to my left were the squatter villages where the many who slipped through our net came to settle and work. In the distance, the peninsula narrowed to a point and, on it, a couple of skyscrapers protruded. Beyond them, over a glittering blue harbour, lay the island of Hong Kong, a dramatic row of steep hills with a few houses scattered on the upper slopes while, on its shoreline, buildings jostled for space.

We took a *sampan* or *walla-walla* – a local, keel-less boat – to Wanchai. Victoria Harbour, though a tourist attraction, was also a busy working harbour: we dodged between traditional Chinese junks with their crimson tarpaulin sails, wove through a brace of Star Ferries in their green and white livery, snuck around the backs of destroyers and troop carriers here on R&R from the war in Vietnam. The toothless coxswain, his face of leather, gave me a grin and a knowing wink as we stepped ashore.

I struggled to walk. Here, on Hong Kong Island, unlike the NT near the base, the girls were dressed in the latest of fashions: miniskirts, high heels and tight-fitting tops, their hairdos in bobs and pageboy cuts. They approached in clusters, giggling and elegant, svelte and adorable.

'Steady on, chum,' said Forsythe.

At that age, a certain body part has a life of its own.

We turned into streets festooned with neon signs proclaiming bars, nightclubs and dance halls. The doors were attended by faded professionals whose job it was to lure in those who wished to be lured – which we did. Within, the specifics of decor, lighting and stench varied, but the two constants were dim corners and girls.

At one I met Lily.

No. 'Meet' is not the right word. She entered my life with the force of a thunderclap. I can still feel the twist of my guts on first sight: tall, willowy, refined. Her face as if crafted from porcelain, her delicate nose, her eyes just ever so slightly askew. On a soldier's pay and a derisory allowance from mother, it wasn't going to be easy.

I saved for three weeks and returned. 'I knew you'd be back,' she said with a smile.

Contact with the local Chinese was discouraged yet most of the bachelor officers, and more than a few of those already married, had their own Lily. For most it was physical relief and companionship, though a some took it the whole way and – fatal to their prospects of a promotion – the army turned a blind eye to a night here and there, but that was the limit – a very few married and started families. But Lily, my Lily. . . .

No fool, she spoke much better English than most. Not the awful 'Heya nice drinkee for you' of the thriving industry near the barracks, nor the similar but distinct pidgin of Wanchai, but fluent English with an understanding of the nuances of the language. Yes, her dialect was of her own devising, unidiomatic, with a flowing sing-song beat – 'Stanley, nice seeing you so a-handsome for me' – but there were also times when it went beyond banter: 'Haven't those communists done enough damage already?'

Curiosity kills and I was the cat.

'Come on,' I said one bleary-eyed morning, waking up next to her in some flea-pit in Wanchai. 'It's Sunday, it's a lovely day outside. Please let me buy you lunch.'

'Stanley,' she said, 'you don't understand, can never understand, how difficult that would be.'

'Nonsense. It's perfectly simple. All I'm asking is that we spend the day together. How long has it been now? I only ever see you at nights.'

There was a pout on her face. 'You implore me?'

'I beseech you,' I implored.

'If you want a date, ask like a gentleman.'

I took my hand off her breast and left her cold for a month. I turned up at her bar, roses and chocolates in hand – along with Forsythe's scroll of love poetry – and swatted away the lowlife who sat pawing her. To much tittering from her colleagues, I addressed her: 'My darling Lily, I request the pleasure of your company,' and named a time and a place.

I'd booked for thirteen hundred hours. I waited for half an hour. I waited another fifteen minutes. By fourteen-thirty, as I was half way down my fourth gin and tonic, I felt a tap on my shoulder. I turned round, ready to rage – and almost fell off my chair.

Her delicate figure was wrapped in a dress that hugged to the curves of her body like mist to a hillside; the sheen of her dress caught the light like dew in the dawn; the smile in her eyes was the rising sun.

'Stanley, you can't be angry? You must never be angry with me.'

Despite all that followed, it's a promise I've kept to this day.

We wined, we dined. Strolling around the higgledy-pig-gledy streets of the old part of town, we stumbled across an antiques shop.

'Oooo,' she cooed with delight, spotting a pot that to me appeared quite undistinguished: dull green and shaped like a funeral urn. It was from such-and-such a dynasty and the seal on the bottom showed it was no fake – and a steal at half a month's pay.

I was about to protest, but she turned those doe eyes upon me and, the next thing I knew, Central Africa became yet more remote.

But her smile, the delight in her eyes that someone cared, more than made up for that.

Boredom became disillusionment. Day in, day out, the same barren hills, the same strip of grass next to the fence. The trudge, the rain, the humidity and the heat. Spring was hot, wet and sticky, summer was sticky, hot and wet. When it wasn't scorching sun, it was torrential rain, when I wasn't gritty-eyed from a hangover, my balls were aching from Lily.

The contrast weighed ever more stark as Forsythe and I immersed ourselves in the colony. At first feeling as though I was an intruder, I stood at the entrance to teeming street markets but Forsythe pushed past me and plunged into their pulsating life. There were hairy red fruits and bitter green gourds; the air was thick with their pungent, flowery odours, an assault on the senses. The housewives and amahs haggled at the tops of their voices, cheery and raucous, in that strange mixture of yelling and melody that is the Cantonese language. There was laughter, a devil-may-care attitude that was so rife it was almost palpable. Hope and optimism abounded.

What trouble there was, came from the north. The Cultural Revolution was raging in China. Those we arrested had fled its madness and Mao's tyranny, leaving their homes and families with a pocket full of small change and a heart full of hope. Many walked for weeks, even months, enduring hunger and risking savage reprisals. Those who slipped through our net were as hostile to communism as we were and, once they'd found a job in Hong Kong – which was easy – they worked too hard to foment any trouble. The trouble-makers were provocateurs, already within.

The arbitrariness of the system began to prey on me. The policy then, though only dignified with a name many years later, was the touch-base policy. Those apprehended in the NT, which were leased from and bordered on China, were sent back, while those who made it as far as Kowloon or Hong Kong Island, which were annexed and thus Crown territory, were permitted to remain. At first sight a marvel of petty bureaucratic logic, it was in practice no more than a reflection of the reality that, while the NT consisted of sparsely populated farms, villages and barren hills, where strangers stood out, the streets of Kowloon and Hong Kong were mobbed night and day, and telling a newcomer apart was a lost cause.

The whole endeavour was futile. For every refugee who lost the lottery of that bloody fence, a dozen swam, tunnelled or were smuggled in. Those squatter towns were not mere clusters of shacks, but sprawling cities within themselves.

'Why not turn a blind eye?' Lily asked.

'Duty,' I replied, but to what? To Queen, to country? The British public school system provides not only the fodder of Empire – me – but also indoctrination: I'd been raised to believe that the Empire was the enlightened bearer of hope, peace and justice to the under-trodden.

A woman sticks in my mind. As she stood in front of me, her eyes, at first blazing with hope that she'd made it, wrinkled in a question. The corners of her eyes dropped, her shoulders slouched. She rubbed her tummy; it was only then that I noticed its taut spherical shape. As I stood in paralysis, a wail started in the pit of her stomach, grew louder and burst. Fear grew in those screams, not of us, but of what awaited her and her unborn child on her return. The cries faded and turned to whimpers; the light in her eyes was extinguished.

It wasn't just her, it was the steady accumulation of hundreds like her. Part of me wanted to turn a blind eye. But I couldn't, not with the troops to bear witness. Corporal Gupta and the men, self-assured and better equipped than I to deal with the routine, rounded them up. Gupta himself was third generation and knew that a soldier's job is to obey without question. Friendly yet never familiar, I may have to send my men off to die, but, as we sat in the grass, sharing tiffin, they'd chat about their families, their hopes for their children, their plans for retirement – open a restaurant, put their sons through education. They seemed unable or unwilling to believe that those we caught may share those same aspirations. Gupta planned to send his eldest to England, yet that was not for the fleeing Chinese. They were the enemy. My troops had been told so, and right it must be.

I envied them the simplicity of their outlook. But, as CO, I had no discretion. I had no authority to turn a blind eye.

Lily said: 'You are drinking like a man who forgets.'

'Correct,' I said, propped up in bed over a morning beer chased down with a whisky.

'Do something.'

'What is there to be done? Army officers have contracts. I can't afford to buy myself out. Not until the inheritance arrives.'

'Then do,' she raised her eyebrows and gazed at me, 'nothing.'

I had no idea what she was talking about. I rolled onto my side and drank her in. She was naked, beautiful. My eyes swept down her voluptuous curves.

'If the tiger knew where the hunter was,' she sing-songed, 'he could take a different path.'

'Clairvoyant tigers,' I mumbled. My hand, of its own volition, reached out for a fondle.

'Maybe a little flower would tell the tiger,' she said. Her hand reached out to guide mine.

What was she suggesting? Tiger? Flower? Lily telling the tiger the hunter's secrets? No—

'You promised you'd never be angry.'

I took a deep breath: 'I can't do it, Lily.'

She pouted: 'Not even for Lily?'

Drinking does not necessarily widen one's social circle, but being an all-round cricketer who happens to drink a lot, does. I was invited to join a club. It had tennis and squash courts, a cricket pitch and, most important of all, a bar. Not just any old bar, and not at all resembling the squalid affairs near the barracks, but a proper room of wood panelling on which were hung photos of sports teams long-gone and current. It had a foot-rail along the bar counter and a counter-top of peened copper.

'Boring,' said Forsythe.

I met traders, civil servants, architects and engineers, expats to a man. I met a banker who arranged an overdraft for me, which I – or rather Lily – used up in a flash. I met Percy the stockbroker who promised the wealth of Croesus if I followed his tips – until he discerned my illucrative situation, from which point on he ignored me. I met a doctor. Thirty years my senior, he had a full head of wavy silver hair. His eyes were blue and piercing – and blood-shot. Every morning on the dot of half-past seven, he'd slip into the bar, order himself a stiff double, and lurch off to his practice. Why? I asked him one night.

'Because, Stanley, when you reach my age you come to realise that everything you thought bad about life when young, is. Conversely, much that you thought to be good, isn't.

'Take the bloody Empire. Look at the horror we un-leashed in Indian and Pakistan during Partition. I was there. Pax bloody Britannia indeed. We set the Hindus and Muslims at each other's throats to control them – yes, of course another whisky – and millions died as a result.

'And China. Bloody hell. Got the whole country hooked on opium, gutted the economy and annexed all the bits worth having. No wonder they hate us. We're a bunch of pirates in cassocks.' He looked over my shoulder: 'Ah, talking of which.'

'Rights for the chinks again is it, Doc?'

'Meet Stanley. Despite his profession, a fine young man. Ron,' Doc turned to me, 'is a pedlar of opium.'

Ron, pedlar of opium, was six feet and two inches tall, groomed like a racehorse, had slicked-back hair and a jutting chin. He was slim, wore a blazer, a crisp white shirt and a Paisley tie.

I wished I could be that well groomed and dressed. But on a soldier's pay. . . .

'No longer opium.' He eyed Doc's safari suit. 'We move with the times. Refined heroin these days.' He said it with such gravitas that it took me a moment to work out he was joking. He turned to me: 'You're with the Gurkhas, I'm told?'

Regimental pride welled up within.

'Good job you're doing on the border. Always the same with the chinks. Let one in and a hundred will follow. Doc here is inclined to treat them as humans.'

My chest fell. Doc wasn't alone.

'I can't anymore,' said Lily.

What had I done? What had I failed to do? Hungover, in the first light of dawn, I had fallen prey to an ambush. My hand groped beneath the bed in the hope of finding a bottle.

'Don't be angry,' she said. 'Mama-san says when I'm with you I don't earn enough.' She turned her eyes on me: big doe eyes. 'Oh Stanley, why can't you be rich?'

'Another few years. What's that old witch got to do with it?'

'How can you be so stupid?'

'I am an army officer.'

My darling Lily, it emerged, had learnt her near-perfect English in a very posh school, paid for by her loving father who, tiring of Lily's natural mother, had taken a second wife (legal in those days and commonplace amongst the Chinese). Wife number two was young, beautiful and sweet – to Lily's father. Behind his back to Lily, she was a bitch. After a year or two, wife number two had her way and threw Lily out.

On the streets, Lily had borrowed to make ends meet, but the usurious interest was used against her: the evil old witch who ran the bar had purchased Lily's debt and most of Lily's earnings went to repay it. Lily was now spending so much time with me that she was falling behind on her payments.

I was in urgent medical need of a beer. 'You want me to pay her?' I rasped.

'Stanley, I'm not that kind of girl.'

I'll never understand them.

She smiled, all innocent radiance. 'Remember the ceramic you bought me?'

I hadn't. It turned out that she was referring to the dull green pot like a funeral urn.

'I found a buyer. Big profit. I only need—' she named a sum.

'You sold it? It was a gift.'

'Yes, it made me very happy. The profit was good.'

'I'll have a chat with your mama-san,' I sighed. 'The inheritance will arrive in another two or three years.'

She rolled to face me. The sheet slipped, now covering only her hips. She looked me in the eye, her hand wandering down, almost caressing her full round breasts, her slim waist.

The sheet fell from her hips. 'It's too much. Too much for Lily.'

Too much for Stanley, more like.

'This,' I said to Forsythe, 'is very bad.'

From behind his wing-like spectacles, Forsythe gave me a look of utter despair. Empty of pocket, we walked away from the stall, our stomachs empty of beer. 'Two months no paying,' we'd been told. At the eighth stall in a row.

'Anywhere new?' I asked.

'I've heard there's a place in Tai Po.'

'Don't we still have credit at the petrol station?'

'Old chum,' he perked up, 'indeed we do.'

We remembered when we got there that there remained one stall at which we still had credit. Like most in the area, it was a wooden shack, its floor of hardened earth. Dusty tins of fruit and luncheon meat lined the shelves. Beer crates acted as stools, boxes, bases for tables, whatever. There was no electricity; what little illumination there was filtered in through layers of unsold goods.

We ordered and watched village life go by, which meant watching very little at all. Dogs lazed in the sun, a man wobbled by on a bicycle: strapped to the luggage rack over the back wheel was a complete pig's carcass, its dead pink trotters dragging in the dirt. One ancient lady used a bull clip to pluck hairs from the face of another.

Somewhere through the third beer in this timeless byway, a car so wide it could barely fit down the street approached. A Rolls-Royce, it transpired. It stopped. A window was lowered.

'You wouldn't know where the nearest petrol station is?'

We told him.

'Thank you. Hear that, Chan?' said the voice to the driver. The car lurched forwards only to stop once more. The window came down. 'Price, isn't it?' said the voice. It was dark inside: I had to peer. 'We met at the club,' it continued. 'Doc was expostulating on the rights of the oppressed masses.'

'Ron,' I remembered, pedlar of opium.

'Borders safe?'

'Absolutely,' I lied.

'Give the man a card, Chan.'

The name meant nothing to me but it did to Forsythe. Ron, it turned out, was very important. He was head of one of the venerable trading houses or *hongs* that had their roots in the early nineteenth century, when they'd shipped vast quantities of opium to China – hence Ron's joke about refined heroin. According to communist orthodoxy, the opium trade was an evil imperial plot hatched by the English to keep China poor. After his quip, Ron had rejoined that the tea trade was an evil imperial plot hatched by the Chinese (let's not forget, also an empire) to subjugate England, which was as addicted to tea. Be that as it may, I'd assumed Ron was a mere functionary. He was, however, the Taipan, the ultimate boss, of a *hong*.

'I have a rich uncle,' said Lily.

I rolled to my side. Beautiful, sensuous Lily. I coiled her hair around my fingers, enjoying its softness. I remembered the green pot like a funeral urn and the thought occurred that what I was doing to her hair, she did to me.

'I'd like one of those,' I said. 'Who is he?'

'My mother's brother, of course.'

I'd assumed it was a new client.

'He's in China,' she said.

'He won't be rich any more then,' I said. 'The communists will have stolen the lot.'

She rolled over, her back to me. So I reached over and offered support – by cupping a breast.

'He wants to come to Hong Kong.'

'Don't blame him.' My hand wandered south.

'He wants to—' she guided my hand '—cross a-the border—' her hand reached behind her '—at Sha Tau Kok urrgghhh at ten o'clock on ah Mon-ahhhh-day—' she shuddered in climax '—oh, Stanley. All you have to do is not see.'

And at ten o'clock on a Mon-a-day morning, with less than two hours' sleep under my belt, it was all I could do to keep my eyes open, let alone to see or not see.

'We've had a tip-off,' I told my platoon. A plausible lie

as we got tips now and then from the police. Though this one didn't come from anyone wearing a uniform. Or anything much.

I pushed that happy thought to one side.

Gupta gestured at the barren hills around us: 'No cover.'

He did have a point: barely so much as a tree or a cluster of boulders to hide behind. Which was hardly a surprise as all I had to do was not see, which meant manoeuvring my troops into a position to not see. And I hadn't told my men a lie; I did have a tip-off. Lily had given me specific instructions about when and where her uncle would cross. So I was taking Gupta and Co. to some other place.

They got farther and farther ahead, I lagged farther and farther behind. At the top of a rise, they stood in silhouette, waiting. As I caught up I saw a kind of collective wry smile in their eyes. Teetotallers themselves, they nevertheless knew what went on in the officer's mess.

In a rush, the many kindnesses shown in my year in their country came flooding back. I had once reeled into a village after an ill-advised walk up a hill in the pre-monsoon sun had left me on the edge of collapse, and was given tea by a woman so infirm she could barely walk, yet who refused payment. Another walk in the forest, the rust-coloured pine needles thick under my feet, the deodorant smell rich in the air, but the night closing in. Every way back seemed to lead in a circle. The panic rising, I felt a burst of sudden relief on hearing the lingering bass of the trumpets and deep rings of the gongs of a monastery sounding across the valley – the Gurkhas are Hindus, but there was a Buddhist temple nearby – and that call to prayer guided me home as the sun dipped behind the Himalaya and the permanent ice on the peaks was turned pink by its glow.

Goodness only knows why, but my men would have tied themselves to the mouth of a cannon to protect me. Call them mercenaries, but never question their loyalty.

What a load of old rot. Instead of beefing up on expeditions to be had, I spent every my spare hour with a whore; instead of saving what little I earned, every spare penny went on her. Arresting Lily's uncle would liberate me. It would see off Lily. I could apply for a new posting and be in those vast plains with the most beautiful of women.

'Bring the map, Lance-Corporal,' I said.

'Chum,' said Forsythe in the officers' mess. 'What about Kilimanjaro?'

Reader, I pined. Far from applying for a new posting, I entered a place of empty and hollow nights, punctuated only by the steady thwack-thwack of the ceiling fan above me and the drone of mosquitoes beyond the net. My mind was consumed with tormenting images of Lily's uncle, pleading and begging, of the fear in his eyes. He was of the landlord class, she'd told me: a particular target of communist brutality. By sending him back, I'd bestowed a death sentence.

Lily was gone now, forever. And all because of a sudden impulse to be clever. Too clever. I'd betrayed Lily, but without being loyal to anything else.

After two weeks, Forsythe could endure it no longer: 'Stop moping,' he said. 'She's only a tart.' And dragged me off to Wanchai.

'Stanley!' Lily screamed down the bar. I braced for a sharp implement; she threw herself into my arms, loosed a volley at the mama-san, who was tending her broomstick, and marched me off to the nearest place with a bed.

'My uncle wants to meet Stanley,' she said.

After five year's of hard labour, so too would I.

'To thank you,' she said.

'But . . . but. . . .' I stuttered.

'I dank-a you very much,' said Uncle Yan. I'd got the wrong person. We'd made it to where Lily had told me he'd cross, and rounded up a load of people. The man she introduced to me now was short, with close-set eyes, a narrow mouth and a mole on his chin. Unlike many Chinese, who tend not to have facial hair or, if they do, a rim of fluff, he had a five o'clock shadow. I'd have recognised him in a stroke.

He must have snuck across before we arrived – I thought at the time.

'You worka me,' he said.

After I'd recovered from my choking fit, Lily explained 'He wants you to work for him.'

'Army wouldn't allow it.'

He slipped a red envelope into my hand. The only gift the Cantonese ever give is money, always in a red packet.

What I was yet to find out is that the colour disguises the strings attached.

Clotho the Fate, spinner of threads, had also been busy:

'Mr P-p-price? Martin MacIntosh. We met at the c-c-club.'

Not all of Doc's friends were pedlars of opium. Martin M-M-MacIntosh was a man with no chin, whose cheeks bore a web of red capillaries and whose eyes were those of a sad, tired dog. He was thin, but so out of shape that at first glance he didn't appear so. He had a limp, clammy handshake.

'Doc said you may b-b-become available soon. You see, after the riots. . . .'

Lily was delighted. Uncle Yan's red envelope contained, in a way I later found out to be very Chinese, sufficient to pay off her debt with her mama-san, with enough and no more left over for me to buy my way out of the army, but not enough to go expeditioning. Martin MacIntosh offered me a nice comfy job with no more stomping over those bloody hills. The pay of course was much better than a soldier's: at the end of the contract I'd have enough to set off.

And so I submitted myself to the Fates. Just as they'd placed Sharon in my path at that critical moment, so too again, they'd done me proud with Uncle Yan: the Greeks, I thought at the time, would have deemed me a fortunate man.

Reader: I hadn't a clue.

Chapter 3

THAT BUREAUCRACY IS A FRENCH WORD is an outrage. Red tape is our invention, not theirs. Though desk-cracy, it must be said, does not trip off the tongue.

I sat at my bureau. It was eight o'clock on Monday morning, my first day on the job. Stanley Featherstone-haugh Price, Inspector of Factories, at the service of the public. Two years at the expense of the Hong Kong tax-payer, pocket the cash and off to explore the world. The inheritance was due by then, too.

I waited.

At about oh-eight-forty-five, the door opened.

'I'm Cheng,' he said. 'Tea?'

I drank some tea.

At quarter past ten, it opened again.

'I'm Sally,' she said. 'Pencils? Paper clips?'

I sharpened some pencils.

At about eleven, Martin stuck his head around the door.

'All ready for b-b-business?'

That was the last I saw of him for the b-b-better part of a year.

My first file arrived on Wednesday. Ten forty. I'd just finished the sports section. As I was reading – the file, that is – I became aware of a face at the door.

'Mr Wong,' said its mouth. 'Neville.'

'Price,' said I. 'Stanley. Can I help you?'

'The opposite. I'm your assistant.'

I had staff?

'May I come in?'

He was dressed in a natty double-breasted number, the stitching of which suggested bespoke tailoring; his shoes were patent leather. He bounced over to my desk, took a seat, smiled and leant forward with the demeanour of someone about to ask for the pleasure of a quick tango.

'Where do I start?' he asked.

I'd rather been hoping he could tell me.

'New on the job,' he expanded.

'And I.'

'Oh.'

'Oh.'

He leant back, waiting.

I leant back, waiting.

I remembered the file.

'Take this and let me know what you think,' I said.

Dismissed.

By Friday, I was reduced to cleaning out my wallet. Amongst the receipts, phone numbers of whores and the reminders of things to do that had never been done, somewhere behind a photograph of Lily that she insisted I carry – as effective at warding off rivals as a pot of menstrual blood against vampires – I stumbled across the visiting card of Ron, pedlar of opium.

'How are you?' he said, when he returned my call the next week. 'Still holding back the hordes?'

'No, government now. New department. Very, er, challenging.'

We exchanged a few more pleasantries and: 'Nice to hear from you,' he said and rang off.

That, I thought, would be that. But a week later a flunkey phoned. I was invited to a party on the Peak, said in the tone of voice that suggested an address of importance.

The government supplied me quarters. A cut above barracks, I was given what real-estate agents term a commodious, well-appointed apartment in the Mid-Levels, an area half way up Victoria Peak on Hong Kong Island, with views over the harbour and the personality of a cigarette wrapper. It consisted of one largish bedroom, one smallish guest room and a closet-sized indentation to accommodate a servant, along with a bathroom, living room, dining room and kitchenette – the first place since leaving Blighty that was bigger than a room and a toilet. It needed a woman's touch, however, so Lily came over. We played an energetic game of hide-and-seek which resulted in a trail of garments scattered around and her departing without a suspender – which I never did find.

The following morning a neighbour accosted me: 'We realise that, as a bachelor, you have certain needs, and what you do with your personal life is, of course, no business of ours, but we do not take kindly to having Chinese house guests.'

A bit rich considering we were in bachelors' quarters, but Lily had ideas of her own: 'A nice apartment for Lily,' she sing-songed. Of course, she needed more than just the rental – 'So I can be beautiful for you' – so I gave her an allowance. She'd always gone through it by the middle of the month. 'You must learn to live within your means,' I'd remonstrate, but she'd turn those big doe eyes upon me and the next thing I knew there'd been an exchange of bodily fluids and cash.

But it wasn't just Lily. I had the costs of my own home and hers and, when I was in the mood, the costs of a bachelor's life which included, thanks to my prudish neighbours, several nights a month in a hotel and – as I was never one to skimp just because my date was a tart – decent hotels. For the first time in my life, I was on a fat salary, yet the overdraft went up rather than down. And my dreams of escape remained tantalisingly out of my reach.

Tantalus was a Greek. I should have known the buggers were scheming away.

I felt so proud of Lily when I picked her up in my new second-hand Rover. She had insisted on a new dress but, contrary to her usual practice of stepping into and out of her new apparel, one item at a time, wearing nothing beneath – and the consequent interruptions – she had shown an unusual coyness about this one. It was her favourite style, the *cheong sam*, a tight-fitting single piece, high-necked, ankle-length but with short sleeves. This one had slits up the sides that showed off her lovely long legs; it was of lime-green satin which clung to her figure. Her hair, her make-up were perfect.

'Stanley, not now.'

'But—'

Despite my best efforts, we were on time.

The butler directed a glance at her, frigid, and then at me. My invitation card was for two, yet he seemed at a loss. For a moment, I wondered if I'd come to the wrong place, but then he bestowed upon us a smile. It went no further north than the lips, nevertheless we were admitted.

Despite my expansive quarters, we were packed and stacked where I lived; we inhabited barracks-like shoe boxes and, although mine was larger than most, our social rituals were orientated, as in the army, to keeping us out of them. We ate out, we drank out. We rented a room in the club for a party, or in a hotel for a larger affair. Home was for sleeping, bathing and the changing of clothes.

Ron's hall was larger than my quarters. We waded through a crimson carpet the thickness of elephant grass, beneath a chandelier of twinkling crystal that sent rainbow prisms skittering across the walls, past a pair of suspended scrolls of Chinese calligraphy beneath which stood an exquisite rosewood table on which rested two porcelain vases.

'Late Tang,' said a voice behind me, 'given to my great grandfather by the court of Chi Hey, the Iron Buddha.' Ron picked up one and showed me the artist's seal on the bottom. 'I'm glad you were able to come,' said Ron. And then, to Lily, '*Lei gwai sing ah?*' in what appeared to be fluent Cantonese.

'Underglaze,' said Lily.

As Ron's jaw bounced off the ground, I suppressed a smile and a small flush of pride: nobody's fool, my Lily.

'It's very rare amongst ceramics of that dynasty.' Lily pointed to the vases. 'Specific to the Cheungsha site in Dongguan.'

Chatting to her in Cantonese, Ron led us out and into the garden. A garden! I hadn't seen one since England. The neon signs of the town twinkled at the bottom of the hill below us. Behind that, the harbour was dotted with the lights of ships, most moored, a few on the move – and I remembered my first *sampan* with Forsythe and how I met Lily. My now radiant Lily.

The only Chinese not in a uniform.

Pools of guests stood in dinner jackets and evening gowns. Servants, in white chemises and loose black trousers wove between us, bearing canapés and – it would demean it to call it mere booze – refreshments. Ron led us to a group, made the introductions and left. The men eyed Lily with a combination of lust and awe, the women with unconcealed disgust.

'How clever to speak English,' said one.

I'd rather enjoyed Ron's shock at Lily's knowledge of things ceramic; now I revelled in the envious if hooded glances directed my way.

Someone said something to Lily in Cantonese. As she engaged in conversation, there was a tap on my arm and 'Word in your ear, Price,' was whispered.

I was good that night. I was sober enough to remember leaving. Lily was ebullient, gabbing away: she'd collected a stack of name cards, this one was interested in ceramics, that one in porcelain, and she'd met someone called Charles, who was very important, even spoke Cantonese. And everyone was so polite – not nice, but polite – and so on.

Why on earth would Lily collect name cards?

I didn't have the courage to tell her of my boss's boss's word in my ear. He'd nodded at Lily, busy wrapping some fellow – probably Charles – around her little finger, and saying – the boss – 'We don't air our dirty laundry here.'

It was only later, much later, that Lily told me the point of Ron's conversation in Cantonese was to establish if she was my servant.

I looked out over the pitch towards the offside wicket. Subra was polishing the ball on his trousers. I'd played him before: a vicious spin bowler. Amateurs shouldn't spin. I checked my bat, gripped it. He ran, delivered.

The ball kicked up a cloud of dust, spun up into my face, forcing me to duck.

Batting is a defensive art: the object is to defend the wicket. Runs are secondary. But, that gloat, that supercilious smile on his face. . . .

I looked him in the eye. He polished the ball and took

the first steps of his run. The ball flew towards me.

To this day, I don't understand what happened next. It was as though an elastic wire within me snapped and, instead of being taut as a piano string, I loosened up. I stepped out of the crease, whacked Subra's ball for a four. Then a six. Two threes. A one. Six. Again. Whack.

I could see the frustration mounting in him: I was doing everything wrong, coming out of the crease far too early, attacking, leaving the wicket undefended. Whack! Another ball went into orbit. Thwack, bang. The harder he tried, the easier it became. I found myself focussing on his hand as he delivered: I could spot the twist of an off-spinner, the twitch of a googly.

Eight overs, ten overs, twenty, went by.

The heat swam in waves over the ground as the sun reached its zenith. Mirages danced over the field. The earth burnt. Sweat ran into my eyes.

One bowler, another, went by.

Ninety runs. Ninety-three-four-six-nine. Could I? A century?

The sun beat down on my head, the skin of my arms tingled under the heat. A bead of sweat dribbled off my face. The latest bowler, a fat old chap I knew to be harmless, rumbled up.

I think he gave it to me. One-hundred-and-three. A century.

Claps. Cheers. Scattered applause. Still I played, my mouth dry, my head thumping. I would not declare.

Another ball swerved through the air towards me. I raised the bat but it became lead in my hands. I pulled – and the ground rushed towards me.

When I came to in hospital, recovered from heatstroke, I still had a smile on my face.

Lily sat by my bed. She'd been watching the match from

outside the pitch, had seen me go down and followed the ambulance: 'Your friends were here. They seemed very surprised to see me,' she said. She faced me directly: 'They do know about me?'

I stood with Lily in an antiques shop. Her favourites were porcelain cups, almost translucent, with exquisite, delicate miniatures painted on the inside. The one in her hands – about the size of her palm – depicted two ladies playing zithers under a willow tree, with a distant snowy peak in the background: the closest my overdraft was going to allow me to get to any snowy peak anytime soon.

'They don't know its value,' she Lily'd me. It was her innocent smile, all the cynicism of her times in the bars stripped away as her eyes looked up into mine and the thought came that, while I'd had a childhood, the latter half of hers had been robbed. She took such joy in being bought presents, in being coddled, that I crumpled.

As always.

The cheque – for those were the days before credit cards and other whatnot – was returned two days later. A bounced cheque in the Hong Kong of old carried a custodial sentence. I sorted it out, but these calls were getting closer and closer.

'How are the factories, old chum?'

'Dreary, Forsythe. Dismal, dreary, dull and horrible.'

'So you miss us?'

'Not for a second.'

He sipped his beer. 'New tour of duty,' he said.

'When are you going to buy your way out and start that pub?'

'When are you going to mount your expedition to Rwanda?'

That made me wince.

We sat at tables in a street market in Kowloon. The tables were fold-ups, and the seats, plastic stools. Shoppers wandered past, some stopping to browse the stalls set out in the road. Behind us was a tank of live fish – when the Cantonese say fresh, they mean it – and behind that, in the kitchen, was a flame with a roar like a space-ship's at which the chef produced food of dubious hygiene and wonderful flavours.

All of sudden, from across the junction, shouts came. A commotion. A man burst out of a neon-lit shop, running. Four others followed. Blades flashed in the air, there was a scream.

Less than two minutes later, an ambulance and a police car screeched to a halt. The policeman in charge, being an expat, was easy to spot. As his lackeys mopped up a large pool of blood, ever the conscientious citizen, I went over: 'Need a witness?'

'Triads,' he said. 'As long as no outsiders get hurt, we leave them to it.'

'That,' Doc later explained, 'is because the police *are* the triads.' He looked at my innocent gaze with the same sad pity that Sharon had when she demanded that first fiver: 'Did it occur to you to question why the police were able to get there as fast as they did? They knew in advance.'

'I think we should pay them a visit,' said Neville.

As a factory inspector who, in four months, had yet to visit a single factory, I'd thought this a splendid idea. Oh dear. We sat in the car in torrential rain, waiting for a bus to move on. Although the middle of the afternoon, the sky was gunmetal dark: umbrellas exploded in flashes of blue, red and yellow, as they opened when passengers jumped off the bus. Mothers dragged their children over puddles, their laughter a chirrup over the growl of distant thunder. Neville, trussed up in his double-breasted bespoke and today wearing a bow tie – which I noticed with some satisfaction was a clip-on – lit a cigarette.

I wound down the window to let out the smoke. The smoke didn't go out, but the rain came in.

Neville snapped at the driver in Cantonese. I waved away a cloud of smoke and rested my forearm on the sill. For all its faults, this was better than pursuing innocents through the grass.

Space was so short in Hong Kong that even factories were high-rises. We took a lift up a dozen floors and entered a vast concrete cavern. The noise hit me first: a constant, mechanical roar of sewing machines. The workers were crammed in, a parade-ground layout of row upon row, the aisles so narrow that only one person could pass at a time. Clouds of swirling white cotton dust hung in the air; it was hot and humid: I burst out in sweat. This wasn't in the days before air-conditioning, but it seemed the owners did not waste money on such fripperies.

I had a sudden flashback to the typing pool in Howard's bank. But here the workers, although silent, did not seem unhappy. Despite the unholy racket, there was a smile here, a joke cracked there, someone standing up to come to the aid of another. A nod from a supervisor when a worker asked permission to take a break. Far from being the oppressed masses, the workers got paid by the piece and, as far as they were concerned, the more pieces the better.

My visiting card fell in the direction of one who was rather pretty. I received a telephone call a day or two later: her English turned out to be as deficient as my Chinese, but that didn't stand in our way. Lily, when she got wind of it, did.

The factory owner was a small man, wizened, with more

liver spots than hair on his pate. His head bounced up and down in servile bows as he ushered us into his office, which was a very tight fit with three of us in it. From his pocket he extracted his own visiting card – the Chinese, pragmatists to the core, call them name cards – which he presented with both hands and another deep bow. I played along and whipped out one of my own; Neville followed suit.

Chinese tea was served.

'Business busy?' I asked. A question of staggering redundancy. Even in the relative quiet of the office, we still had to raise our voices.

I tried a few more pleasantries then got to the point. 'We're here because, as you may be aware, as I'm sure you know, the purpose of our visit is to, er, ah. . . .'

'. . . to ensure that the safety improvements detailed in this –' Neville whipped out a copy of some letter '– have been effected.'

Well, said the boss, they were going to make them as soon as they could but being so awfully busy—

'So you haven't made them?'

I let him wriggle. If I could spin it out for another half hour, I could skip a return trip to the office and go straight to the club.

'You do understand the penalties for failing to make the improvements?' I asked.

He did. They weren't up to much.

I looked at my watch: another twenty-three minutes. 'Neville,' I said, 'would you mind taking a look to see how much is outstanding?'

He was far too efficient. Thirteen minutes and he already was back: it was all outstanding.

I sighed – no bunking off early – and we returned to the car. As we set off, Neville turned to face me and said, in tones of offended innocence: 'Do you know, Mr Price, I was offered a bribe?'

If Hong Kong had a national sport, it was being on the take. Expat policemen arrived at work on a certain day of the month to find their hush money awaiting them in the top drawer of their desk, and those who left it there enjoyed dim prospects of promotion, or even a renewal of their lucrative contracts. The triads, officially branded as organised criminals but, to the Chinese, their own form of Freemasonry, complete with secret rituals, initiations and hierarchies, albeit without the goats, ran the prostitution and drugs and, for a minor payment, would keep a shopkeeper safe and even forbear from setting his children on fire.

Even firemen demanded a bung before they'd switch on the hoses. A Chinese social contract, one wit described it, yet never a truer word was said in jest. It greased the wheels, maintained an orderly society and kept the girls clean. I didn't object to the principle; it was rather that being British and military had left me ill-equipped to march up to a factory owner, hand outstretched in greeting and introduce myself with a breezy 'Good morning, Stanley F. Price, inspector of factories. I've come for my squeeze.'

Sally the secretary resigned. She'd hit the jackpot on the stock market – the other national sport of Hong Kong – and was off to a new life in Hawaii.

'So,' I asked Percy the stockbroker who, now that I was no longer a poor soldier but an exalted civil servant, acknowledged my presence at the club, 'only blue chips?'

'Absolutely,' he nodded. 'Though perhaps a flutter on the Overseas Trust Bank. It's small and aggressive, with great prospects.'

The markets were soaring, the Cultural Revolution was

a distant memory, China was stable. I had to do something about my finances.

A sudden image of Howard flashed through my mind. 'Well quite—' I said.

Ron's again.

'The Factories' Inspectorate?' asked the group to whom I'd been introduced. Their dinner jackets were immaculate; mine grew tighter every day that I sat at my desk. They talked of the cherry blossom season in Japan, of Jim Thompson silks from Thailand, of the dawn over Borobudur. They talked of cruise liners, exclusive hotels and French chefs flown in for the night. They talked with the ease that comes with knowing that no bill will ever be left unpaid, no hardship ever endured.

Of not being up to their eyeballs in debt.

I looked around for Lily, only to stop myself. I'd learnt my lesson: Chinese were not welcome. But without her and without the envious glances of the men – and the spiteful ones of their wives – the envy was all on my side.

I wandered off through snippets of overheard conversations: '. . . got lucky on the markets and bought his yacht. . . .' – ouch – '. . . fresh off the boat, married a chink, a gold digger, got what he deserved. . . .' – no, not Lily – '. . . brown-paper envelopes: it's how business is done in this part of the world. . . .' and found myself alone – and relieved to be alone – standing at a balustrade.

The night was clear, a half moon shimmered off the harbour's water. The lights of the city glittered below me, its rumble ascended but didn't intrude. In the moonlight, the range of mountains behind Kowloon was shaped like the back of a dragon. Indeed, the name means 'nine dragons': it was said to have been bestowed by some toady when a visiting emperor of China had counted eight and the toady, preferring to keep his head attached to his shoulders, had included the emperor in his own count.

That first moment of revelation, as Forsythe's car emerged from the tunnel, came back to me. After only a few years, the skyline was heading into the clouds. The isolated skyscraper on the tip of Kowloon was now one of many and reclamation works were underway to fill in more harbour and create more land for homes and factories. Though many people had been resettled into public housing, more came from China each day and those squatter villages still carpeted the hills.

They came to this city of dreams, industrious and willing to give things a try. All around me were people who took being wealthy for granted. And I was sharpening pencils.

Another view came to mind, of the mighty cone of Kilimanjaro, the permanent snows glittering on its summit. Would I see it again? With Lily? Burton, Speke, Livingstone and my namesake had hacked through the heart of Africa with baggage trains of provisions and a hundred bearers – but a baggage train of Lily's *cheong sam*, her collection of *objets d'art*?

One means to an end had led to another, yet between Lily and debt, there was no end in sight.

'Price?' came a word in my ear. 'Sorry to see Miss Chewy isn't here.'

'Miss Chewy?'

'Lily. Lily Tsui.'

She used her surname so little, and it was so difficult to pronounce, that it took me a moment to put two and two together. He meant Lily, my Lily.

'She found the most exquisite piece for my collection. Pass on my thanks.'

What on earth was he talking about?

My inheritance arrived. Inflation was then rampant in England: between that and death duties, the best it enabled me to do was, in modern parlance, reschedule my debts. All that remained was a house which I would have sold were it not for the tenant, my mother.

A friend from school appeared one day. I took him to all the usual places: the Peak, the club and a spin around the NT.

Strolling around the back streets, we stumbled across an antiques shop, Tsui's Ceramic and Porcelain Antiques.

'Zoy,' he rolled the name of the shop around his mouth. 'Joy?' he tried once again. 'Anyway, just what I was looking for,' he said and opened the door.

'Hello, how can I—' the assistant stopped in mid-sentence.

The assistant was Lily.

'Sorry, we're closing,' she said. And shut the door in our faces.

I played cricket every weekend, except when it was too hot – when everyone in the team lied to their wives, girlfriends or both and hid in the club – except if there was a typhoon, when there was nothing for it but to get quietly sozzled at home. Only this particular typhoon had turned out to be a damp squib, fizzling out in the afternoon and leaving a beautiful evening in its wake. 'Come,' said Lily, 'I'm meeting my friends for seafood. Join us.'

A dull horror gripped me. Her friends were from her old days in Wanchai. But, while Lily had left Wanchai behind, on the nights when I wasn't with her, as a sewer draws rats. . . . 'Your friends hate it when I'm around,' I floundered. 'They all feel they have to speak English.'

'Why can't you learn Chinese?'

It was the tones. What to English ears is the same sound

can mean a whole range of things to the Chinese ear. Depending on the way it's pronounced, their word '*see*' can mean shit (as in Fireshit or Forsythe), a thing, to give, and many more. I couldn't get the hang of it.

'Easy,' she said. 'Like your name in Chinese, See-daan-lay. Means "up to you".'

Which, coming from any woman anywhere, is both a threat and a command. And we'd been at it all afternoon. And the bars would be shut.

And I ended up paying.

Neville and I called on the honourable premises of the much-esteemed Kwong Tat Plastics Manufactory. They had a file about a foot thick. In an organisation in which requisitions for paper clips could run to six inches, this was notable though far from exceptional. But the Kwong Tat was exceptional. The file listed one violation after another and not a jot of progress.

'I think, sir, we should deliver an ultimatum.'

To spank their botties?

The Factories Inspectorate, despite the genuine desire of Neville and similar starry-eyed innocents, was no more than a sop, implemented after the riots of '67, to hoodwink militant trade unionists into thinking that *things* were being done. The factory owners were having none of it, bullied government and, as a result, the penalties for violations were mere fines. No owner would ever have to serve time and quite a few regarded the fines as a business expense.

'Yes, Neville,' I replied, suppressing a yawn. 'I quite agree.'

As long as I could be in the club by lunchtime.

On inspection, though, the Kwong Tat lived up to its file. Filthy. Unsafe. Dickensian. Almost certain employment of minors.

We delivered our ultimatum, that we'd be awfully upset if something wasn't done, and legged it before we choked on fumes.

It dragged into autumn.

'Marry me,' said Lily.

'I shall,' said I.

She rolled over and faced the wall, her back to me.

'You won't.'

'I will.'

'You never take me to your friends'.'

'I took you to Ron's.'

'Or your club.'

I remained silent on that one.

'Because I'm Chinese?' She rolled over and looked at me, a sob in her voice.

'They won't let you in.'

'Why don't you go somewhere else? Why do you always go there? Why be stupid, like a cow? Marry me. I can make you happy.'

That was the rub of it. Yes, she could make me happy. But, while there were many routes to success in the civil service, some even tangentially related to merit, the one sure route to failure was to take a Chinese wife. And I needed that job if I was ever to save enough to explore.

'Because of the shop?' she interrupted my dissembling.

The rumour mill if the club found out that she was a shop assistant—

'I'd sell it for you.'

'Sell it?'

'My shop. Tsui's Ceramic and Porcelain Antiques. I'd sell it if you wanted.'

Chewy. Zoy. Joy. Tsui. Lily Tsui. 'It's . . . it's yours?'

'Oh, Stanley.'

Hong Kong's first topless bar, *Bottoms Up*, later to appear in a James Bond film, opened. The street sign was a marvellous collage of sixteen girls' bottoms in a four-by-four grid. With an invitation like that, I was first through the door on opening night. Their girls were young and fresh; I experimented with combinations. Moreover, it was in Kowloon, out of Lily's orbit and away her friends' spying eyes.

I soon had a tab there, too. Which soon also became unpaid.

'The Overseas Trust Bank?' I asked.

'Safe as houses,' said Percy the stockbroker. 'The government wouldn't dare allow a bank to go broke.'

I sat, squirming.

'The dividends alone make it worth doing.'

I squeezed away another sudden image of Howard. He was smiling in approbation. His smile, I should say, was ghastly: a condescending grimace of yellowing, jiggledy teeth. And I still wished I'd punched him in the nose for disparaging my friends as fuzzy-wuzzies.

'You can sell them anytime. Easy as picking a phone up.'

I had to do something.

'Alright,' I said.

'Stanley,' said Uncle Yan – my aspirant wife-to-be's relative of the border crossing, still with his five o'clock shadow, and now owner, it transpired, of the Kwong Tat Plastics Manufactory. 'Your department make me very trouble.'

His English was still execrable, but the improvement was astonishing.

'The law's the law,' said I. 'Anyway, the improvements won't cost much.'

'But we have to stop work. No work, no money. Big cost.'

I shrugged.

He pressed a red envelope into my hand: 'Stanley. Remember before, I help you. Now you help me.' He paused, his eyes locked on mine: 'Nobody knowing.'

That's when I found out about the strings attached to Cantonese red packets – strings woven by Clotho herself. The first one he'd given me had paid my way out of the army and Lily's way out of her bondage. If that became known, my reputation was sunk.

Nobody knowing. A veiled threat: if I turned this second red packet down, everybody would know.

Anyway, it was Hong Kong's national sport. And I was a sportsman, wasn't I?

To put it another way: if you've ever been had by the balls, you'll know how quickly heart and mind follow.

The club, the bars, even the overdraft. Remarkable, the difference a red packet makes.

I stood in an antiques shop with Lily.

'Are you sure?' she said, her eyes wide with surprise.

'Lucky on the markets,' I lied. 'Promise you won't sell it. Dinner?'

It wasn't just one red packet, though. And it wasn't just Uncle Yan.

'Neville,' I summoned him one bleary morning. 'Come hither.'

He came bouncing in, all natty pinstripes and patent leather. Rather than face him across the desk, I sat down beside him for an avuncular chat.

'You seem a little unhappy of late?'

'What makes you think so?'

'Just a feeling,' said Uncle Stanley.

'There was just one thing, sir. It was Kwong Tat plastics.'

'Refresh my memory.'

He did. '. . . so, sir, I don't understand why the case was dropped. It was iron-clad. We could have made an example of them.'

The factory wouldn't have been the only thing to have been made an example of. Uncle Stanley wouldn't have come out of it covered in glory. Conspiratorial tones were in order. 'Between you and me, it came from higher up. You see. . . .'

'No?' he said, when I'd finished what was a complete pack of lies.

'In the greater interest, though.'

'I suppose so, but—'

'Now listen, Neville. There's another reason I wanted to have a chat. Part of what we hope to achieve in government is to find fine young men such as you and develop their talents. Ready Hong Kong for the day when – well,' I glanced at the floor, coy but frank, 'when we leave.'

'Sir?'

'When it's your turn. To rule.'

His face lit up like a whore's offered breakfast in bed. (I should know.)

'Now,' enticed Uncle Stanley, 'we have recently started a scheme. . . .'

He swallowed every last word. Three years out of the way in England at university, then back to help the govern-ment for the good of the populace. People everywhere believe what they want to, but our sheer credulity as a species will never cease to amaze me.

Or maybe I'd found the right bribe.

Neville was bright, young, efficient and honest – and chosen by others. I devoted considerable care to the choice of his successor. I looked for and found a human being of the lowest order. Stupid, lazy and, like myself, perpetually broke, he was not intelligent in any pleasant sense of the word but nevertheless possessed a low animal cunning that made him a sterling negotiator. I won't name him: what would have been a character flaw in any normal organisation was an asset in Hong Kong's bureaucracy and, although he's now retired, libel is tiresome. But, damn, he was good: 'Two accidents last month,' my reptilian side-kick would hiss as the bosses squirmed in their chairs. 'Make department look very bad.' The next thing I knew, I'd find a brown envelope packed full of notes in the top drawer of my bureau and a glowing report to the effect that the factory was now a shining example of rectitude and safety would follow.

Lily and I had such fun. Earning a multiple of my salary, I showered Lily with all the toys and baubles she wanted. We went to the best bars and restaurants. 'Wait over there' became 'Good evening, Mr Price'; we even made appearances on the society pages.

Where did I find the money? people would ask. The stock markets were booming, the Overseas Trust Bank had proved a great punt; I'd come into some family money, Lily's uncle doted over his niece, her shop was going from strength to strength. But what tickled me most was that my beat had the best safety record of the lot.

'Ex-ex – marvellous job,' said Martin.

When I entered a meeting in one of my bespoke suits and patent leather shoes, people's backs straightened. When I voiced my opinion, it became the voice of record. When I submitted a memo, it was answered in days rather than weeks. At factories, they would send down a lackey to open the door of my car; the owners would cease whatever they were doing and negotiate in person.

Up went the bribes; the Fates their web to spin. Did the Chinese have their Icarus, I wonder?

'It's a bloody disgrace,' Doc had said one night, 'that having a Chinese wife should be an obstacle to advancement in this, a Chinese city.' Several loud howls of derision were his answer; 'Word in your ear, Price,' came to mind: sod 'em.

Lily looked at me, refulgent. In the candlelight – not at the club but at a Gaddi's French Restaurant, the poshest in town – I saw only her face: the pearly glow of her teeth as she smiled, the light from her eyes, her thin, aquiline nose and ruby lips. The high collar of her *cheong sam*, the lustrous glow of her hair.

She put on her Wanchai accent: 'You mean it for Lily? Really?'

I did. What about Stanley, world explorer, you ask? Now that I was rolling in cash, albeit ill-gotten, and with all the fun we were having, exploration had fallen off the agenda.

'What about your friends? Your job?' she asked.

It was the seventies, for goodness' sake. Having a Chinese wife should no longer be an obstacle to advancement. And, if I committed the act and marched her up the aisle, the rumour mill would cease.

'In that case,' she said, 'Yes.'

Being a willing submissive comes at a price: you can't do it by halves. Appointing my sidekick had violated the terms of my arrangement with the Fates.

I was promoted.

I am sure that he was behind it. I cannot prove it; I have no evidence, but my sidekick wanted it all. The cut I allowed him covered his vices but not his avarice – and there was far too much money. During my time in the army, Hong Kong's economy had crashed. Now, it was booming. Its factories were producing goods for the world:

plastics, textiles, electronics, you name it. Fortunes were made, men who ten years ago had been in the rice paddies of China were driving Rolls-Royces; the skyline was shooting heavenwards. In the crush of factories and houses, in the swirling mass of workers, those with the brains, luck and wherewithal to keep Stanley sweet could succeed.

My sidekick came to see me as an unnecessary expense. He contrived to have me posted to the single department of the Hong Kong Government which offered no opportunity for self-enrichment: Social Services.

I hadn't saved so much as a penny. As to my stocks, there was the small matter of the Organisation of the Petroleum Exporting Countries, who decided to switch off the oil taps. The whole world suffered, but Hong Kong suffered the worst.

'You said they'd be easy to sell,' I raged at Percy.

'You can sell them,' he said. 'But no matter how little you offer them for, no one's interested because they'll be cheaper tomorrow.'

'No money no talk', they say in Cantonese. Lily and I fell off the cocktail party lists; those at whom we had sneered by flouting social norms, now resumed their sneering at us.

Lily stood by me. She tried to encourage me, tried to clip her wings, even sold some off of her own *objets d'art* as the crash had hurt her business, too.

'You promised you'd never be angry.'

If only I'd saved, I could have been looking at the distant peak of Kilimanjaro, the lions at their kill, the wide skies of the Serengeti: 'I'm not angry at you. I'm angry at myself for being an ass.'

She knew me too well: *I could have been. . . .* Not *We could. . . .* She was not telepathic but, as her gaze stretched out and our history hung in the air between us, from the early days in Wanchai to her devious Uncle to the whirl of the past couple of years; to all those times I'd neglected her for cricket or pretended she wasn't mine, to the part of me that blamed her for my own profligacy, she knew.

'You don't want what I want,' she said. Her back straightened, her eyes creased at the corners. A wan smile graced her lips: 'Remember Charles from the party?'

Lily, my Lily, was gone.

The trouble with the Chinese social contract is that, beyond a certain point, it stops working. Between the police, the triads, half-a-dozen government departments and Stanley, no profits were left over for businesses' owners. By the early seventies, one could barely cross the road without someone demanding his squeeze. The crash didn't help. Rather than gambling every spare cent on the markets – which had fallen to a sixth of their value – businesses had to work for a living.

The Independent Commission Against Corruption, also known as 'Interference with Chinese Ancient Custom', was founded. It was not expected to live, but its gainsayers were wrong: I was senior enough to be an embarrassment, but not senior enough to be hung out to dry. I was silenced with the offer an amnesty if I resigned, which I accepted with alacrity.

I tried Ron, I tried all those people I'd met on the cocktail circuit, but it was Doc who explained: 'It wasn't that you were on the receiving end, nor even that you were caught. It was that you took bribes in person from a Chinese.'

In the end, it was down to one choice.

'I won't give you money,' said Uncle Yan, now in possession of a starched English accent. 'I'll give you the agency for my products, exclusive for one year. Generous credit terms, renewable subject to reasonable performance.'

We closed the deal with the only form of contract he ever entered into and which was his absolute bond: a handshake.

Chapter 4

S TILL VENUS AND ERIC ARE LATE and I wonder, as I look at the men, now playing backgammon in their booth, and the two elegant ladies on high stools: will she have forgiven me? For what happened, what followed?

I look down the bar. I met Eric because of a drink at a bar. And Venus.

She'll arrive soon.

I don't blame Lily for Charles. Deep inside she knew that, while a side of me revelled in the high life alongside her, the other was marking time until I had the means to escape and explore the world. That other side of me was a closed book to her. Charles, I found out, was a captain of industry, steadfast in a way that I never could be. He forgave her her past; he and she married, moved to his native Canada and, to judge from our correspondence when Lily stumbled across me on the Internet, she has been a wonderful mother to their three children. The antiques shop she founded has morphed into a successful auction house.

Lily, my Lily. I soon came to realise that her combination of beauty, charm, wit and libido was unique. She was glamorous, tasteful and had a flair for the arts; she could be funny, charming and gay. She would look the other way if I was wayward for a night, though for no longer and, indeed, regarded fidelity as being unmanly.

So I pined once again – Lily's the only woman I've ever pined for – but part of me was relieved to be off the hook. And, despite her views on male hormonal urges, my peccadillos had been only moderate. After another period of moping and another blunt shock out of it by Forsythe, I was like a Rottweiler slipped from the leash.

I had always been more of a quality than a quantity man, but those first few months after Lily saw me rebound in the opposite direction: round, slim and athletic; frigid, insatiable and the inevitable quota of actors; Filipina, Chinese, English, a memorable night with two Koreans and once, and sadly but once, a random stranger with a predilection for quickies in public: in our case an upmarket department store where I'd been shopping. We caught each other's eye, played hide and seek through household goods and lingerie; I thought I'd lost her in bedding only to have her hand snatch me from behind a curtain whence we beat hasty but necessary post-coital escapes in opposite directions before I could get her number.

They introduced me to strange parts of Hong Kong. Once, after working up an appetite with a girl who laughed without ceasing, we kicked awake a taxi driver and she took me to the Aberdeen fish market in time to see the catch being landed: in the half-light before dawn, the boats moored and a small army descended, slick yellow oilskins catching reflections of strip-neon lighting, a deafening chorus of cheerful yelling as the catch was hauled away in blue plastic barrels, escapees flapping and slithering across the floor. It turned out that she was one of the Tanka people, easy-going folk with a reputation – of which she seemed unabashed – proud if anything – of being promiscuous. Together with her family, solid people, well-tanned, with ready smiles and the mist in their eyes that comes from a life on the waves, we sat at a large round table as the sun's first rays sent shafts of light through the struts that supported the tarpaulin awnings, eating all sorts of wriggling creatures from the sea. They taught me that one should never turn a fish over on its plate as this symbolises a boat capsizing. Instead, one has to hollow it out from below: a habit I've kept to this day.

I got back in touch with the girl from the factory. She'd followed my advice, taught herself English and had found a job as a secretary. Before I could say 'missionary or doggy?' she'd introduced me to mum, dad, granny and four siblings in the public housing unit they shared, which was about the size of a garage in England. Everything served at least two purposes: beds had drawers beneath them and doubled up as seating during the meal; when I entered, the dining table was in use as an ironing board and after the meal transformed into a *mahjong* table; the wardrobe acted as a partition between one set of beds and another. 'Luxury,' they said. 'You should have seen the shanty town before this.' Yet, despite the cramped surroundings, there was – it was more than hope – a certainty that things would work out: her father had qualified as a doctor in pre-revolutionary China, so was not licensed to practise in Hong Kong, but one brother had just started his own real-estate business to take advantage of the booming market, another was working two jobs to save up for college, and the whole family had pitched in to help a friend start his own business. Yet, despite their welcome, leave her I did: she'd invested such hope in me, but only as an escape route. She'd never thought about love.

One morning I woke to infantile giggles. Thinking the window had been left open and a school nearby, I rolled over only to see two children in school uniforms standing at the end of the bed. I shrank back, pulling the covers over myself. My conquest couldn't have been more than twenty years old, yet the two brothers looked to be seven to ten. 'I'm thirty-four,' said the mother later that morning. Asian women again: I'd got her age wrong by a decade.

I employed a girl, when the agency for Uncle Yan's plastics picked up, who developed a crush on me. She would stand behind me when I was reviewing her typing, but by less than was proper. As the weeks passed, she started brushing by me. Once, as she stood behind my chair while I was signing letters, she shoved her crotch into my shoulder. She had to go. A male relative turned up a couple of times and lurked outside the office in a threatening manner, but nothing came of it. I wonder what she had told him.

Ah yes, the office. Uncle Yan's agency turned out to be a goldmine. Excellent though his English had become, he suffered from a communication problem not of language but of concept. A customer would approach him with a design, he'd quote and get the job done. But Uncle Yan didn't consider the use to which the product would be put. The result was a simmering dissatisfaction. Customers would come back but only because he was cheap. He'd still make lots of money, but from volume, not quality.

I changed that. One of the first customers wanted a toy aeroplane: a tailplane, fuselage, wings and the landing gear. The designs he sent were detailed almost down to the rivets – and this was a 1:100 model. It was to be moulded in two dozen parts and assembled.

I pointed out that the most a five-year-old wants from his toy is that it stay airborne for more than three feet. Out went the scoring representing metal panels, the exquisite wheels and the trim. We got it down to five pieces, which cut the cost of assembly by three quarters, albeit for a small increase in the amount of plastic.

'Too much trouble,' said Uncle Yan.

In those days before facsimile machines, let alone email and smartphones, we had no option but to post samples. Sometimes it took months to get right.

'Wait and see,' I told Uncle Yan.

Nine months later, the customer phoned to rave about the great new design. The customer was not the only one delighted. As we'd reduced the cost by almost half, but only passed on half the savings, we increased our profit as well.

It was then that I received from Uncle Yan the first and I think the only red packet which wasn't a bribe.

I made new friends.

Leukemia Pete was so-called because once, during the banter that drinkers mistake for conversation, someone had declared themselves to be of blue blood. Another claimed red; Pete white. 'What, do you have leukemia?' Doc had asked. The name stuck. As with most nicknames, it was inappropriate as he was the fittest amongst us by far, tall lean and blond, tanned golden-bronze, and lacking a beer gut because he never stayed for more than three pints. More unusual yet, he was a policeman. Many, grown fat on bribes, had shared my fate at the hands of the Independent Commission Against Corruption and been forced into early retirement. Leukemia Pete – later abbreviated to plain Luke – had not only steered an honest path through a labyrinth of temptations, but got employed by those same crime fighters who had been my own nemesis. We treated each other with wary civility until we found out that we had two things in common: the same birthday, and childhoods in the colonies. I confessed my crimes, he asked me if I'd put that behind me and I truthfully answered in the affirmative.

'Godber's Chinese name translates to Kudzu-Cypress,'

he said, referring to a policeman of prodigious venality. 'Really quite interesting.'

And that was the last we ever said on the topic.

There was an Austrian called Max, short for Maximilian. Just as Scots hate being taken for Englishmen, he hated being taken for a German, and at six foot four and twenty stone, it was inevitable that the diminutive Max became short for Maximum and then Minimum, so we called him German Min, later contracted to Germin. He always had a deal on the go – shipping parrots from the jungles of Indochina to collectors in Austria, a salvage operation for a ship full of gold sunk during the Vietnam War, a coconut farming monopoly in the Philippines – but never seemed to have the wherewithal to advance them. He consumed two beers for each one of ours and was sober as we slid to the floor. 'Vot, you leaf so early, you English sissies,' he would say in a mock German accent as we beat a retreat.

One night there was a knock at the door of my apartment. There he was, swaying like a twig in a storm. 'Stanley,' he slurred, 'tomorrow an appointment I am having. You must at seven wake me.'

His vord order in English a barometer of how far gone he voz being and, in this case, fully Teutonic, he was very far gone, so it came as little surprise that, by seven, he'd found his way into the bathtub.

I shook him. I shouted. I slapped.

I sprinkled him with water from the shower.

He shrieked, leapt to his feet and made it to the couch before passing out cold.

'He pours acid on me,' he announced that night.

Thus I became Stan, Stan the Acid Man.

Nitric for short.

Clotho the Fate, my web she was spinning.

We were at the club one night, Luke, Germin and I, when a fellow walked in. He was of medium height, wore large, round horn-rimmed spectacles over a round, jovial face, and was stout in a muscular, compact sort of way.

He was also Chinese.

He sat at a high stool and ordered a drink.

From the shadows of the bar, an elder member arose, wraith-like. His gaunt features, his raptor nose, honed in.

'You,' he said. 'What are you doing?'

'George Wang. New member.' He offered a hand.

'New what?' A vein in the elder member's temple started to throb as his face turned beetroot. 'This. . . . This is a decent club. We don't permit chinks.'

An inner part of me groaned. The etiquette of clubs is such that elder members are not to be questioned. But I needn't have worried.

'It seems to me that there are quite a number of chinks here,' said the new member. 'The serving dish my dinner arrived on, for one. A couple of the cars outside are positively dented.'

A thermonuclear device exploded in the elder member's head. His lips twitched, blood vessels stood out, eyes bulged. 'We'll see about this,' he said, spun around and strutted out with the posture of a man who's just had rectal surgery without anaesthetic.

George withdrew his spurned hand of greeting.

Germin looked at him, the floor, and said: 'Standards are falling.'

'Indeed.' I replied. The best I could muster by way of a welcome was to make a joke of it: 'Was the porcelain really chipped?'

'The word porcelain derives from the Italian for a cowrie shell,' Luke chimed in, 'which,' he jutted his chin in the direction of the departed and outraged elder member, 'is said to have the same root as the word for a young sow on account of its resemblance to the porcine cunt. Really quite interesting.'

Hong Kong was later to develop – and lose – a reputation as one of the world's safest cities. Back then, though, things were a little less lawful.

'I've just escaped being taken a hostage,' said a very shaken Germin one day.

I thought he was drunk, but he'd been in a bank when some armed robbers had burst in and, unable to clean the place out before the police arrived, had taken hostages. Germin would be a large chap anywhere but in Hong Kong, he was a giant. They looked at him, one of the robbers said 'Fuck off, now' – in a Cockney accent – and Germin had bolted.

Bank? Hadn't I had something in banks once?

'Po Sang Bank,' he said.

No. Didn't ring any bells.

Business, club, cricket and women. It was a whirl. But something was missing. My flat was like a hotel room: too clean, too neat. It lacked clutter, lacked familiarity. On the rare nights I spent in, there was nothing to do.

I avoided spending nights in. But there wasn't much new to do when I went out. We played snooker. We drank. I turned up at the office, often hungover though rarely late, dealt with what had to be dealt with and, before the mere thought of exploration could enter my mind, the day was over and I was down at the club once again.

As to the women, the professionals were paid off and kicked out in the morning, which suited both parties, but my multi-headed, multi-bodied replacement for Lily didn't come close. I'd take them home once, twice, thrice at a push, but there was always some flaw, some incompatibility – and often trivial things: if it wasn't bad table manners, it was being finicky in her diet; if it wasn't too long in the shower, it was insufficient attention to personal hygiene; if it wasn't preserving their maidenhood, it was that they'd relinquished it all too quickly.

It occurred to me one Sunday morning that I should try somewhere other than bars. But there were no concerts, no art exhibitions or shows. I'd never been one to make a cuckold of another man and that exhausted the possibilities for respectable ladies. But this was Hong Kong:

> *Onwards Christian soldiers*
> *Marching as to war. . . .*

I'd chosen St John's Cathedral: the same area as a couple of tennis courts, inside it was white-walled and had a vaulted wooden ceiling, stained-glass windows and suspended ceiling fans that did little to stir the sultry air. I stood at my pew, the sweat from my hangover pooling around me. It was a marvel it didn't etch a hole in the floor.

Most men were in suits, most women in hats. Small boys and girls stood, groomed and sweating. There was a man over there, handsome, fit and athletic, attached to a woman who was none of the above. A few rows in front was a woman with an hour-glass figure and long, brunette hair. The back view proving more than pleasing, just as I was wondering about the front, she twisted around in the act of swatting some insect away. There was a flash of creamy white skin and the curve of a very generous bosom.

After the service, as I stood drinking tea and ogling her, I was bumped from behind.

'Oops,' said a young lady. She was short, had freckles and

blond hair and her pursed lips invited a kiss. I may have seen wings sprouting from her back, and a halo. 'Your shirt,' she said.

'Quite alright,' I stammered.

A brown tea stain was spreading around my nipple. She dabbed it with her handkerchief.

I took a very deep breath.

Her name was Jo. From Southampton. Visiting friends. Arrived from India two nights ago. I'd been there? Kathmandu? She'd love to have gone, but visas were difficult (back then, they were) and she was pushed for time. Wasn't it fascinating and how could I have spent a year on the subcontinent without seeing the Taj Mahal? And the Gate of India? Oh, I was in the army? Business now? No, not at all boring, it must be fascinating. And I played cricket? Imagine, England being beaten by the West Indies (which we'd just been). No, she hadn't seen much of Hong Kong, but she'd love to. I must be so busy – but look, there was Molly, come to collect her.

'You're not really Christian?' she asked me a day or two later at a Chinese temple.

'Um, yes.'

'You believe in hell?'

'Not as such, er—'

'Eternal life?'

'Well I think—'

'God?'

'Yes.'

'You don't act like much of a Christian. I'm Hindu, you know. Don't look at me like that. It's not funny.' And, later that day, 'I think this one-on-one thing is possessive you know. I mean – could I get on top? – the object of physical love is – oh yes, that's better – physical love is to bring you closer to Brahma, the Atman. I mean – slow down – the

Atman, yes, as long as both people are working – ahh, yes – working together – oh fuck, yes, faster now. . . .'

George Wang, now christened Legal George after his calling, was locked in mortal combat with me over the snooker table. It was the last red and the side bets were mounting.

'Ten on Nitric.'

'Ten says he fouls.'

A red in the opposite corner was hanging over the pocket. There was fifteen feet of table between the cue ball and it. I drew back the cue and hammered its tip into the cue ball just beneath and to the right of its centre. The cue ball hurtled down the table in a wide arc, smashed the red out of the way, bounced off a cushion and into the black which met the original red and knocked it into the pocket.

'Serves you right for calling me Nitric,' I said.

'Flukes don't count.'

Flukes were all I had ever counted on – and not just on the snooker table.

'As your legal counsel—' George began. Germin rolled his eyes and parted with a ten-dollar note.

Back in the bar, George drew me to one side. 'Stanley,' he said *sotto voce*, 'small favour to ask. Nephew returning soon from America. Trained as an engineer. Your sort of thing. Could you help out?'

And so it was that Eric – yes, that Eric – entered my life. He came to the office a day or two later and sat for two hours unnoticed at reception while I sat fuming that he'd arrived late. That resolved, my first impression was of something missing, that Eric had been created to fill a human-shaped void in the firmament, that Brahma had had a bad day and couldn't think of anything better to do with that particular five-foot-three, seven-stone chunk of the cosmos.

'Your Uncle George tells me you're interested in plastics.'

'Yes,' he whispered.

'It's a challenging industry,' I said, scratching my crotch and wondering if I could make it to the club by four as I listened to myself rabbit on about the wonders of plastics.

'It sounds very interested,' he said.

'Interesting,' I corrected him. 'How long did you spend in America?'

'Four year.'

'Years,' I corrected him. 'Could you speak up a little?'

'Four year.'

'In?'

'MIT.'

He was something *cum laude* – don't the Americans love the affectations of Latin? I looked at him sitting there, hunched, knees pressed together, as if trying to suck himself out of existence.

'Tell you what. We'll try things out for three months. If you're comfortable, we'll keep going. Five thousand a month?'

'Four thousand enough.'

Silly bugger.

I told Jo about him: 'Don't be so mean,' she said. 'But beware of employing friend's relatives. They can be difficult to get rid of.'

Sage advice, though it was years before I realised it was also prophetic. But, away from the club where all was bravado and cheer, Jo had insights about things in the office that I didn't notice. And, when in the club, she astonished my teammates by being better informed about English cricket than most of them were.

Heady stuff: we seemed to be becoming an item. We even went on holiday together to Thailand, my first since arriving in Hong Kong. The exploration I'd had in mind wasn't of Bangkok's sex shows, but Jo's enthusiastic participation changed that.

Forsythe never bought that pub he was going to retire to. On patrol one day, he stepped on a snake and died of its bite. He'd requested a funeral in Hong Kong: I could imagine him lying there, dying, 'Don't make a fuss, old chum. Don't make a fuss.'

There is a small chapel set in the Stanley peninsula on the south of Hong Kong Island, the pine trees surrounding it framing the view of the azure ocean to both sides, and the graveyard of those who made the ultimate sacrifice during the Japanese occupation of 1941–5 a mile to the south. (The chapel itself was the site of the rape and murder on Christmas Day, 1941, of dozens of innocent nurses and doctors.) Within, the fans suspended from the ceiling turned in lazy circles, stirring the turgid air. Forsythe's wishes had, by a greater power, been allowed to override those of Wogeh, so I was one of the pallbearers.

I was too stunned to cry. Forsythe and I had drifted apart through circumstance, but those early years had made us brothers, and that's a bond that time and place can never diminish. Now, he was no longer.

As the regimental chaplain droned on about He giveth and He taketh away, my gaze drifted around the chapel: the small, stained-glass window, the alpha and the omega, the Christ and the crucifix – *Oh merciful God* – with the nails through his feet and INRI on his chest – *We say together, Our father, who art in Heaven* – and, as I mouthed the prayer, I remembered a small boy holding his mother's hand at a service like this. The mother was swaying – 'How unexpected' – 'cerebral malaria' – her make-up running as tears coursed down beneath her veil and, when it was over, she needed support as she was led from the pew. The little boy was too young to understand.

I was nudged. Dressed in my uniform, I took my handle and hoisted the coffin. In a military slow step, we started on the path to the hearse – and again I saw that same little boy, still watching, as understanding dawned on him that someone had died but without him comprehending who it was.

The rain started but brought no relief from the heat as we marched through the mud. One of the pallbearers slipped, the casket jarred. We struggled to catch it.

That rare laugh, those wide-mouthed, asthmatic hoots of Forsythe's – Fire-shit's – came to me. I recalled hands in the air like fluttering doves scrambling for the glass he threw before he dived into the swimming pool that first night; the lap of the waves as we drank beer, his scroll of love poetry, the night of the chopper attack. I remembered nights, mornings. Dawns.

I saw again that little boy, wondering why Daddy wasn't there to comfort Mummy when she was crying. '. . . gathered here today to celebrate the life of William Richard Forsythe. . . .'

He never would be.

Then, I cried.

Jo seemed to have moved in. At first it was a night once in a while, then a weekend. Next thing I knew, in the words of a then current song (of hers – she acquired a stereo, too), I was buying me a washing machine.

My flat acquired character. Persian rugs appeared on the walls, statuettes of dancing Shivas with many arms and entwined legs lined the shelves, large potted plants adorned the sideboards. Candles flickered as joss sticks sent spirals of sickly sweet smoke to the ceiling. Beef went out; vegetarian curries, lentils and yoghurt came in. My weight came down, my libido soared.

Free love was Jo's creed. Drunk, in the wee hours, I staggered from bar to bar looking, but none of the girls fitted the bill. *Her* smile, the way she wore *her* hair or the shape of *her* nose; that *she* had small breasts and that one there, fat legs.

A standard evening: I of course found *the one*. I slobbered over her in the darkness, believed what I wanted to believe as cash changed hands. She took my hand and conducted me outside – she had no choice as my legs were no longer mine to control – and the thought occurred to me. Must have occurred to me. Jo and her free love. Did she mean it? Tonight was the night to find out.

'You crazy?' my new friend asked.

At the door of my flat, the dread hand of sobriety stroked me. Perhaps a hotel room. Perhaps sending her home. A quickie on the stairwell.

The door opened.

Uncle Yan decreed that I was to go on a sales trip to America.

'Find an American,' I pleaded, but international telephone calls in those distant days cost an arm and a leg, had to be booked in advance and lacked the personal touch.

'Quite unnecessary,' he said. He was going through his Winston Churchill phase: 'I think . . . that you . . . are the man . . . for the job.'

The trip was exhausting, expensive and lonely. The Americans were as insular then as now. Some regarded Hong Kong as part of Japan or Korea; one asked if we rode camels over the desert (I told him we did). The only part I came close to enjoying was New York.

'You're de English guy wid de plastics,' said my contact

there, Axel.

As it wasn't a question, I didn't answer.

'Goddamn stuffed-shirt limeys. I got some stuff I wancha to do. Follow me.'

He put me in a limousine the size of a tea clipper and we sailed off through the Big Apple's traffic.

'My goddamn son of a bitch father God rest his soul gave me dis stupid Guyman name. Ran away from the fuckin Nazis and still he gave it to me. Fuckin guy could never leave Guymany in his head, know what I mean. Son of a bitch. But it ain't fucking nothing compared to Feather . . . stone . . . how? Goddamn fuckin—'

'Fenshaw.'

'Fen . . . fuckin . . . what?'

'My middle name.'

'I'll be goddamned.'

His car was better equipped than my flat. The booze cabinet was full, there was a car phone, a television and, for all I knew, a double bed and sofa suite in the boot. Or trunk. He produced and poured a whisky.

'You a goddamn Jew with that name?'

'Strictly C-of-E.'

'What the fuck is that? Some kinda Japanese kinky thing?'

I tried explaining the reformation but Axel, unlike his father, had put Europe firmly behind him.

'Did Joe tell you what we do?'

Jo?

'Thought not. You'll see.'

Axel's warehouse was near some docks, red-brick. A sudden image of my own execution and subsequent reuse as part of someone's foundations flashed across my mind as Axel marched me inside.

'We're in a kinda fuckin delicate business,' Axel said. 'Joe, fill 'im in.'

'Yeah well Mr Prithe,' Joe lisped. 'Our buthineth involves the manufacture and distribution of aids of an intimate nature. A very intimate nature, if you get my meaning.'

I didn't.

'We sell sex toys,' said Axel.

That perked me up. After two months of replica cartoon characters and bicycle seats, something worthwhile.

'Yeah,' Joe took up the story. 'We carry a full range of accethories for people with all types of . . . needs.'

'Perverts,' Axel clarified.

Joe nodded, looked at me as if he hoped I'd be shocked, and went on when he saw that I wasn't. 'Our manufacturing standards are very high. Product liability claims are on the rise and the intimate nature of our line necessitates special attention—'

'Our customers get mad if the dildos fuck up their pussies.'

Helpful, this Axel chap.

'Costs stateside have been rising and so. . . .' it went into the usual stuff.

Axel, I might add, was the only host in that fine country who showed me the kind of hospitality to which I had become habituated in Asia. 'This is Priscilla,' he introduced a delightful young lady. 'Help her test this,' he said. And gave us a dildo.

No sooner had I returned to Hong Kong than Jo whisked me away on another holiday, this one to Indonesia.

Since Thailand, we'd been to Malaysia, Japan and Australia but, rather than hack through jungle, scale the heights of Mount Fuji or take a camel train across the Outback, we went in style: first-class air travel, swish hotels and the finest dining.

On this holiday, I found myself standing one morning at dawn at the ancient Buddhist temples of Borobudur. Java is an island of stunning beauty: the soft amber light made the statues glow and, in the distance, the peaks of volcanoes were as sharp as if etched into the sky, the shrill cacophony of insects rose with the heat.

I had a sudden urge to walk away from Jo, from plastics, from threesomes and beer, and into those hills.

'Right,' Jo burst into the moment. 'We have to be at' such-and-such place for such-and-such thing. My shoulders slumped. We never seemed to leave the hotel without a tour guide. Jo's itinerary was as precise as an army's invasion plan: she'd tick off one temple and museum after another, acquire a meticulously itemised list of knock-offs at designated street markets and, to ensure an aura of outrageous conduct amongst her own circle, nibbled at insects, reptiles and other peculiar delicacies. And, of course, there was ever more sex.

As to exploration: 'No, Stanley, we can't go there.' She'd brandish a guide book: '*Fodor's* says it isn't safe.'

I sighed. Forget exploration; it was barely even a holiday. Almost a chore.

'This time,' said Germin, back in the almost domestic familiarity of the club, 'I will be rich. We will be rich.

'It goes like this. Air tickets are expensive because. . . .'

The details flapped past me but the gist was that he could obtain air tickets on the cheap, sell them at well below the retail price and make a tidy profit in the middle: 'It's not illegal?' I asked.

'Absolutely not. I checked already with Luke and George, they both say it is alright.'

I had my doubts.

'You are not sure? I show you the figures.' Never my

thing, the numbers blurred past. 'This is the cost of the ticket, this the selling price. We still sell at half the official price. Price?'

Droll.

'How much do you need?'

He told me.

I shook my head. He'd drink the lot.

'Stanley, it is good business. I only ask you because you are a man I can trust—' A hearty slap on the back restored me from my choked cough – 'More and more kids are coming from Europe, backpacking. They need cheap tickets. Business people from Hong Kong fly more and more overseas and are careful with money. With your connections, this can work. And since you left to America, I have stopped drinking. Three months already.'

He had, too, the bugger. With the order books full, I had an embarrassing surfeit of cash and, having been bitten once, the stock markets were out.

'At least it doesn't involve a country at war,' said Jo.

It seemed I had no choice.

Those were the days when couples 'lived in sin', but the sin was starting to spin out of control.

My flat resembled a Himalayan jungle. Large green plants sprouted from the gloom, the Shivas and incense sticks seemed lost behind a confusion of fronds and leaves. I half expected to see tigers and snakes in the foliage. I had started avoiding the place but had forgotten something there, so I stood at the door, ten in the morning, juggling the keys with one hand while holding the post with the other.

The door opened. A man with the proportions of Hercules stood there. He wore only a bath towel. He smiled at me.

I double-checked the number on the door. 23A. My flat.
'Who are you?' he enquired.
'The bloody postman.'
'Oh. Thank you.'
He took the letters and moved to close the door in my face – but I got my foot in the gap.
'Mind if I watch?'

Eric, like a mouse approaching a cat, entered my office. Not that many mice carry with them a twelve-inch dildo.
'I not very like this,' he said.
'Few of us are, Eric, few of us are.'
'I mean, I not very much want to work this.'
How had he made it through MIT with such dreadful English?
'It's a piece of plastic, Eric. Nothing more. Some people use a broom handle. A beer bottle. Heaven only knows.'
'It's immoral.'
'That depends on the purpose to which it's put.'
He looked at me.
'Eric. Business is neither moral nor immoral. It's a-moral. These items are likely to be very profitable so long as we can make them to specification.'
'I need think it.'
Despite his outward appearance and indisposition towards prepositions, he'd proved himself a fine engineer. I had neither the time nor the inclination to find another. Besides, he was George's nephew and George would be disappointed if I sacked Eric. 'I need a mould design. I understand the discomfort you may feel, so I'll give you a bonus.' I named a figure. 'Think about it.'

Eric said yes to the dildos; I said yes to Germin. Uncle Yan was pleased, though not enough for another red packet; my friends at the club got wind of my new product line and for a while chorused Stan Stan the Dildo Man whenever I entered the bar.

That left Jo. The thing about a relationship founded on adventurous sexual experimentation, I realise now at the distance of decades, is that, once that experimentation has reached its limits, so too does the relationship. We'd worked our way through all possible permutations of participants and positions, and further repetition became just that: repetition, mechanical and increasingly dull. The novelty was no longer in it. And that left a gap that grew between us.

But it wasn't only Jo. Seven years had slipped by; all of a sudden, instead of being in my late twenties, I was in my mid-thirties. The business, started in desperation, then interesting as I learnt my trade, was now an activity that filled the time between waking and passing out drunk. No longer the pursuit of a dream, one order followed another with never quite enough profit accumulated to cash out and explore. Mountains were conquered, records were set, but my orbit shrank.

I needed change. All it took was a dinner.

Chapter 5

'I CAN'T BELIEVE YOU would do that,' Jo started. 'How could you be so exploitative?'

'I'm a businessman.'

'You know what I mean.'

I had no idea what she meant. I contented myself with pouring stiff G&Ts for us both.

'She has a degree, you know. In philosophy.'

I sliced a lemon.

'I just can't believe you'd do such a thing,' she said.

I was about to point out that she was repeating herself, however, her pursed lips and defiant pose suggested an alternative tactic.

'No.' She brushed my hand off her breast. 'Not after last night.'

Ah. She was upset that the young lady we'd shared had a degree. In philosophy.

'She was only here for the money.'

'Her and the other four million of us.'

'Here, in this flat, Stanley. Not here in Hong Kong.'

Another stiff one.

'How could you?' she spat at me.

I'll never understand them. All the stuff about free love. Her men. My women. Was I to be confined to the uneducated?

'How could you pay?'

'Wasn't that difficult. Opened the wallet, took out the old banknotes—'

'It's immoral.'

'Steady on. She was hardly an unwilling participant.'

'But—'

'But nothing. I didn't tell her to come from the Philippines and go on the game here. She made that choice.' I trotted out all the usual arguments, take 'em or leave 'em.

I took 'em, back then.

'My dear Watson,' I addressed the wall opposite me at half-past eleven the following morning. 'We detect here the classic symptoms of a hangover. The victim arrived late, having missed two appointments, cannot concentrate on his work and his breath smells like – Yes, Stella?'

'The man's here for his interview.'

'Thank you, Stella.'

'Coffee?'

Cheeky cow.

'Mr Price?'

'Sorry, Stella. Daydreaming. Oh, reschedule my appointments and—'

'Already done. I told them you were at the doctor's.'

'Angel.'

The latest lamb shuffled in behind her. Only this one didn't shuffle. He bounced. He stood straight, posture erect. He wore his hair in a ponytail and had round, wire-rimmed, pink-tinted spectacles.

'I'm John,' he said.

'Er, Stanley. Stanley Price.'

'Cool. You like beetles?'

I'd never heard of some odd diets in Asia, but beetles?

'The band. The Beatles. My friends tell me I look like John Lennon. Man.'

'Really.'

'Yeah.' He nodded his head and assessed my office. 'Good vibes, man.' He inserted a digit into a nostril and, after due exploration, withdrew it, examined the sample and wiped it on the underside of the chair he'd flopped into. 'When do I start?'

I wondered what job he'd applied for. Didn't much matter.

'Monday.'

Germin had another business proposition.

It had been years since I'd been to the posh part of Kowloon, Tsim Sha Tsui, on the tip of the peninsula. My, it had changed. When I first arrived it had been an area of relaxed boulevards and two-storey houses standing in private gardens of lush green. Now, we pushed our way along crowded thoroughfares lined by skyscrapers limited in height only by jets flying so low that, on their final approach, they seemed to skim the very roofs. We battled through a crowded, narrow corridor lined by buildings on one side and, on the other, construction hoardings, behind which lay a cavernous pit at the bottom of which coolies slaved away in knee-deep mud wearing only shorts, flip-flops and conical bamboo hats: the government were building the stations for underground railway, the MTR, by the simple expedient – rather akin to Stanley's technique – of tickling open a hole, dropping the payload inside and closing it up again.

'Surely not?' I protested as we came to a dingy entrance from which chopper-wielding thugs could at any moment appear. A blur of people swept past, their voices a Tower of Babel over the roar of construction machinery; the smell of curry wafted out of the shopping arcade. Shops lined the street, their windows cluttered with cameras, watches and jewellery, all tax-free, a Mecca for tourists – and smugglers. 'Tailor?' a voice echoed in my ear. 'Copy watch?' I brushed a hand off my blazer and made sure my Omega was still attached to my wrist.

'Nitric, it is quite safe.'

We entered a half-lit shopping arcade, took a lift and emerged. The top floor was caked in filth, cobwebs hung from the ceiling, the wiring was a fire waiting to happen.

'Max,' I whispered. 'How on earth did you come to know of this place?'

It was a hotel for hippies. They stood in aimless clusters or sat, smoking, gazing off into the distance. Emitted grunts. Some wore kaftans, some jeans. Some had long hair, for which the most common fashion was: tangled. My blazer, cuff-links and tie took on a distinctly tight feeling.

'Do not judge by appearance. They're just kids, Stanley, exploring the world.'

That stung.

'It's appalli. . . .' My voice trailed off as one floated past wearing a translucent smock through which a pair of pert breasts showed. My back straightened, my chest puffed out and my right foot, of its own accord, stepped off in pursuit—

'Stanley, pay attention,' said Germin.

The proprietor of this fine establishment was Sonny, Sonny Chan. He had close-set, gleaming eyes and was thick-lipped; his salt-and-pepper hair was permed into an Afro. His florid Hawaiian shirt was unbuttoned to the navel revealing a heavy gold chain with a pendant sporting a lump of green jade against the deep tan of his solar plexus while, on his wrist, a gold bracelet jostled for space with a gold watch. A minor waft of cheap aftershave or perhaps cannabis competed for attention with the prevalent BO.

'So,' said Germin, 'we recruit kids who want to go to

Korea. We give them a haircut and dress them in suits so they don't get stopped at immigration. We put them on a plane to Seoul, and they deliver your dildos.'

'Don't they have them in Korea?'

'Your toys are illegal in Korea. These kids will smuggle them in and give them to Mr Kim's man. The kids get a free flight and Korean women get—'

'Quite. But what if the kids get caught at the airport?'

Sonny shrugged. 'Sent back, lose dildos.'

'How much is Mr Kim willing to pay?'

He gave me a figure.

'That's almost their weight in gold,' I said.

Germin's cheap air tickets were already raking in cash; he'd been sober since he'd started that business. A bit of focus and capital behind him and he was coming into his own.

We had a deal.

'See-dan-ley,' Uncle Yan parodied his own Chinese of a mere decade ago, 'you make-a me very trouble. My secretary resign, say: "No can do la".' He emitted a loud chuckle, looked around and said, his accent reverting to the West-coast American that was his current favourite: 'But I can tell you, it's the most profitable plastic we've ever made.'

'Maybe she should try the six-incher, not the eight?' I ventured.

More self-parody: 'No can do. Number two wife, after she use, say no more Uncle Yan. Too tiny, not satisfy like big plastic.'

Even I laughed at that.

We were in a restaurant the size of the Oval. It was packed. The tables were crammed in, the hubbub was deafening, cigarette smoke billowed in the air. Women pushed along trolleys laden with steaming bamboo baskets containing *dim sum*, the local speciality. Some of it was quite palatable: prawn dumplings were one of my favourites. 'Don't be so unadventurous,' Uncle Yan chided me, stopped a trolley, and a collection of chicken gizzards was plonked down in front of us.

Was he punishing me for the hangover? What had I employed John to do?

As the waiters were clearing away the last of it, Uncle Yan's accents regressed through Californian to Churchill to stockbroker and then disappeared altogether. Which meant he was getting to the point: 'I heard from Lily the other day. She says she's very happy. New life. Loves her husband.' He shook his head. 'Love. Stupid word.'

He should know. He had half-a-dozen regular girlfriends (he scolded me if I used the word 'concubine') on top of his three official wives, or *tai-tais* in the vernacular – polygamy had only recently been outlawed and in any case, with a sound three-millennia celebration of bonking, the Chinese didn't give a hoot about Victorian English morality. '*Tai-tais* for sons, girlfriends for fun, Stanley.'

He paused; he looked at me: 'I know Lily too well. She still misses you.'

I missed her.

I also missed Forsythe, I reflected as I stood outside in the early afternoon sun. There was a hole where he'd been, an area filled with joy and good cheer, that Luke, Germin, George and Doc could fill neither as individuals nor collectively. I missed his thirst for adventure and the novelty he brought to all that he did. I missed his smile.

I missed that I hadn't been on an adventure since leaving the army. I missed the quietude of the countryside, the unchanging rhythm of life in the NT, a stark contrast with the city's unrelenting buzz. I missed drinking beer at a shack watching the world go by, chatting about nothing in particular or sitting in silence.

I imagined him tumbling through the whatever-lies-beyond-ness that, to him, would be just another gregarious riot, swooping up on other dead souls, his too-wide spectacles glinting in the light, his asthmatic hoots of laughter leaving them – as he'd left me – with confusion and joy.

To this day, I miss him.

I also missed that, without his gentle cajoling, exploration had diminished from being an immediate goal to being a pipe dream.

I debated knocking off for the day, taking my stomach full of unnameable food and last night's gin back home to sleep it off. But home? Home had Jo and the jungle. Home had sexual experimentation and arguments. Arguments about everything. About my exploitative capitalistic life-style – the lifestyle that supported her jungle and cannabis habit. About the way I was always out with my friends and never paid any attention to her, about the creepy way I was always hanging around and should not be so possessive.

Jo, Jo, Jo. There were times when the magic was there, a spark of her eyes, a flash of her smile. But mostly it wasn't good enough to want to remain without being bad enough to break off.

I hailed a cab to the office. There was a newsstand on the pavement outside the building next door; the owner sold newspapers, fags, soft porn and, when she'd started to recognise me and worked out I wasn't a grass for the cops, hard porn too (that being outlawed in Hong Kong). As I was alighting my taxi, a Rolls-Royce drew up. A man popped out and gave her a bag of take-away food, got back in and drove the Roller away.

'My son,' said the stall holder with a toothless grin.

'She owns the building,' the security guard explained. The stand was her way both of passing the time and of keeping an eye on her tenants. I wondered how she'd react to our products. 'She thinks they're funny,' Stella told me, up in the office. And we expats think we keep secrets.

I went to my desk and stared at the pile of telephone messages. Modern communications are marvellous, but there were times when I yearned for the age before the infernal machine, when one could reply in a confident, copperplate hand: *Dear Sirs, With respect to your enquiry of 13 August, 1849 for the leather-clad assplug. . . .* In this modern age, we must make our excuses, like all else, on the fly.

I remember reading a book of Jo's – my only book was the cricket *Almanac* – which dissected the routines of normal office life. The novel was supposed to be clever but, from the first page, it was obvious that the author had never set foot in the real thing. No matter how hard he tried, reality was duller.

Eric knocked and entered, bearing an artificial vagina. 'What's this?'

What did the man do at nights? 'Bring me a dildo,' I said.

'So, as you see, the product range is educational,' I concluded my demonstration.

'You should tell me early.'

'Earlier,' I corrected his English by conditioned reflex. 'I'd rather hoped your father would do that.'

'My father not doctor.'

Oh dear.

Stella came in, glanced sideways at Eric who remained on the spot, hands occupied with interlocked plastic genitalia, and said: 'We should go now.'

'We should?'

'To the hotel—'

Stella had long legs, a more than adequate cup size and a sense of humour that was about the only thing to look forwards to in the morning. If she hadn't been such a good secretary, I'd've—

'—to check the room.'

Was I blurring fantasy and reality? Hong Kong had a more than adequate supply of hotels, of varying levels of salubrity, which offered accommodation on an hourly basis, no questions asked. Indeed, one building, the 'Four Fs,' had a dance hall, restaurant and hotel respectively on the ground, first and second floors so one could find, feed, fornicate and forget, all in one convenient package. Should I take Stella up on it? Would she be as good in bed as—

On no. I remembered. Tonight was the annual staff party. That meant two Chinese meals in one day. It meant polite conversation with my staff for the first half, followed by brandy races for the second; it meant a gargantuan hangover.

It meant no way out.

'Of course,' I said.

Like a good boss.

I girded myself with a couple of quick ones. The points of intersection between Chinese and expat orbits were commerce and concupiscence – woe betide any who mixed them – and the artifice of these obligatory celebrations was as much a strain on my staff as on me. They had to force conversation in a language which many barely spoke; I had to feign jollity when I'd rather be potting the cue ball or cuddling up with Jo in front of the telly – it wasn't all bad between her and me.

Mahjong tiles clattered, cigarette smoke clogged the air. It would be dinner time soon. Everyone bar Eric was here. He was late, as usual. I paused to admire Stella's long legs and recalled her miniskirts of the summer just past: cockteaser or innocent? Ah-Wing, his baldness a narrow gorge along the centre of his crown, slammed down a *mahjong* tile, flipped over the rest of his hand and smiled with triumph; Ah-Kin giggled as he pulled a banknote from his wallet and mouthed a long series of Cantonese expletives which, even with my rudimentary grasp of the language, I knew referred to sexual congress with the winner's mother. Raymond, our slick salesman in his double-breasted, gold-buttoned blazer and polished but not patent leather shoes, extracted a cigarette from his silver cigarette case and squirted, as was his habit, a spray into his mouth to neutralise the smell – and I recalled one rainy morning he'd come into the office and said: 'Good news, bad news. Good news the order. Bad news you don't got enough fucking money to pay my commission.' (He was correct.)

Somehow, I'd built what would now be termed a team. They had their fights and no doubt their intrigues, but they were tight-knit and worked well together. Our designs were shipped on time and on spec, and not only the sex toys. Torches, light fittings, umbrella handles, lids and containers, knobs for cookers: look around your own home: there's little that doesn't contain plastic.

I saw them all, laughing, chatting, the Cantonese hub-bub rising and falling in waves. I saw their teeth flash with laughter and their eyes sparkle with mischief.

I felt far, far from home.

There was a hiss of escaping air: 'Mister Price?'

I turned to greet him: 'Yes, Er—'

I stopped dead in mid-sentence.

'My friend,' he said. 'Venus.'

Chapter 6

I TRIED TO PUT HER OUT of my mind. I'd been to any number of cocktail and dinner parties where I'd been introduced to women of jaw-dropping beauty, excruciating sensuality or just plain had-to-have voluptuousness, only to find them spoken for. I'd shrugged off the lust and moved on. What had Uncle Yan said about love? Stupid word.

Venus was a stunner: so what? Tall, taller than Eric, coming up to my nose. Her face was long, her eyes a dark hazelnut, in almost perfect symmetry and a little slanted up at the edges. Her smile, when she'd shaken my hand, was wide and her teeth a perfect straight row. The slight kink in her nose set her apart from the plastic-surgery beauty of models and film stars. She was slim without being skinny, the curve of her bosom was adequate without being distracting, her waist was slender and her hips narrow. But it was more than her looks: it was the way that she carried herself, the confidence of her poise, the relaxed, self-assured posture. The jut of her chin, the vitality.

Everything that Jo used to be. In the five or so years that I'd known her, Jo's tummy had gone from washboard-flat to pillow-soft; her breasts were no longer firm. I told myself that she and I had grown comfortable together – but she the more so. Amateur cricket isn't up there with prizefighting or sprinting, but Jo took taxis everywhere, walked nowhere; if it wasn't pot for breakfast it was gin for lunch; her male visitors – there were never any secrets between us – left her frustrated rather than satiated.

But it wasn't only the physical. 'Funny thing at the office today,' I'd start, only to meet a blank stare. 'Good chance against Australia,' I'd predict, only to receive a dismissive shake of the head. 'Coming along?' I'd invite her, only to hear 'What, to watch you get drunk with your friends again?' The fact that she'd slept with most of them didn't help.

I couldn't dislodge Venus from my mind. I tried my usual cures: finding an approximation in the shadows of Wanchai, fantasising that it was Venus rather than Jo with me when on the job, but to no effect. That unsullied smile, the way her hair bounced, the glow of her dusky skin, the echo of her 'Pleased to meet you', the song in her voice, anchored themselves in my psyche. Yet all we'd done was exchange a few pleasantries before she sat next to Eric, Eric the hunched-up, sucking-himself-out-of-the-cosmos Eric; she'd spoken only when spoken to, and they'd left together as soon as the brandy came out.

I tried to put her out of my mind.

'I don't know about this, man,' said John. The ponytail into which he had crushed his hair at his interview was, it transpired, his idea of formal grooming; he now wore his hair loose. It fell as evenly on his face as it did on the back of his head, like a wigwam balanced on his scalp: had he turned his head to face backwards – anatomically improbable, I grant you – I wouldn't have noticed. 'These instructions, man, I mean, the presentation is, well, second-rate—'

I waited.

'—man.'

Had he learnt his English from pop songs? I wondered. 'What would you have us write?' I asked. ' "Open legs, insert, orgasm" is about all there is to it.'

'It's the simple things. The typeface, just typed. And mimeographed. Like school lessons. And the diagrams. They're ugly. Man.'

'I thought they were clear enough.'

'This one? Changing the battery? It looks like a giant chicken's foot putting a sausage into a roll.'

'They get the idea.'

'Yeah, if you could power them from sausages.'

'Seems clear to me.'

He looked at me. He paused. A light came into his eyes. 'You drew them. That's why you're so sensitive.'

'I am not,' I barked through clenched teeth.

'Be cool.' He raised his hands. He tried a smile as his finger wandered, with no apparent volition, nosewards. 'I'm not saying they're bad or anything. Just maybe a professional could do better.'

'Maybe.'

He leant back, resting his ankle on his knee.

'So what do you want?' I asked.

'All that I'm saying is, you know man, I'll do this if you want me to but, you know, I think it could be better—'

The phone went.

'John,' I said.

Ring ring.

I'd found out what I'd employed him to do: 'You're the technical writer. Take responsibility for the whole thing. And do get them printed.'

Ring ring.

'For real, man?'

'All yours.'

Ring ring.
It was Jo.

There was a gasp on the line. I shut the door behind John with a smile on my face – Jo sometimes phoned so that I could listen in, a pleasant intermission from work – but the gasp became a sob, then a wail.

By the time I'd got home, the ambulance that I'd called had arrived. These were the days before paramedics and Jo was being whisked away on a stretcher as I got to my door, leaving me in a scrum of leering policemen, surrounded by splintered furniture, shattered glass, upended flowerpots and – the oddest details remain – a dancing Shiva with a joss stick up its arse.

I still hadn't the faintest idea what had happened, and the police, spotting a cluster of Price's pleasurable plastic playthings, seemed more interested in extracting lurid details than in illuminating me. I extricated myself and, by the time I arrived at the hospital, the doctors had patched her up and I was allowed into her room.

'Jo—' the name burst from within me, becoming almost a cry. One of her eyes was so badly swollen that it was already shut and blackening fast; the other was a mere slit. Her nose had a splint and a bandage, her wrist was in plaster.

She was too sedated to make any sense. I spent an hour or two by her side, but was ejected at the end of the visiting hours.

On the way out of the hospital, in a quiet corner, my fists balled so tightly that the nails dug into my palms, I couldn't keep it in any longer. A word that I never use burst from somewhere deep, deep inside, and I punched the wall so hard that it left a dent in the plaster.

'It must be karma,' Jo said in a whisper a few days later, her voice a quiet vestige of the forthright, no-nonsense diction that I knew. 'My body . . . my body sensed something my mind didn't know. It just wasn't reacting. So I said no.'

'Tell the police. A man who raises his hand to a woman once will do it a second time. What about his next victim?'

Her gaze rested on mine. I'd stopped touching her as she met my touches with an involuntary flinch. But this time her hand ventured with caution to me. One fingertip then another touched my cheek, then her palm cradled it. 'Stanley,' she bit back a sob. 'I'm so sor—'

A rattle, a slam and Legal George stood there, all flowers and smiles.

He'd stolen the moment. But Jo made her statement.

It was three in the morning but sleep wouldn't come. My mind was a maelstrom of vague fantasies in which Venus presided and, every time I reached for Jo, Venus stood in my path, her glowing smile luring me away. Meanwhile, soft snores emanated from Jo's side of the bed. In a day or two, Jo would be home and those snores would be hers.

I hauled myself out of bed.

In the toilet, the sudden brightness of the light stung my eyes. A fortnight ago, these tiles had been spattered with Jo's blood, a coil of her hair with the skin still attached lay in the bathtub.

I forced my fists to unball, my jaw to relax, and splashed cold water over my face. There was grit in my eyes: I opened the cabinet. My eye drops were in their place, alongside my regimented instruments of coiffure – grooming goes much farther than looks with the ladies and the razor-sharp parting, plucked ear and nose hairs and a clean shave demand a certain attention to detail. Jo's half, by contrast, was a jumble of sanitary pads, nail varnish and remover, eau de Cologne – what is so special about the water there? – foam bath, shampoo and pills.

I flipped up the toilet seat and directed my jet, first at the water and then around the side of the bowl. Shook, flushed. Only the flush water was off once again.

Back in the bedroom, I lay once again in the darkness. I tried to conjure an image of Jo that first time in the church: the wide blue eyes, sun-bleached hair and the freckles on her cheeks. But, wherever I focussed my gaze, I saw instead Venus's glossy black curls, upturned eyes and the kink in her nose.

It was absurd. Jo and I had our tiffs, our differences of opinion, our habits that annoyed one another, but we were a couple. When, in a week or two, I'd nursed her to health, we could take a holiday—

'No, Stanley, not there. *Fodor's* says it's not safe.' Damn it. Jo and I were history. We'd followed the path to its end. The fling had become passion, but the passion had faded away and all that remained was inertia.

The phone rang. At four in the morning, it could only be the hospital.

'Price speaking.'

'Uhhh,' said a voice. A woman's voice.

'Who is this?'

A buzzing sound came on the line. 'I like your products very much.'

Splendid. A customer endorsement. And my companion, tousle-haired and the sheet in her hands concealing one breast and not a thing else, had awoken and was approaching.

A threesome. 'Please,' I said. 'Do tell me about it.'

A crisis meeting was convened. Sonny looked worried – which in his case was all the concern of a Buddha contemplating a flea taking a crap: his permed hair was flattened in one or two places, sweat stains showed under the armpits of his shirt. The jade on his gold-chained pendant was a millimetre off-centre. He lit his third cigarette of ten minutes and glanced at his Rolex. The air-conditioning unit growled.

Germin was late. 'Another five minutes?' I asked.

Sonny fidgeted with his cigarette, I without one. It occurred to me that I knew nothing about him. 'What got you into this?' I asked, waving at the hostel.

'Make easy for young people to see the world. If more people see the world, we have better understanding,' he said. 'Better understanding, no wars.'

And my fellow expats held with deep conviction that Hong Kong people care only about money.

Germin arrived. 'Sorry,' he said. 'The traffic late was being. Mr Kim from Korea is to me telling—' he belched loudly, '—that the bribes to customs what we are paying is not enough.'

A smell of not so stale beer permeated the room.

'How much do they want?' I asked.

His head lolled, his gaze wandered around the room. It landed on me. He shook his head, which seemed to jog his memory. 'Not how much but who. Why do you at me look like this?'

I shrugged and looked away.

'We must a person find and inform the customs in Korea.' He paused for another resonant belch and continued. 'They catch him, put him in jail. Their bosses the pressure take off. Everything normal again.'

'We're going to set someone up?'

'Problem,' said Sonny, though I couldn't tell if it was a

statement or a question.

'Big problem,' said I. 'I'm not going to send one of these' – a young lady bounced past, all bra-less and liberated – 'one of these people off to a jail in Korea. Not for a few pennies. I don't like them, it's true, but—'

But—

'What problem?' asked Sonny.

Germin's attention had drifted. Behind his head hung a photograph of Hong Kong. It had been taken from the very place where I'd asked Forsythe to stop his car all those years ago, my first glimpse of this town that had now become home.

'Give me a few days to think about it,' I said, my eyes on the photo. Hong Kong: different rules.

Jo was released from hospital. I made it my habit to arrive home sober and early rather than my usual snooker and beer at the club. I cooked her the favourites we'd both allowed to lapse: lentil curries and such-like; we'd snuggle up on the couch, chat about cricket and she'd do her best to offer sage counsel on the affairs of the office.

After a couple of days, I started to realise I rather looked forwards to going home sober and early. After a week, though. . . .

'Come to my listing party,' Uncle Yan insisted, still in West Coast American. 'It's awful. Great. Awfully great – ha ha. I make more in a week than this goddamn factory does in a year. And property—' he rolled his eyes in glee.

So he'd decided to list the Kwong Tat Plastics Manufactory on one of the stock exchanges.

'Won't the shareholders mind the dildos?' I asked.

'The shareholders won't even know what we do. And anyway, as soon as I've listed I'll use all the money to buy property, which is what they'd expect.'

'Property?'

'I have a couple of new pads. My new shareholders will pay a good price for them.'

I must have looked at him blankly.

'Stanley, you don't get it. When I list the company, I get lots of money from the new shareholders. The company uses their money to buy my property from me at inflated prices. The property goes up sooner or later, the company sells it at a profit, everyone's a winner.'

And here was me thinking about blue chips and a steady chain of dividend income to fund my someday exploration. But Yan's way was the Hong Kong way. While I'd been beavering away, turning up at the office, manufacturing things that actual people used – or enjoyed – and collecting a modest profit to pay my staff, with enough left over for Jo, her cannabis habit and my own diversions, the rest of Hong Kong had moved to what would now be described as a different business model: make a quick buck in plastics, garments or consumer electronics and plough all the profits into real estate. Once one had enough property, list that on one of the stock markets. The punters would go wild with glee, pile in with their own savings and, the next thing everyone knew, they'd all become even richer without an honest day's work in the picture. It was a casino in which no one ever lost.

Jo made an effort on the night of the party and did she ever look stunning! She'd had her hair done at my insistence – 'Stanley, you know I prefer to be who I am' . . . 'It will make you feel better' – put on a smudge or two of mascara and dressed in a one-piece suit that put all the best curves on show.

A Silver Shadow awaited us downstairs. The only other time I'd ridden in a Rolls-Royce, it had been Howard's; this was Uncle Yan's. His uniformed chauffeur drove us to some vast pile on the Peak. A butler glanced Jo up and down and then we were in.

Almost a racial mirror image of Ron's all those years ago, this party was full of those who were creating the new Hong Kong. Hong Kong people have never considered ostentation a sin and enough gold and gems were on show to fund a war on a small kingdom. Uncle Yan was stopped by a woman – a *tai-tai* by the hallmark hairspray hairdo and haute coiffure – who was wearing on her wrist something so encrusted with diamonds that I had no inkling that it was a wristwatch until Uncle said: 'Nice watch. A Piaget?'

Legal George was there, too, horn-rimmed spectacles reflecting the general glitter. Hong Kong's a small place and it turned out his firm had handled the legal aspects of Yan's listing. A night with the great and the glamorous was amongst his rewards. He and Jo started chatting, drifted off, and I found myself alone.

'Mister Price?' I heard the sucking sound of a vacuum.

'Eric?'

He was dressed in a dinner jacket. Rather than being smart, it looked as if it had a coat hanger inside it suspending both him and the suit. His collar was two inches too wide, his bow tie was not only a clip-on, but was clipped on askew.

'I wasn't expecting to see you,' I said. 'Hello.'

'My uncle invited me.'

Legal George, of course.

'Well anyway,' I said, scanning the horizon for other people to talk to. 'It's good to see you.' My scan detected no one but Jo, who was chatting to George, albeit in a jerky, forced way. I was about to rescue her when there was a swish by my side.

'Remember Venus?' asked Eric.

Her dress billowed out at the shoulders, gathered in at her waist and out again at her hips to come down to her knees. The material was of shimmering black and white stripes, vertical and wide, which extenuated her figure while emphasising the glow of her skin and her hair; a wide red belt at her waist and red stilettos completed the picture.

She smiled at me and the party chatter was banished as a waft of her perfume carried me away on a magic carpet, as a rhapsody floated its way up my larynx.

'Ah, um—' The rhapsody jammed up against an obstruction. My mouth opened and closed like a goldfish's swimming a four-minute mile.

'Stanley,' she said, and extended a hand.

My own jerked out. Her hand in my palm was like warm silk. Part of me registered how small it was, yet how strong was her grip. 'Ve-Ve-Venus?' I Ma-Ma-Martin-MacIntoshed. 'How nice to see you.' I cringed inwardly at my own cliché. I was a man who could proposition a woman from forty paces with a raised eyebrow, charm her with exotic tales laced with subtle innuendo and have an assignation before hors d'ouvres. Yet here I stood, struck dumb in the face of perfection.

'Hey,' an American accent came out of nowhere. 'Venus Lim, is that you? This is so wild. . . .'

All of a sudden, he was between me and her, I facing his back. Another joined and another, a wall of brimming bonhomie, wide-shouldered and butch, American football types cracking jokes and desperate to impress – 'Berkeley' this, 'Harvard' that and 'Chuck here, a senior partner already.' She smiled, a small frown crinkling her brow as she nodded. I was about to beat a retreat to Jo when a startled, apprehensive expression flitted across her face, a fleeting mixture of panic and fear.

Over her shoulder, I saw Jo, now standing alone, awkward,

abandoned and out of place: ostentation and glamour were not for her. Yet Venus's eyes were on mine and, before I knew it, I'd spotted a gap in the scrum. I inserted a hand, an elbow, a shoulder. 'Excuse me,' the rest of me followed. I offered my forearm. 'Your Uncle George asked me to find you.'

It's the military bearing. Venus looped her hand under my arm, rested it there with a stroke of silk on steel and I swept her away before they had time to react.

She looked up and I down. Our eyes met and we laughed. The moment stretched out: the glowing whites of her eyes, the slight upwards curl of her eyelashes, the half-crescents of her eyebrows; the dark maroon of her lips, the pink of her tongue; a sound like chimes as she laughed, these all etched themselves on my mind.

A sudden clatter of tinkling glass brought us back to planet Earth. Jo still stood there, alone. I deposited Venus with Eric.

'Early night?' I asked Jo.

'Not your usual type,' she said, nodding at Venus and forcing a brave little smile.

Hong Kong is all about who you know, and Luke was in law enforcement. He made a phone call or two and arranged for an informal chat in the police mess. The booze is cheap there, which would go some way to explaining why so many policemen were drunk so much of the time. The inspector in charge of Jo's case was sober, however.

'His word against hers,' he told me. 'He says she slipped.'

'Have you read the doctor's report? Seen the state of my flat? There was a coil of hair in the bathtub with her scalp still—'

'No need to shout.' He took a sip of his beer. 'I know it may be difficult for you to accept, but this type of thing happens a lot. A girl takes a man home, consents, decides it was a mistake and calls it rape. No, Mr Price, listen. With the victim's promiscuity, the defence would have a field day. Were you there? Are there any witnesses? From the point of view of getting a jury verdict, there isn't a chance.'

'Where does that leave her?'

'What about the possibility that she's lying? Do you have any idea what happens to sex offenders in prison?'

I all but threw my beer in his face.

'Mr Price, if he's scum, sooner or later we'll get him for something and, believe me, when we do, we'll get him good and proper. But for now, this case is closed.'

Hong Kong rules: I'd see about that.

Jo and I slept in different rooms. Her body was healing, but she still lived with a mixture of guilt, fear, self-repulsion and anger. I did my best to turn over a new leaf and rekindle the flame, but there were telephone calls at ungodly hours with Axel in America and other clients both there and in England and Europe, and a quick bite at the club became a bite and a pint, two pints and more, snooker and then the seedier haunts of the city.

'Stanley, it's alright. I understand. But I'd rather you brought them back than I lie awake worrying where you've got to.'

So I stayed home, to appear gritty-eyed at breakfast. Jo thought I lay awake squirming with unrequited desire.

I was. But it wasn't for her.

I tried not to remember the way Venus's radiant eyes had sought out mine in her moment of panic, tried to dismiss the touch of her hand on my forearm as I'd swept her away, tried to discount that moment when we'd stopped and we'd shared an innocent giggle at my audacity.

That second meeting with Venus had stifled the spark

with dynamite. *Rubbish*, I'd remonstrate with myself. I was misreading the signs, making a romance out of an encounter, mistaking an incident for interest. Yet, also, in the wee hours, she came to me in my dreams, naked – save for the red belt and stilettos, so it wasn't all bad – and yet I resisted until we were wed. I imagined children, a flaxen-haired Stanlette and a kink-nosed Venusy.

Never once had I contemplated children with Jo.

I turned up in the office and functioned – 'Mr Price, you were saying?' – 'Sorry, Stella. Daydreaming.' I processed orders, allocated tasks and cracked the whip. I arrived home to find Jo, small and vulnerable, curled up on the couch; I'd cook her a meal or gently cajole her to come out of the flat.

'You seem so distant.'

'Trouble at the office,' I'd say.

'Tell me.'

But there was nothing to tell her. A moulding gone wrong, an order misdelivered, a customer had run off with the goods. All part of the rough and tumble of business and nothing Jo hadn't heard before.

'Germin's started drinking again,' I tried, thinking of his late arrival and un-Teutonic breaking of wind at Sonny's.

'He never stopped. You just didn't see it. Or didn't want to.'

And we'd snuggle and cuddle and go to our separate rooms, she with her sleeping pills and I with a resolution to set aside my puerile nocturnal fantasies.

They refused to be set aside.

'Your friend has an exemplary eye for detail,' I told John.

John's friend had prepared diagrams for our instruction booklets and, though my own efforts had been quite competent – stylish, even – those of his friend were splendid: no room for doubt about which end the business one was. There was, however, something a little stilted in the portrayal of the receiving orifice. I couldn't quite put my finger on it. Abstract? Tasteful?

I pushed the thought to one side as John leant back in the chair and commenced a digital inspection of his nose. This, I had come to learn, presaged announcements of Delphic profanity.

'I'm concerned,' he said. 'The vibes here are bad, man. Very bad. I mean I just have this. . . .'

'Premonition?' I tried.

'No. Nothing religious. Just something. . . .' he waved his hands, stuck for words.

'Is it me? The company?'

'Don't know. I mean, I really don't know. Don't pressure me, yeah?'

'No problem. Stay,' I found the word, 'cool.'

'Uhhh,' said the voice on the telephone. It was three in the morning. 'I want to come.'

'In your mouth.' I whispered, so as not to disturb Jo. Silly, as she was out cold with pills.

'I like it when you talk dirty.'

'Let me put my big cock in your pussy.'

Buzz.

We seemed to be coming to an understanding. I wondered how she'd react to our new instruction leaflet. I still couldn't quite work out what it was about the depiction of—

'Gently,' the voice urged.

'Call from America,' I told Jo at breakfast. 'Time zones. Damn inconsiderate.' Silly, as she'd slept through the lot.

It's handy what one picks up in that great recruiter of low life, the army. Low life is, if nothing else, predictable. It frequents certain places, certain pubs. Pubs where the beer is cheap and the music loud. The Chinese do their public drinking in restaurants, so there were no more than a dozen pubs – plenty of nightclubs, dance halls and outright brothels, but few actual pubs – in the whole town. Those on the island were decent; those in Tsim Sha Tsui were hell holes, their table tops sticky with stale beer and the taps never cleaned.

Never go for the tourists. They're always in groups, full of curiosity and cheer. No: dress cheap – the clothes will be ruined – and find the solitary man, nursing a beer in a glass with no condensation because it's been there so long that it's warm. Look for the cheap cigarettes, the dirt under the fingernails. Do not sidle up, but approach like a man with a business to be there. Take the seat next to his – which will always be empty because no sane man would take it. Drink half of your own pint and:

'Quiet night?'

'Yeah.'

'Been 'ere long?'

'A while.'

'Me, just got 'ere a couple of days back,' I said. Voice training in Cockney didn't number amongst Sharon's talents as such, but our relationship had gone far enough beyond the physical – just – for words to come into play.

I'd piqued his interest. 'Where you staying?'

I named Sonny's squalid flea pit as I knew he was staying elsewhere. 'But not as a paying guest,' I added.

'No?'

'Nah. Picked up this Swedish bird in India. She thinks I'm mad about her. Am'n all. She pays my 'otel and food. Fucks like a rabbit on 'eat. Put me on to this great way to earn a quick bob.'

'Oh yeah?'

'Don't know if I should tell you.'

Of course I told him – and five days later, sure enough, the phone rang.

'Nitric?' said Germin.

'None other.'

'They got him.'

'Did he resist his arrest violently?'

'How did you know?'

Hong Kong rules: 'I did my research.'

'Research?'

'Yes, Germin. That's why *I* am here and you are there. I gave the police identikit to the proprietor of a certain backpacker's hostel, asked him to make enquiries at his competitors and so was able to track down a chump to be detained by the good customs and immigration officers of Korea. A chump with a past. Of beating women. A certain woman. Please see the word gets to him.'

There was a pause on the line, an intake of breath. 'This,' said Germin, 'I shall be delighted to do.'

We said goodbye and I sat in the empty office, surrounded by the halo of my own devious brilliance. I spun around in my swivel chair and said to the vacated desks: 'Don't ever mess with Stanley Featherstonehaugh Price.'

The doorbell went.

It couldn't be, could it? They wouldn't bail him out so soon? Even if they did, he was in Korea. And I'd been so very careful to act out my part: there was no way he could trace me to here.

I laughed, a strained he-haw in the darkened office. Barely seven o'clock. What had I to fear?

I steeled myself and went to the door. It was glass: whoever was outside could see me on the inside. But it was locked after office hours and, if it was the scumbag who'd raped Jo, I'd be able to make it to the phone before he broke the door down.

I stopped in mid-pace.

'Hello, Venus,' I said.

'You remember me?' She smiled; the sun shone in the gloom. 'Is Eric here?'

'He left a little while ago. Was he to meet you?'

'He said he would.'

'Do come in. I'm sure he won't be long.'

'Too trouble.'

'Too *much* trouble – and it is anything but.'

She smiled again, this one a shy smile. Oblivious to the chorus of angels that burst into song, she sashayed past me and into the office. I realised she didn't wear perfume: the aroma was her.

'It's a shame we've never had the chance to speak with each other,' I said. 'There always seems to have been so much happening.'

She smiled once again. *Jo!* came a voice in my head.

'Venus? It's a lovely name,' I said in spite of myself as I led her to my office and ushered her into a chair – the one that John didn't sit at, which I suspected ought to be burnt out of hygiene concerns.

'Thank you,' she said.

'Did you choose it yourself? Your name, I mean.'

She replied slowly this time, choosing her words with care, trying to be correct rather than fast. 'Eric told me that Venus is the goddess of love.'

'Indeed she is.'

We smiled at each other.

'What do you do, Venus?'

'I want to be a painter.'

'Of houses? Landscapes? Portraits?'

'I prefer the Impressionists, but I want to paint abstracts.'

'Want to be? So you're not yet?'

'Soon.'

We smiled at each other again. She had the poise, but her hips were narrow and her legs were thin. A discomfiting possibility was dawning.

'Do you live with your family?' I asked.

'Yes.'

In crowded Hong Kong, they all did until they got married – and often after.

'But I want to leave soon. When I finish school.'

I stifled a choke. I remembered the old woman near the base in the army days and the morning I woke up to the sight of two children at the end of the bed. I never could tell the age with Asian women – 'How old are you?'

'Eighteen—'

Thank goodness.

'—next year.'

White-knuckled, I gripped the arms of my chair. I was alone in an office – an office full of sex toys – with a seventeen-year-old. Half my age. And Eric! My junior by only two or three years. What was he thinking?

'Is there anything wrong?'

'I . . . I thought you were older.'

'What does your company make, Mr Price?'

'Stanley, please.' No. Call me Mister Price. Sir. Your Highness. 'Um nothing much. We're just traders. Plastics. Toys.'

'Like the ones I drew the pictures for? The educational ones that Eric showed me? Are you alright, Mister— Stanley?'

'You . . . you did the pictures?'

'You didn't like them?'

'They were—' It struck me: that was what was amiss about the diagram of the vagina. It depicted plastic, not flesh. '—splendid.' I suppressed a sigh of relief that the diagram wasn't of the real thing. 'Super. I mean excellent. The best.'

She smiled.

Help.

'Mister Price, do you mind if I practise my English with you? You speak very clear—'

'Clearly.'

'—very clearly. Next year I go to England to study and I worry my English is very bad.'

There was a clatter and rush of air out of the room created by Eric's arrival.

Seventeen and a bit. Eighteen soon. I'd thought she was twenty. Twenty-something at least. Much too young. It was improper.

'I'd be delighted,' I heard myself say.

The Daughters of Night were odd in their choice of oracle, but John's premonition was spot on.

The following Saturday was Jo's birthday. After work (a six-day working week was the norm in Hong Kong in those days) I opened the door, flowers under the elbow as I juggled keys and a cake.

The door opened. You could have cut the silence inside with a chainsaw.

'Happy—' The words died on my lips as I noticed the haversack and suitcase at her feet. 'Holiday?' I ventured. 'Splendid. . . .'

The words trailed off as she thrust a piece of paper at me. The writing was not hers and not mine, but a barely literate scrawl:

Jo,

Bet you think your clever. I'm in prison in Korea. Stitched up by your Mr Price. When I get out, I will kill him. You next.

'How could you?' said Jo as the letter fell from my hands.

'It's bluster,' I replied. 'He won't come after us.'

She shook her head, more in despair than anger. 'I didn't mean that. How could you stitch him up?'

'Connections,' I said, about to proudly explain—

'It's so wrong.'

'Oh.' She meant why, not how. 'He raped you.'

'You can't take the law into your own hands like this. When does it stop? No. You're not going to charm me with talk of "the next victim". Maybe he should have gone to jail, maybe not. But it should be in Hong Kong and after due process.'

If I'd ever loved her, it was in that moment. All the fire, the principles, the fury. 'They – the police – they—' I floundered.

'Maybe I led him on. I did lead him on. I don't know.'

'A woman's "no" is a no.'

'Stanley.' She came to me, the tears coursing down her cheeks, her lips pursed, her bosom heaving. 'I know you were trying to do what you thought was right and I know that what I'm about to tell you will hurt you, but I've thought about it a lot. . . .'

The Fates, the jealous Fates. Just as I'd overstepped the line when I'd taken on my reptilian sidekick in the Factories Inspectorate and Lily had left me, this time I'd trespassed by stitching up the scumbag. And now, at the moment I'd realised how special, unique and wonderful Jo was, they'd taken her from me.

'I have a flight to catch,' she concluded.

Ring ring.

'Let me—'

Ring ring.

'Stanley: Goodbye.'

The door shut behind her. I picked up the phone:

'Come in my mouth,' came the voice.

The knot in my stomach of tension and guilt that had been there since I'd first met Venus at the staff party: that knot was no longer there.

'On your hair, all over it,' I shouted in glee.

Now I could shout. Now that the Fates had delivered.

Chapter 7

'TELL ME ABOUT YOURSELF,' I started. Only Venus had little to tell. She wanted to paint. (John denied all knowledge of her, by the way. Just said that he had given the diagrams to Eric. Who had a friend. Man.) Her father owned a trading company; she lived in Stanley, on the south side of the island, with umpteen sisters, brothers and other relatives. She told me their names; I looked at my watch. It had taken fifteen minutes, with corrections, to get through that.

She smiled and a voice in my head clamoured *Get out while there's time*. It was not what she said, but the way that she said it, it was something that transcended common interests and small talk; it was something shared, unsullied and pure; uplifting, unselfish and bright.

'What hobbies do you have?'

She wanted to paint.

'Any sports?'

No.

'You won't earn much painting, you know.'

'I not care. I—'

'I *don't* care, not "I not care." '

'My English so bad.'

Was she threatening tears? A sudden rush of compassion enveloped me, the urge to take her in my arms and comfort her. 'That's why you're here,' I stuttered. 'Just keep at it and you'll improve. I had to learn it once, too.'

She was looking at me.

'What do you think of the cricket?' I tried.

'Ask Ah-Ping to deliver this,' I commanded the latest of our secretaries, the delectable Stella having been talent-spotted and become a *kung fu* movie starlet – the improbable becomes mundane in Hong Kong.

The secretary looked at me, uncomprehending.

'Ah-Ping, the messenger.'

'He doesn't work here any more.'

Messengers came and went: one had turned up fresh to the job one morning and had never been seen after lunch the same day. 'What happened this time?'

'He won on the stock market,' came the reply. 'Rich now. Never come back.'

'Won?'

She named a sum: six times what my little empire made in a year. 'Traded margins,' she explained to my drop-jawed response and, on seeing me unenlightened, launched into a long explanation that would have left a merchant banker (this was a decade before the industry re-invented itself as investment banking) gasping for air.

'How much?' I repeated my question.

She repeated her answer.

It seemed to happen to everyone but me.

'It's goddamn motherfucking late and I do not like late.'

'Axel, for once—'

As I listened to him vent his spleen, I was thankful that he and not I was paying for the call. It would have cost half the amount without the expletives.

'You fuckin' listening?'

He hadn't run out of steam yet. 'Bad connection,' I said, to let him get it out of his system.

Another tirade of Biblical proportions came down the line and, like one of the those pathetic creatures who apologises when the trains are running late, I explained to him that we were working hard to make sure the dildos would run on time and could he please bear with us while we rectified the system—

'Rectify my fucking ass.'

Which offered interesting surgical possibilities.

The army left me an early riser for life and Hong Kong people, who drift in after 9:30, eat breakfast at the desk, and don't get up to marching speed until after lunch, are anything but, so I was accustomed to having the office to myself first thing. However, John lay waiting in ambush. He flopped down in the chair on the other side of my desk. So disaffected was he that his finger didn't even venture nosewards.

'Good morning, John?'

He stared through me. More unusual yet. Staring at me, mostly with hostile intent, was normal, but through me? He hadn't done himself an injury with the new cock rings for the Koreans, had he?

'Man. . . .' came a melodramatic sigh.

Even by our standards, the conversation lacked a certain élan. I picked up and started to correct one of the letters the typing of which Stella's replacement was responsible for.

'God,' he said. 'How can you think of work at a time like this?'

'The club bar doesn't open for another four hours.'

'I mean, man. . . .'

'What is it?'

'Don't you read the newspapers? I mean, this. . . .'

I did read the papers – but just from the back, starting with sports and normally losing interest about the cartoons – so had missed the headline: *Superstar Shot Dead in New York*. Even on a good day, few combat zones can hold a candle to that fine city; I was about to head for the inner pages when I noticed a photograph under the headline. Long hair. Round spectacles. Thin. A member of some pop band. John Lennon.

I breathed a sigh of relief: John's bad vibes, his premonition were explained. It wasn't the company, it was just one late shipment. And some pop star was dead.

I'd have done well to remembered the date of another murder, Julius Caesar's: the Ides of March.

John aside, the newspaper was the inspiration I needed. There's only so far the rules of cricket and the state of the national team can advance one's relationship with a young lady who has no interest in either, but I now had a source of topics for our bi-weekly conversations.

'What do you think of this?' I asked, referring to some chap who had mounted the dunghill that is communist politics. 'Deng—' I twisted my mouth around the letters '—Xiao ping.'

She giggled, a free, innocent giggle, her body vibrating like no seventeen-year-old's should, and, as I gripped the armrests of my chair like the vertiginous to a trapeze, she corrected me: 'Not say like this. *Shee-ow* ping, not *Eks-ee-ow.*'

Once my pulse had stopped hammering in my ears and she had completed an explanation of the violence our alphabet suffers at communist hands – 'x' pronounced 'sh' and 'q,' 'ch,' for goodness' sake – we got back on topic.

'I don't trust those communists. My father came from Indonesia after the liberation—'

'Revolution. There is nothing liberating about communism.'

'—revolution. He wanted to help them. He is very proud to be Chinese.'

'Structure, Venus. You must decide what you want to say before you say it.'

Her hand went to her lips in sudden distress.

'Let's write it down,' I said.

My father, she started. But Chinese are taught to grip pens differently from us: we hold them between the last joints of our index, forefinger and thumb at almost the nib, while the Chinese hold them with the index finger almost completely encircling the shaft, pushing that against the outside of the first joint of the middle finger, while the thumb rests on top of the arrangement, with the effect that the pen is gripped a full couple of inches up from the page. I'm sure it works for Chinese characters, but I wasn't having it with the Latin alphabet and certainly not with my fountain pen.

'No, like this,' I said.

She tried it. The pen went flying. She giggled.

I retrieved the object, came round to her side of the desk and – 'Do you mind?' – manipulated her fingers into position. Only – 'Sorry' – we were both right-handed, which meant I had to stand behind her to place my right hand on hers.

Her body was warm in the cup of my torso. As my right hand guided hers in a large letter V then e-n-u-s, my unoccupied left hand wavered between a gentle grip on her shoulder, the back of the chair or, where I forced it to go, the small of my back.

Her upturned face when she'd finished, her lips so close that her breath tickled my cheek—

'Are you alright?' she asked as I sat.

I, who never blushed, took a long swallow of water in

the hope of forcing the crimson flush from my face. 'Never b-b-better,' the stammer came out, my knuckles comfortably white once again on the arms of my chair.

The story was this. Venus's father was a third-generation Chinese living in what was then the Dutch East Indies and is now Indonesia. Being Chinese, the Dutch hated him for being yellow and thus rich, and the Javanese for being industrious and thus rich. To the extent that I could grasp this, the Dutch considered Chineseness, and the Javanese industry, unfair.

He became irked by this (Venus had difficulty with the pronunciation of 'irked,' so I taught her 'cheesed off' with a caution not to use it at school), and, to add to the unpleasantness, Indonesia was in the mid-sixties in the throes of becoming independent which, for reasons seeming no better than that the opportunity had arisen, involved the slaughter of such large numbers of Chinese that killing one had become on par with swatting a bug.

Daddy Venus contacted some relative in China and volunteered to pop back to the motherland and help with its reconstruction. Rousing stuff: he sold the business before marauding Javanese torched it, chucked the family into a boat and set sail for China *via* Hong Kong.

They departed one week before, and arrived in Hong Kong one week after Chairman Mao unleashed the Great Proletarian Cultural Revolution, found out the relative had omitted to mention that he was a fully-signed-up member of the Communist Party, decided that patriotism had a time and place, and that the time was not ripe and the place not the motherland.

'Do you think you'll go back? To Indonesia or China?'

'Hong Kong is my home.'

'You see?' I said. 'English works so much better with verbs.'

She was bright and getting the hang of it, and the smile she gave me was reward enough for the night.

'Bloody Poms,' Yan said, fresh back from Australia. I dreaded the day he visited Scotland: 'Hoots mon the nights are fair drawin' in' and I'd have to stuff a butt plug into his mouth. 'You know the amount of duty the bastards want to charge me for importing bits of fucking plastic?'

'You still make the stuff?'

He looked at me. Askance, one could say.

'Uncle, I don't mean to be rude, but the quality is not what it used to be. We're getting complaints. And shipments are turning up late.'

Nothing.

'You know what we make,' I said. 'And the Americans are very keen on litigation.'

Still nothing.

'I know property is easy money, I know the stock market's booming, but I'm not the only one who relies on this stuff to make a living.'

He burst out crying. I had to steady myself on my chair. A few words of criticism, spoken with a gentle if firm frankness, and he was weeping.

'Stanley mate,' he stuttered through his tears. 'It just ain't easy.'

'No please, I'm—'

He waved a hand. 'It's all going tits-up.'

'Listen, it doesn't mat—'

Once I'd calmed him down, it turned out the problem was three-fold: first, he ran his entire plastics production off a single injection-moulding machine, and that machine was running at capacity.

'Buy another,' I said.

This, he couldn't do, because – second – he was borrowed

to the hilt in the property market. To compound things – third – the individual bits of plastic that came out of the machine needed to be filed, trimmed and assembled to produce the finished products. The industry norm was for factories to distribute kits to the masses, mostly those in shanty towns and public housing, who would be paid piecework rates for their filing, trimming and assembling – so there was family Wong having dinner, with dad, mum and the children shovelling rice into their mouths, while the plastic testicles, penises and the other intricate and intimate components of Price's Plastics' vibrators lay in wait, neatly stacked to one side. This was all very well, but Hong Kong had a shortage of labour and the miserly rates Uncle Yan paid were no longer enough to induce family Wong to assemble the toys.

'Pay them more,' I said.

This, he couldn't do, because he would savaged by his peers in the industry – or so he insisted until I pushed the point and he confessed he wasn't having it on principle.

'If you paid them more, they could afford the houses you're building,' I said.

Anger, resentment, confusion flickered across his face. For a moment I feared he would ram a chopstick down my throat.

And then: 'Stanley, I think you've just made me a billion dollars.'

Which he did – he bumped up the wages and people now had enough money to buy the tiny apartments he built them. And, to this day, all the thanks that I got is the nod that followed that moment.

'In control I am being,' Germin said, fully Teutonic in the order of vords. 'It happens again. Along the road I am walking and a bank they are robbing. Bullets all over the place.'

Robbery, along with kidnapping, whoring and incomprehensible writing, was a solid Chinese tradition. (Food was more than mere tradition; the Cantonese live to eat.) But Germin did seem to be making a habit of this.

'Sober I am,' he declared. He gestured at a fellow standing close by. 'This Peter is be—' he caught the word order 'Peter is an accountant.'

Peter the accountant was tall, thin and gaunt. But, when he offered his hand to shake, I was caught out by his smile. It was as wide as his face and his teeth were massive. 'You support Nottingham Forest?' he asked, his accent Liverpudlian: 'Not'n'am Forest'.

I'd no idea about his accounting ability, but he knew his football to a T. Hired.

Eric approached. The toy in his hands had a jagged spike, which would bring pleasure to no woman, sticking out of the middle.

'It's the plastic,' he said, verbs, articles, the whole nine yards. Venus must have been passing on pointers. Eric: 'This dildo.' Venus: 'No, this *is a* dildo.'

'What can we do about it?'

'Change suppliers. We make in China much more cheaper.'

'Much chea— never mind. China's closed.'

No longer. It not being a Venus day and with nothing much happening in the world of sports, I'd summarily binned the paper. I retrieved it. It transpired that Deng had decreed that Shenzhen, a cluster of hovels amidst rice paddies and pig farms, just across the border and behind that damned fence, was now open for business.

'It'll never work,' said I with a snort.

I was becoming worried about Uncle Yan. 'You've lost a lot of weight recently,' I said at one of our regular lunches.

'Don't be ridiculous,' he said, back to stockbroker-belt English after his nasty bout of Australian. 'Fit as a fiddle. Ask my new friend.' He gestured towards a woman entering the restaurant.

No wonder he was losing weight. His latest was two inches taller than I, had a bustline like a battle cruiser and a face adorned with an expression of utter vacuity. Tight-fitting and shiny was the latest fashion: a series of other male diners suffered whiplash as she breezed past their tables, their womenfolk rolling their eyes in resigned dismissal at their husbands' unconcealed lust.

Uncle Yan said something to her and she directed at me a smile with the emotional punch of a damp rag.

Her job, as was the practice amongst floozies of wealthy Chinese, was to pour tea, pick up morsels with chopsticks, deposit them in Yan's bowl and otherwise to keep her mouth shut. This, she did with aplomb, although once in a while I caught a glance that suggested the vacuity was but a mask. Oblivious, Uncle Yan rattled on about the rising price of property and other injustices the rich have to suffer.

'So you'll invest in China?' I asked. 'Cheap labour there, my staff tell me. Deng and all.'

He gave me a withering glower: 'Have you forgotten your history? They'd lock me up if I were to step foot in the place.'

I smiled. I hadn't been keen, either. Though I wished he'd buy a second moulding machine.

Battle-cruiser boobies said something.

'She says you have a nice smile. I think she may fancy you.'

I pooh-poohed him but, on the way out, swallowed my words when she slipped me her phone number.

Only in Hong Kong, I reflected as I sat with Peter the accountant, waiting for Germin, could one find a Chinese Scouser who supported Nottingham Forest, who could barely stitch together a sentence in Cantonese and who consistently won our ten-dollar bets. His knowledge of football was encyclopaedic and I'd learnt rather fast not to take him up on the outcome of even major past matches, let alone obscure second- and third-division games.

Peter's crowning moment came, however, a few months after Christmas. Back then, he'd bet a substantial sum that Liverpool would win the league. Easy to say now, but at the time, no one gave them a chance.

'Shouldn't we look at the accounts?' I asked, handing him a large-denomination note, when Liverpool came in at the top.

'It's all mine now anyway,' he said with a laugh. Then, just for a moment, an expression of triumph flitted across his face. At the time, I supposed it was the bet. 'What about the European Cup?' he covered it up.

'Ten dollars and ten only,' I said. 'Against them.'

Venus was *hors de combat*. I could wait, would await, her coming of age. At some point I'd have to detach Eric, but he was the finest engineer in the business, so stabbing him in the back would have to wait, too. With Jo gone, however, I found the flat rather empty.

'I'm going to move house,' I told Venus.

'Where to?' she asked, and inflicted on me another of her devastating giggles. Why couldn't she be twenty years old? Eighteen and a half?

'Don't know. Any ideas? Repulse Bay?' I tried a pun. 'Stanley?'

She was leaning over the desk, her chin cradled in her hands. She reached forwards and touched the back of my hand: 'Repulse Bay is nicer.' She looked up at me and smiled: 'Better for swimming.'

The electric touch of her finger; the thought of her in a swimsuit—

Margaret Thatcher, staring up from the front page of the paper, came to the rescue. A sudden vision came of the Iron Lady with her steel hairdo, now with a dildo strapped to her forehead. My pulse wandered down to under two hundred, 'I'll get a flat there and you can come over to swim,' I heard myself say.

Doc had had a bad morning. He'd needed three stiff ones to settle the delirium tremens, and two after those to get the colour back to his cheeks. When I arrived at the club for lunch he was, according to the barman, on his eighth.

'Repulse Bay,' Doc said in the tone of an officer to a soldier contemplating desertion. 'Why?'

'Fresh air. Sea breeze. Anyway, we're half way there since they moved us from Central.' The government was extending the MTR, the underground railway, and the club had been moved uphill to make way for a new station.

'Miles from the nearest damn pub.'

'Have car will travel,' I replied.

'You're too pissed to drive half the time,' he slurred.

Doctors and women. I never will understand them.

'I may drink now and then—' he started.

'*Freuden.*'

We looked at each other.

'*Freude, schöner Götterfunken. . . .*'

Oh no. Though a fine tenor.

'What brings you here at lunch time, anyway?' he asked.

'I was going to go over some figures with Germin.'

'Now there's a man with a problem.'

No longer the slightest pretence voz he having, not even

the vord order trying. So I joined him for one, we ended up in our old haunts and didn't talk a word about back-packers, tickets or the uses to which Korean housewives put our toys.

'Like the old days,' he said with a broad smile as we stood in the first light of dawn eighteen hours later.

My own smile was my answer.

John sat at his desk, listless, as he had since his idol had been murdered. I thought it odd that the death of some hippy pop musician from the other side of the planet and a culture alien to his own, should so affect him. I wondered, as I often had over the years, if he was one of those who believe themselves to be someone else.

'The instructions for the twelve-inch double-ender are needed this week,' I said.

'It's all so pointless. Life. Death. All that stuff.'

'Do you have any plans, John? Marriage, children, career?'

'Convention. Don't believe in it. The whole marriage thing, like ownership.'

'It may be convention, but a child needs a secure environ-ment.' God, I sounded like Emma's parents.

'You sound like my parents.'

Ouch. But had that throwaway comment contained a deep truth?

Venus skipped into the office. Before I could sit at my desk, she grabbed my forearm with both of her hands and looked up at me, half-child, half-adult and fully adorable. For a moment her eyes locked on mine and it was all I could do not to bend down and kiss her. She giggled and gave my arm a playful tug.

'You've been accepted?' I asked.

The grin on her face was answer enough.

'Well,' I said, 'I think we should celebrate.' But Eric was lurking and put paid to any rejoicing.

Aspirations, joy, the hope of youth: it all came back to me that long night as I lay contemplating her admission to the Royal Academy of Arts. I'd acquiesced to my domi-natrices, the Fates, in the hope that my own dreams of exploring the world would be the reward for my willing submission. Yet, they freed me of Emma only to ensnare me here, where, when I had money, I was tied down by Lily, and when I had the leisure to leave, I was broke. Then there was Jo and the plastics and I wasn't one to leave my customers and Uncle Yan in the lurch, so was in a gilded cage of my own making. Only there wasn't much gilt.

Venus and I were of a separate kind. I felt a link with her, a bond that went far beyond mere sexual attraction. Where other youths had shifting dreams of fads and fashions, fuelled by television or magazines, dancing one week and nursing the next, my dreams had remained constant even if unfulfilled. For her, likewise, it had always been painting.

I rolled over in bed, covered in sweat. The rainy season was beginning, the air was turgid, the temperature nudging a hundred. I got out of bed and walked to the window. On the other side of the harbour – I hadn't done anything about moving to Repulse Bay – the lights of Kowloon twinkled under the mass of dark cloud that obscured the stars. The dull roar of the city echoed up. In the distance, headlights twinkled, orange streetlights glowed, neon signs flashed. The tourist agencies entice with 'Come to colour-ful Hong Kong' but in the figurative rather than the literal sense. Yet, even from my apartment in the Mid-Levels, with Kowloon a few miles distant over the harbour, I could make out the red, yellow and green of signs advertising Chinese restaurants, Japanese electronics, a thousand dif-ferent things that people buy, sell and make.

Not dildos.

I poured a whisky and glanced at the phone. It had been a while since my nameless companion had rung. At the peak of our strange affair it had been once, twice, sometimes more per week. I had no idea what her name was, or if she knew mine. Was she a bored housewife? A whore? Old, young, fat, thin, ugly, a stunner? She was whatever I wanted her to be and I, whatever she asked. Gentle, rough, caring, abusive: we'd been all of these to each other.

The Royal Academy. It was such an achievement. As I stood there, a strange feeling arose. Starting in the pit of my stomach, a glow radiated out, forcing my posture erect, my chest to swell.

The feeling was pride.

Chapter 8

I'D NEVER BEEN WITH AN ARTIST at work. Venus had set up her easel outside a tumbledown abandoned house in a village in the New Territories. I had driven most of the way, but we'd had to walk the last mile or so, I lumbering along under the weight of her easel and other materials, while she sauntered ahead in a pink tracksuit that was far too tight, without a drop of sweat showing.

The village was inhabited by a few ancient women who sported traditional wide-rimmed bamboo hats, black pyjamas and golden-toothed smiles. I think Venus must have been the youngest to enter the place in a decade: even during my time in the army, exploring with Forsythe, these villages were dying. In the New Territories, all residents had a full British passport as birthright, and most took full advantage. Peter, Germin's Scouser accountant, for one.

Venus painted away, so absorbed in her inner world that the outer ceased to exist. Yet she pulled that outer world through herself, as if through a strainer, and put the good bits on paper. I remained for long enough to be painted, was banished, so pottered about and recalled the sense of novelty Forsythe brought to all that he did. I'd vowed to remain sober around Venus so, unlike those days with Forsythe, the stall selling beer went unpatronised.

As I wandered down a lane of derelict houses, a sudden

image from my African childhood came to me: the plantation workers' houses, too, were tiny shacks, but unlike these deserted structures, those of my childhood had been full of colour and laughter, of the steady beat of gospel music, of the gleaming smiles of Jemima and her family. To take Venus there. . . .

I shook the smile from my face and looked up. For just a moment, the image of Zimbabwe still fresh in my mind, I saw something different from what lay before me. Instead of lush green, the hills appeared brown from the winter. The sky became the pale blue of a late spring afternoon. The path on which I stood was dun rather than grey; behind it lay the lighter tan of the fields and, behind those, the coffee colour of the brick houses. Interrupting the brownness was a ribbon of dark blue where a stream cut through the village.

I shook my head and the world again became green.

'Stanley.' Her eyes were no longer lost in her inner world. She smiled that Venus smile and I almost wept.

I had promised not to look until it was complete. I suppressed a gasp of astonishment. Her painting was almost exactly like the scene in my mind's eye, but with one exception. Balancing the browns and blues was a splash of colour: in a calculated contrast to the pop-band T-shirt and jeans of the day, the grey flannels, white shirt and red cravat of Stanley's jaunty casuals.

'It's perfect,' I said.

She was looking at me, expectant, her hand poised in front of her. A smile erupted of joy; she reached out with both hands and took my forearm, the touch of her fingers glancing yet urgent.

That's when I told her of Africa, of the spontaneous joy and lurking danger, the animism and deep Christian faith, of the indelible memories those early years left on me. And, as I spoke, the corners of her eyes creased in a smile or widened with wonder, amazement or shock; her mouth would start to open in a smile, or her lips would purse when I lost her in the language of reminiscence; the skin above the bridge of her slightly-kinked nose would crinkle and her nostrils would flare in empathy. When I told her of hippos spreading their dung, she giggled with a mixture of embarrassment and disbelief; when she had a question, her hand would reach out to touch my forearm – sometimes lingering for an instant longer than needed to catch my attention.

The sun dipped beneath the hills in the west. I picked up her easel and other materials and we strolled back through the lengthening shadows. We passed the journey in silence and I had her home at a respectable hour.

'Thank you,' she said.

I hadn't had such a joyful day since my childhood.

I had fallen out of the way of meeting new people. The cricket team of which I was part numbered, including reserves, eighteen; most were civil servants, lawyers, accountants and other professionals. I didn't see much of them away from the oval. My established drinking partners were – well – established. My customers constituted a crowd in which the individuals came and went but the crowd remained the same.

Hence, I find it mysterious that I cannot recall how I met General (retired) Samuel G. Foswitz or, according to his other name card, General (retired) S. George Foswitz. More mysterious yet, as he was a teetotaller.

Being a teetotaller is a novelty in the West; in colonial Hong Kong, it was an aberration. What else was there to do? No concerts, the local *kung fu* productions crowded out English films, and no one but no one read books. I

could have understood if he'd had some other compen-
satory vice – gambling or gimp suits – but, apart from a
heroic intake of cigarettes, he lived the life of a monk.

He was my height but cadaverous in build and with a
monk's pate of white hair; he had a beak nose that propped
up wire-framed square glasses. His accent had a twang from
the deep south of the US. Not some awful hillbilly, but a
drawl nonetheless, and he had a habit of prefixing stories
with 'Well, Stanley, as you know. . . .' which I most often
didn't. I suppose it was his way of getting attention, rather
in the manner of older composers who, to gain their
audience's attention at the beginning of a piece, would
launch into their tunes with a crash and a bang that had
nothing to do with the theme. (A Luke – Leukemia Pete –
item of trivia, by the way. Really quite interesting.) Anyway,
it must have worked because I remember half the rot that
General G. told me.

'Stanley? Or Featherstonehaugh?' he said on the phone,
pronouncing my name correctly. 'Samuel G. Foswitz.
Remember me?'

I didn't.

He mentioned some cocktail party and, 'After our conversation of that very pleasant evening, I got to thinking I
may have a little business I could be putting your way.'

It happened all the time. Nine times out of ten, they
wanted to sell me something. But I wasn't busy.

'Well, Stanley, as you know,' he told me when he came
to the office a few days later, 'before I joined the military,
I was at college and up there at Harvard. . . .' Having
dropped the name, he then proceeded to a rambling yarn
about an American missionary who'd escaped China
during the Japanese invasion in the mid-thirties, who'd
looked back down the Huangpu River as he fled the
country and 'he got to thinking that, after the goddamn

Nips went back to their own country, the Chinese would have nothing left to rebuild with.'

By this point, there was cigarette smoke down to the floor with no end in sight. On the pretext of summoning coffees, I stepped out for a quick breather. When I stepped back in, however, he ramped up the pace: 'As you know, a military pension ain't worth a goddamn in this day and age and that's why I came to you with this. It's not often I come across a man of your ability, Stanley, and they're ain't many folks in this town who've got your level of integrity to go with it.'

Once I'd wiped the spluttered coffee from my shirt, he continued: 'Now what I'm about to propose is that, as you know, the stock markets are booming, but the expats are on the outside looking in. So we're going to sell to them.'

Stock markets once more. I suppressed an inward groan. But I thought of Sally in the Factories Inspectorate all those years ago, the girl from the factory floor whose brother's friend had just made a killing, and of our messenger, Ah-Ping, who'd made more in two months than I did in a year. I thought of Uncle Yan's business philosophy: make a bundle in something, put it in property, and list the whole lot. Property in those booming days was beyond my reach, but the general's idea wasn't that I buy and sell shares on my own account, but rather to broker them.

For a horrid moment, I had a vision of Howard. Smiling.

'You make money when the market moves up,' General G. slipped in, 'and on the way down. Boy, do you ever clean up on the way down.'

I'd learnt my lesson: what the Fates put in my path was not mine to dispose. And so that is when, to my little empire of sex toys, cheap air tickets and smuggling, I added stockbroking. I don't know to this day which shames me most. The backpacker's travel, I think.

'Jesus goddamned Christ, Price, she was in surgery for two fuckin hours getting the bits out of her pussy.'

'Axel, good morning.'

'Whatchya gonna do about it?'

'Flowers?'

'Smart guy, huh? One more fuck up and we're through.'

He rang off without saying goodbye, but that, I'd learnt, was the American way. I put the receiver down and waited for the laugh to fade from my face, then phoned Uncle Yan's secretary.

'He's in hospital,' she told me.

'He can't be. I saw him the other day and he assured me he was fit as a fiddle.'

Silence roared down the line.

'Which hospital?' I asked.

'Cannot tell,' she said and rang off.

Venus laughed when she saw me.

'Where shall we meet?' I'd asked.

She had told me and said: 'Don't be late.'

I wasn't – never am – and neither was she.

'You look so strict,' she said.

Eric was late. 'I just wish he'd be punctual.' I wished he'd be absent.

It was hot and windless; humid, but not enough for a storm. Cumulus towered in the sky without moving. A few expats lay on the sand, beached morasses of flab, turning from grey to pink in the sun. A man wearing a minute pair of trunks swaggered out of the water, his gut swaying before him, his shoulders so red that they glowed. I hoped it hurt.

'He's ten minutes late,' I said. 'How can you stand it?'

'Ten minutes is nothing.'

She was standing beside me. She turned her head and smiled, and I felt a sudden moment of innocent delight that here, now, we were friends. Ten minutes late was ten minutes more with her to myself. The frown fell from my face. My eyes lighted on the Repulse Bay Hotel, a luxurious affair. I was on the point of inviting her in for a treat – they did a wonderful afternoon tea – but it was also a favoured venue where the gossiping if monied classes met their mistresses, concubines and lesser flings. There was a café over the road: I was about to suggest a tea there, but a bus chugged up, stopped, and, over the hiss of air brakes, I heard the hiss of a vacuum.

He half-walked and half-ran towards us, his arms by his side, palms facing backwards: 'Sorry I late Mister Price.'

He was dressed in trousers too large for him, his shirt was ironed by the mother with whom I assumed he still lived, his belt hung loose on his hips: groomed without being smart. I again was in my jaunty casuals. Venus wore a simple frock, ankle length, pleated and pastel pink. Her hair wasn't flattened down like Eric's, but bounced in glorious, shoulder-length curls.

I took a deep breath. Thought Thatcher and strap-ons.

As we trailed around Repulse Bay inspecting flats, I couldn't help but speculate on the nature of Eric and Venus's relationship. The diagram Venus had drawn depicted the toys themselves, but had little need to dwell on the anatomy. Nevertheless, she can't have been wholly unaware of the body parts they represented. Yet here they were, pawing each other in the manner of—

But wait. It was Eric who pawed, not she. When he held her hand, she didn't return his grip; when he put his arm around her waist, she moved a little away. And here, away from the office, it struck me that Eric was much older than her, almost enough to be a guardian rather than a boy-friend. He took her to school – she'd told me – every morning before work, and returned her home before nine on the evenings they went out. He had even hovered around the office during the English lessons until I asked him 'Would you rather I didn't help out?' after which he lurked outside.

Yet, with me, her touch was so ready.

We entered yet another flat. The lounge happened as soon as we opened the door. It was large and airy. To the back, it looked out over mountains verdant with foliage which, for a fleeting moment, recalled the army days. The front looked out over the bay.

'Hate it,' I said. 'Let's go.'

Venus had told me to say this as a ploy if I liked somewhere but wanted a better price. It didn't work. The agent quoted a price that was ludicrous and which I accepted without hesitation.

'You very bad negotiate,' said Eric when I took them for a celebratory dinner (not at the Repulse Bay Hotel and finished by eight thirty).

'I *am* a very bad *negotiator*,' I said. 'You must try a little harder.'

'No matter. You understanding.'

He had a point, I suppose.

'We have a small cash-flow problem,' said Germin, sober in his word order.

'Cash flow?' I asked.

'We must pay the salaries and the rent.'

'So, pay them.'

'We don't have the money.'

'I thought business was good.'

'Very. The Koreans love your dildos. More and more backpackers are coming to Hong Kong.'

'So . . . cash flow?'

'Ah,' he said. And explained that cash-flow was business-speak for money coming in versus money going out.

'And more went out than came in?'

Business had been good. Very good. There had been a large pile of cash in the bank. Peter the Scouser accountant had talked Germin into investing a chunk in the stock market. The markets knew no gravity in those heady times and soon the pile of cash was even huger, so they invested yet more.

In Peter's name.

'And Peter is. . . ?'

'Nowhere to be seen.'

I remembered Peter's momentary expression of triumph and 'It's all mine now,' when he'd relieved me of a few hundred dollars for a bet. It struck me: he hadn't been joking; he'd been confessing. And the bugger hadn't even paid the one and only bet I'd ever won against him (Liverpool had been knocked out of the European Cup early on).

'Of course I've informed the police,' Germin cut into my thoughts.

I needed money and dildos, fast. Uncle Yan had both. Where was the old bugger?

It was three in the morning. The telephone rang.

'I am sitting on a stool in the kitchen. It is upside-down and one of the legs is in my—'

'Let me be your chairleg.'

Must remember to give her the phone number of the new flat.

That triggered a thought.

She smiled at me. Her battle-cruiser boobies were trained upon me, her scarlet lipstick twinkled in the light. The perfect vacuity of her eyes inspired: nothing.

Having found the phone number she'd slipped me, I was on a mission. For it, I'd chosen tea at the Mandarin Hotel. Posh, but not overbearing.

'Delighted you could make it,' was my opening gambit.

'My English name Matilda,' she said. 'After the hospital.' There was one on the Peak by that name.

'How are you?' I enquired.

'Good. You?'

'How about Uncle Yan?'

'Not so good.'

'Dear me. Where is he?'

'It is secret.'

Knowing a girl's heart, I changed the conversation. 'Would you go to bed with me for a hundred dollars?'

'I'm not that kind of woman.'

'Two hundred?'

Matilda deliberated for a few seconds. The most remarkable transformation occurred. That carefully studied vacuity melted away. Her facial muscles became taut, her indifferent slouch mutated to a poised and matronly posture. 'Stanley,' she said, her vowels rounded and consonants articulated, 'a lady must have some principles.'

'We've already established those,' I said. 'Five hundred?'

Doc hadn't been seen at the club for almost a week. I employed Leukemia Pete's law enforcement skills to bully the address out of the membership secretary, flagged a taxi and knocked at his door.

His skin was a pallid yellow, the whites of his eyes were jaundiced. His movements were slow and small; he shuffled rather than walked, pausing for breath, clutching his side.

'You're looking well,' said Luke.

'Been under the weather.'

Why is it that doctors refuse with such venom to go and see one of their own profession? Luke and I sat there, pleading with him. He'd been putting back a bottle of whisky a day for forty odd years. Cod liver oil and a hot water bottle – well, it was now the middle of summer, but you get the idea – was not going to cure it.

'I'm alright, do you hear me?' he said. But the wheeze in his voice made a lie of his words.

'Look at yourself,' I said.

'It's the light.'

'If you're so fit, let's go for a walk,' Luke insisted. 'Socrates recommended it. Really quite—'

'Alright,' said Doc.

Doc's wardrobe was splendid: a dozen safari suits of identical cut. Clatters and bangs emanated from the bedroom as he changed.

'Maybe you're right,' he conceded, less than a dozen paces from the door of his flat. 'Let me pack. Collect me tomorrow.'

'Doc—'

'A night won't make a difference. Grant my medical knowledge at least a modicum of respect.'

'Oh-eight hundred hours?'

'Roger.'

'Stanley,' said Uncle Yan. 'How did you find me?'

'A little birdy told me.' The money was a means to an end: a little pillow talk unlocks most and it had unlocked Matilda – but Uncle Yan had no need to know.

The twinkle was still in his eyes, but his eyebags were heavy and blue. His five o'clock shadow was more of an eight o'clock smudge. Most of his chest was wrapped in bandages. His neck, once double-chinned, was a wiry tangle of sinew.

'I don't want to be seen in this condition. Trussed up like a goose before roasting.'

I'd come to beg, for money, for dildos. I'd rehearsed in my mind how to dissemble, to work around to the point. All of a sudden, none of it mattered; I told him the truth.

He smiled. 'Some of my sons and daughters were here earlier. I could see it in their eyes: they were already dismembering me. It's the first time I'd seen some in years. "Daddy,"' he parodied an American accent — he'd sent them all there for schooling — '"Are you comfortable? Is there anything we can get you?"' He shook his head and managed a bitter laugh that ended in a series of wheezes. 'I'm in bandages from my neck to my arse, down one lung and they ask if I'm comfortable. Of course I'm not bloody comfortable.'

He shook his head.

'If you think that's bad, you should see their mothers.' He laid back against the pillow. For a moment I thought he'd drifted off but, when he spoke, although he was no longer looking at me, he was addressing me. 'You're more of a son to me than any of them, and if you were one of them, I'd lie right back to you.' He eyed me from the corners of his eyes. 'Remember when I came over the fence to Hong Kong? You tried to catch me, didn't you?'

What could I say?

His gaze returned to the ceiling. 'From what Lily told me, I thought you would. That's why we paid the others to be caught by you.'

That moment of confusion from long ago came to me: not when we'd picked up the crowd, but when I'd first met him with Lily and realised that he hadn't been amongst those we'd picked up. He was cackling, too.

'Don't be embarrassed. It was your duty. We Chinese fear chaos above all. We like order and you British keep it. And

I wouldn't have trusted you otherwise. A man who'd betray his own country would have no problem cheating his friends. How much do you need?'

I told him and added, 'You see, I've—'

'If you need the money, you need it. It'll be with you tomorrow. And I've told the factory to fix the issues.'

'Thank you.'

'No need.'

He sighed.

'Shall I go now?' I asked. 'You look shattered.'

'Would you keep me company for a while? It gets lonely, you know.'

'Of course. Anything I can get you?'

'Don't mother me.'

I sat.

He said nothing for a while and I wondered if he'd drifted off, when the word 'Chocolate' rang in the air.

A sign above him said *Nil by Mouth*. I was about to remind him, but: 'Chocolate,' he repeated. 'That's what first brought me here. I was nine at the time, living in China, and a relative had joined us from Hong Kong. He gave me a bar of chocolate. It was the best thing I'd ever tasted. In China, the chocolate was brittle and tasteless, like cardboard. This was rich, smooth and tasty. Right then I decided.' He laughed, then winced with the pain. 'The money helped too, of course. . . .'

It was a strange thing. I'd known him all these years, yet it was only as he lay dying that we came to know each other. Before, it had always been business. Convivial but perfunctory. We'd shared a few jokes and the common bond of Lily was always in the background, but the public schoolboy in me had kept his distance and so too, it occurred to me as I sat by his side, had my awe of his sheer prowess at business. But – and my visits became part of my daily routine – what I knew of him was superficial.

I hoped I hadn't left things too late.

Luke and I pushed open the door of Doc's apartment.

His was the flat of an entrenched bachelor. No pictures on the wall, no ducks over the fireplace, the fridge void save for a row of eggs, a carton of milk and a pat of butter. The plates were stored on a rack by the sink and, judging by the layer of dust with which they were coated, had not seen use for many a week. The toilet seemed clean but, on closer inspection, there was grime around the edges of the floor and some mould on the grouting between the tiles.

He was in bed, on his back, dressed in a safari suit. His hair was washed and combed, he was shaven. His shoes lay by the bed, polished; his gold watch caught the sun's rays. The bed was made, the blanket tucked in and the sheet folded down; a glass of Bell's whisky stood on the bedside table, half-finished.

Two packed suitcases stood at the foot of the bed.

He'd gone on ahead.

General G. needed a 'flashy office, to wow people'. It was in Central, Hong Kong's imaginatively named central business district. Flashy was not the word, however, that sprung to my mind. Spotlights shone down on a goldfish tank. The Cantonese are wildly superstitious when it comes to numbers and eight is a good one, so eight goldfish swam in the tank. The name of the company was also in gold.

No, not flashy, nor even gaudy, but vulgar.

He'd moved fast and had already recruited some salesmen. They were white to a man – 'The expats are racists and won't trust a Chinese.' They wore ill-fitting suits and, at ten in the morning, there was a distinct whiff of alcohol – 'You got to take clients out and show them a good time.

And young guys can kick ass.' I recognised one from Sonny Chan's hostel – 'Give 'em a chance,' said General G. 'They don't know what can't be done.'

This was the official opening, at a specific time on an auspicious day in the Chinese calendar. A couple of monks, here to bless the opening, entered. We allowed them to move us to our designated positions: me first, then General G., then assorted others. An entire roast pig was delivered along with various other offerings. The smell of joss sticks filled the air and the head monk, dressed in grey and with the most ageless face I've ever seen on a man, chanted a blessing that to my ears sounded like a funeral dirge.

He had a string of worry beads. Half way through the ceremony, the string broke. Beads scattered, bouncing over the floor, rolling under the desk. The monk shook his head: this was a very bad omen.

General G. thought otherwise. He'd rounded up some hacks from the local rag: 'Great publicity,' he said as the hacks snapped away with their cameras. Sure enough, some wit used it in a column on the back page of the business section in the following morning's edition, and Fat Golden Finance was launched.

'Germin?' said Legal George. 'He's behind on his bar bill.'

So he'd stopped using the club and didn't know about Doc's funeral.

We found him in a bar in Kowloon, his bulk towering over a gaggle of tourists. His left hand gripped a bottle of champagne, his right, a Chinese meat cleaver. 'If the bottle not damaged is being,' he lurched, 'you pay. Otherwise, I pay.'

'Do you think they understand the bet?' asked George.

'Do you think he does?' asked Luke.

Germin swayed. A frown crumpled his brow. His eyes

pointed in different directions. He raised the cleaver. Before I could step forwards to stop him, there was a flash of steel, a pop and a sudden intense pain. The cork had buried itself in my eye.

And not a chip on the bottle.

'I never saw you in a fight,' he said when he saw me the following evening.

I attempted to remind him.

'You are making this up.'

'I wish I were, Max.'

'A new client has a lot of business, so as soon as you can get the money to me—'

'I don't have any.'

I tried to explain about how my own spare cash was tied up with Fat Golden Finance, but he cut me off in mid-sentence: 'You don't trust me.'

It was a statement. And true. He tried so hard, but the scales had been stripped from my eyes. His suit was over-worn, the grime under his fingernails was embedded. I'd hoped that, by supporting him in his ideas, I'd give him hope. All I'd done was slow the decline.

It's a dangerous thing, going into business with friends. Bad feelings, lost tempers, unkind words. Germin thought I'd concocted the champagne cork story as a pretext to deny him the money he needed. I suppose his own guilt didn't help. He shouted, he ranted, he raved. Begged.

'You still have the travel business,' I said.

Venus giggled. She brushed my black eye with her finger – a stroke as painful as it was gentle. 'Eric says you *gwailos* are always fighting.'

The more I protested my innocence, the more it confirmed in her eyes my guilt. Then I looked to the floor and a loud sigh escaped. 'I lost a friend,' I told her.

She looked at me. Her brow creased with concern, a slight pout formed on her lips and the bridge of her nose crinkled: she was curious, but wasn't sure if she should ask.

'Trying to tell him the truth was pointless,' I said. I was putting the cart before the horse: I confided the whole history. 'He refused to believe it.'

'That's why you look so sad,' she said.

In two days she'd fly to England. 'And,' I said, 'because you're leaving.'

She smiled her Venus smile and the sun popped out from behind the clouds. 'I'll be back,' she said.

'To this backwater? The art world is in London and New York.'

'I know.' It was her turn to look downcast. 'I need to come back. To marry Eric.'

'You're far too young to be thinking of that. Do you love him?'

'I don't—' she tried, but struggled to find the words to explain. What does love mean to a seventeen-now-almost-eighteen-year-old? But, then again, how many seventeen-year-olds had such a clear idea of where their lives were going?

The seed of doubt planted: 'I'm sure you do,' I let her off the hook. 'Let's go out for a happy meal together.'

It probably would have been, but Eric inserted himself.

I looked at my empty flat. How long had it been? The memories, Jo, the procession of others, the mysterious telephone girl. And here I stood, moving out to Repulse Bay for the sake of a girl whose flight, in a few hours, would touch down in England.

I'd told Venus things I could never have told Emma or Lily or Jo: with them, I'd felt compelled to be the man in their lives. With Venus, I'd spilt the beans about Africa, Forsythe and Germin, and, for want of something to talk about in our classes, of my own adolescence – though not, I hasten to add, Emma's spectacular cleavage. Now, there was no one in whom to confide, no bi-weekly lessons to look forwards to.

No Germin, Doc gone.

And, on the material side, at the very time I wanted to amass wealth to live the life I wanted to live with Venus, Uncle Yan's falling quality and tardiness was costing me customers, the travel business had run out of cash and the Koreans had legitimised dildos. Things couldn't get very much worse.

Quite.

Chapter 9

Dear Mr Price,

I am arrived in London two days ago and I find I am very exciting. London is very beautiful and hot. Not raining like you always telling me. My aeroplane flight make me very tiring. The film showing not very interested to me. We change plane in Dubai. A fat man sit next to me. He look at me very much and make me to feel very uncomfortable and smelling very bad. He always wanting talk with me, so I pretend sleeping and when he sleeping I ask for new seat. I sit next to window so when we landing I see London very good. It is so big. Really, I don't believe. And everything is so old.

My room so big. To school is very far, so take bus is not very long. Tomorrow we need registration.

I am so tired. Maybe jet-lag. I writing you again soon,

Yours Sincerely,

My heart burst forth. I had not expected so much as a postcard; I had expected two years of silence followed by a gradual conquest on her return. To the contrary, I now had a pen pal. And, what was more, what I couldn't do with flowers and candle-lit dinners, I could do with words.

There was more to London than *The Sound of Music*

and loitering ladies. There were museums and art galleries, concerts and plays, parks and palaces. I, I hasten to add, had barely glanced in their direction. But I knew where to point Venus.

And then, there was her English. I went to the photocopier and returned, armed with a red pen.

'How's the patient this morning?' I asked.

'Bored,' said Uncle Yan.

The doctors had removed the *Nil by Mouth* sign, but whether he was on the mend or they were allowing him a few final meals before he popped his clogs, I had no idea.

'Bloody awful food, too.'

'Anything I can get you?'

Wasn't there just. The list started with abalone, beluga and champagne, whizzed past oysters and smoked salmon and into the latter reaches of the alphabet with whisky, at which point he ran out of steam.

'I'm not sure they'll allow me in with all that.'

'They bloody well will because I'll bloody well tell 'em to. They keep trying to feed me congee. Told them no more. Had my last bowl of the stuff the night before jumping the fence and vowed I'd never touch it again. Hate Chinese food.'

Not that I'd ever seen him refuse shark's fin or snake soups, and, as to the *dim sum*, he scoffed it down.

'I'm paying good money for them to cut all these bits out of me and they will let me eat what I bloody well tell them.'

He paused for breath.

'Sorry. The rantings of an old man with a foot in the grave. I'll eat whatever I'm told and, if that doesn't kill me, I will survive some passing flu.'

'I'd hardly call lung cancer a flu.'

He didn't like that one. But after a silence he said 'No,

it's not. But it's attitude. Look at me. I'm far from being the most exceptional man that I've met. I'm not frightfully stupid but I know many who are more intelligent than I. Yet I am rich and they are not. You know the difference? I plan. I research, I plan and I plan for success. Have you any idea how many people fail because they're frightened witless of success? Attitude, that's the difference.'

Planning. Success. They were hardly words in my lexicon. Yet, if I was to conquer Venus and she and I were to live the life that I'd planned, perhaps it was time to take a leaf out of Uncle Yan's book.

'Attitude—' his voice commanded me back '—in the face of adversity. I haven't smoked a cigarette in my life, yet do I lie here complaining? No. I face it with determination and let the doctors do as they must.'

He winced.

'No, don't mother me.' It was becoming a stock phrase.

I was about to leave.

'By the way,' he said. 'I hear the new moulding machine's arrived.'

As it happened, it had. No more unfortunate breakages.

The stock markets, the markets. There was no need for casinos. Crowds spilt out on to the streets, maniacal in their tracking of numbers. Young and old, men and women, they fought for space and, in those days before smartphones and the Internet, hollered their orders. It's hard to believe in this day and age but, when I first arrived, there had been half-a-dozen stock exchanges in Hong Kong: to the government, they were just another type of business – plastics, shirts, stock exchanges, brothels, etc. Plans were underway to consolidate the exchanges but, in the mean time, the carnival danced on, fortunes made and lost in an hour, any and all invited to make a quick buck, put their company on the market and throw up yet another skyscraper.

And the exchanges themselves: General G. took me to one. The din was louder than even the garment factories. There were no ticker tapes but chalkboards lining the walls, and the stockbrokers were armed with binoculars to see them. It was all done on trust, all done on memory and worked like a charm.

'Well, Stanley, as you know,' General G. said, his voice a military boom, 'there are many innovative products in the financial markets and it's taken us some time to get the message over, but we're getting there. Where we are failing is . . . well, the expatriate market is good – overpaid civil servants and cops are dumb suckers – but we're getting nowhere with the Chinese. They're too sharp for us. So I got myself to thinking that we should offer a broader portfolio of services. Instruments they can't buy in Hong Kong'

'Instruments?'

He looked at me. 'Financial instruments.'

I shook my head.

'Shares, stocks, warrants.' He paused for effect. 'Derivatives.'

'Ah.'

'Seems to me the market's only going to up, and I've been in touch with my alumni from Harvard. The latest thing is junk bonds. No one sells them in Hong Kong.'

Two packets of cigarettes later, he got to the point. He'd arranged it all.

'. . . up front. As a sign of good faith.'

> *Dear Mr Price,*
>   *Thank you for your letter. Your life so interested to me. So many things you have to say! And so many places in London. I go the places you say. The British Museum*

is too big, really, in one life, cannot see all! I like the National Portrait Gallery very much. I have big shock in Hyde Park, where some women lie in sun, not wearing anything on their top. I cannot imagine.

This week too busy. Really. You wouldn't believe it. On Monday, phone call comes. His voice is too difficult to understand, makes me very confused. Not like your voice at all. My things come. He told me to come to docks to collect them. I decide to take Underground, but it is too confusing. Really, I don't know which line to take. There are so many. But the map is very pretty. I like the colours very much, I think that maybe I can paint like this. When I go to the godown it already closed for lunch. The building is very old and dirty and all the men are very fat. Much fatter than you. But I feel very uncomfortable so I take taxi home and Tuesday go back. When I reach, the man had a big beard and very interesting face so I think maybe I can paint portrait. He was very nice. He help me carry my trunk to the taxi. When I give tip he become very angry but I told him I had never been before and I don't know.

Living next door to me is a girl. She is called Mary. She is very friendly and is coming to study industrial design. Her hair is very long and curly and beautiful and she is very thin and elegant. She is very kind to me. I think she is very kind person. When I come with my trunk she help me carry to my room. It was so heavy, really, you wouldn't believe.

Yesterday we go to society day. There are very many societies here and I don't know which one to join. Mary says I must learn to defend myself, so together we join karate. The first time is next week. Also classes start. Already I am buying all books and materials. There are so many, and I must walk very much to find shops, but

it is nice.
       Mary waiting outside. I will write again soon.
                                                Yours Sincerely,

I put the letter down with a smile as I recalled my days with Forsythe and the novelty of that situation to me. Venus's eyes too would be open wide with wonderment, soaking up new sights and sensations – topless sunbathers included – and trying to make sense of it all.

I brandished my pen but this time, paused. The post in those days, even by airmail, took weeks to get from Hong Kong to London: between the first letter and this one – I didn't keep any copies of my replies, by the way – almost two months had gone by.

There was no need to rush. And there was still a hole in my diary where my bi-weekly meetings with Venus had been. So I decided to keep up the lessons at the same times, but to use them to compose my replies.

In any case, the thought of Venus wheeling around the floor in white pyjamas, wearing goodness-knows-what beneath them, throwing karate punches and kicks, had me quite ruffled; I needed time to calm down.

'Nitric, my old friend, I knew you'd come through with it.'

'It's not that simple, Germin. Business is business and friendship is friendship. I had to borrow this money and I will need to pay it back.' Not an untruth, though Uncle Yan wouldn't pressure me on the repayment.

'Yes, of course—'

'What about the drinking?'

'It will stop. It has stopped. Look, I am drinking a Coke. This time I've quit for good.'

Better and better – until the barman ratted on Germin: his Coke had been half full of vodka.

I looked over the race course. A man can nurture only so many depravities, and sex, beer and cricket were mine. But General G. had a client in town, a certain Louis V. D'Arcy the Third – ah! those American affectations of generations – who was 'old money' – which amounted to mere century or so – and wanted to be treated as such.

He was one of those film-star types with a jutting chin, square jaw, dense blond hair and manicured nails. He was dressed in a suit that seemed to have been sprayed on, his shirt gleamed, his cuff-links were of solid gold. 'Got a good thing going on here,' had been his assessment of Fat Golden Finance. My role in the conversation had become ornamental as General G. and he launched into talk of leveraged buy-outs, debt, junk bonds, margins and similar arcana. I'd drifted off into a pleasant daydream involving the double-ender, Lily and Jo, but was jolted out of it when the talk turned to matters equestrian. Leukemia Pete went without fail to every meeting, so I arranged for us to tag along.

Beneath us, down in the cheap seats, *hoi polloi* milled around making a great deal of noise and exhaling vast billowing clouds of cigarette smoke. The green oblong of turf was radiant under the floodlights. The first race of the meeting was yet to begin, but the air was thick with tension.

The horses were brought out to parade. I saw half-a-dozen nags, indistinguishable save for their colours. Luke and Louis, finding a common interest, saw anatomy, form and all the other fine things that turf-goers discern.

'Leveraged whats?' I emerged from my daydream.

'Give me ten dollars, now, and I'll lend you a hundred at twenty per cent for a bet on the favourite,' commanded General G. The notes changed hands and I went off to teller to place the bet. I had no idea which horse I'd bet on but, to much cheering and booing, they galloped away, did the circuit and crossed the finishing line.

'Now, go and collect your winnings,' said General G. The favourite, he told me, had won. I returned with the hundred dollars he'd lent me, now doubled. He took back the hundred he'd lent me, helped himself to twenty dollars interest, and returned my original ten dollars.

'What's your profit?' he said.

Never one for mental arithmetic, I fumbled with the notes. It seemed I was up eighty dollars.

'That's leverage,' he completed the lesson. 'If you'd bet the ten dollars unleveraged, you'd have won ten dollars. By borrowing from me, even after interest, you're up eight times as much.'

Duly impressed, I pocketed my winnings and sat tight for the rest of the race meeting.

Luke, however, far from sitting tight, seemed to be well ahead – and without borrowing a penny from General G.

'Didn't realise you knew so much about horses?' I wondered as we left for the night.

'Case I was working on,' said Luke. 'Did you realise that almost every racehorse on the planet traces its lineage back to a single horse, Darley Arabian, imported from Syria to seventeenth-century England? The lucky stallion must have shagged himself silly. Really quite interesting.'

Louis had a good night and insisted we celebrate. I was all for the club, but General G. drew me to one side: 'Stanley, this guy is after some pussy.' He named a place. I recoiled, but was trapped.

I'd always considered discotheques to be corrals for the vulgar. I'd been to a couple with Jo, under duress. However, if it was my obligation, it was also Louis's treat. He suggested one that turned out to be full of stunning women, and the gyration that passed for dancing was easy after the first few martinis.

As I staggered out, it occurred to me that the new flat was unchristened.

Venus flashed across my mind as I opened the door and, with that thought, a sudden surge of guilt. I had taken the place for her and was already, in a sense, cheating. And with Venus, I wanted to turn over a new leaf. *Tai-tais* for sons, girlfriends for fun may be alright for Uncle Yan, but the woman I wanted – the woman I'd found – was wife and girlfriend rolled into one.

'Anything wrong?' asked my bundle of fun.

She had golden skin and hazel hair, and the figure of – I had to suppress the thought – a Venus.

'Why would it be?' I managed a smile.

Venus would never find out.

They picked up Peter the larcenous Scouser, Germin's accountant, at immigration.

'Splendid,' I said. 'Home and dry.'

Not so.

Peter had invested our money under his own name, so I thought it was a matter of getting my signature onto, and his off the share certificates. But it turned out that he'd sold all the shares when he'd done his bunk. Gambling, bar the horses and stock markets, is illegal in Hong Kong, but in Macao it is not merely legal but encouraged. He'd gone there and, hoping to double his booty, had lost the lot.

'Happens all the time,' said Luke. 'That's the story, and there's no disproving it.'

'You mean he's lying?'

'Nine times out of ten. But the money will be stashed overseas and chasing it down is nigh on impossible.'

'But he'll go to jail.'

'Two years for half a million or a year and a half if he returns the money. Six months less in jail for all that money,' he shook his head as if calculating: 'not worth it.'

'Are you saying I'll never see it again?'

That's what he was saying. Though what dispirited me most was losing a fellow sports nut.

'Did you realise the word Scouser comes from lobscouse, a sailor's stew made of meat, vegetables, and hardtack? Really quite interesting.'

A man entered my office. He had short hair that stood up on end like a toothbrush, he wore baggy slacks and a shirt that looked to be silk. He flopped onto the chair opposite mine.

'I'd like some answers,' he said. The voice sounded familiar.

One of his fingers, of its own volition, drifted towards a nostril. 'John?' I asked.

He looked at me.

'It's all over, ma—' He swallowed the word. 'I'm not John any more. I'm Duran.'

'As in the fruit?'

'Fruit?'

'Durian?'

'If you weren't so completely out of touch I'd think you were trying to be funny.'

'Heaven forbid.'

'Duran Duran. New Romantic.'

'Oh,' said I.

'Music.'

The pause became pregnant.

'So,' John-Duran gave birth, 'what's going to happen?'

'We're launching the new line of vibrators, and—'

'No, the money. We all know this place is broke.'

'Who told you?' Wrong answer. 'Listen, I know we went through a rough patch with Axel, but—' I changed tack. 'Just because I dipped into my own pocket to pay the salaries last month—'

'It's that general guy, isn't it?'

Greek deities sometimes assume human form. Looking back now, it had escaped me that John was one such.

From the window of my apartment, I looked out over Repulse Bay. On either side, the horns of the bay extended, covered in grass that would soon, with the end of the rainy season, turn brown and dry. Over the sea, the beer-coloured sea, the sun rose and fishing boats on the horizon were caught in silhouette. Breakfast all those years ago in the fish market came to mind: where was she now? I could barely remember her appearance and, as to her name. . . .

The sea. Over there, Venus would be studying or, more likely with the time difference, settling down to bed. Would it be raining, snowing? Cold? Here, now, it was cool but, as the sun rose, so too would the heat.

The patter of feet came from behind me. Louis V. (for Verner, of all the preposterous names – one other little improbability that escaped me) D'Arcy the Third had left the previous night. I'd committed to investing a sum in leveraged thingamajigs and, before he headed for his flight, he and I had repeated our celebratory tour of after the races.

This catch had the figure of a goddess, long hair and slim legs, teeth of pearl, and had proven last night to be as sensual as she appeared. It was all there yet . . . hollow. A simulacrum of what I was after.

How did Eric do it?

She came to me, now, a sheet wrapped around her. Silent, she stood in front of me and looked at the bay. She took my arms and folded them around her.

'Take me,' she said. 'From behind.'
I seemed to be making a habit of this.

Dear Stanley,

Thank you for your letter and the corrections. So many mistakes! I feel very shame when I get it, but Mary says I am lucky to have a friend like you. When I think, I know she is right. So thank you. Really. Also, I'm sorry I don't write for so long. I have been so busy. You wouldn't believe.

College is very interesting. I am so happy to be here. I met lots of new people and they are very interested to me. I don't like all of them. There is a man called Tomas who is very arrogant, always looks down on me. I know, really. I can tell. The reason is because he looks so handsome, like Hermes God in British Museum. But I find his second name so interesting: Krèméry, how to say it? I do not know. There is a girl called Sandra. She comes from Scotland and I don't understand what she says. Her accent is so difficult but she has very long and beautiful hair and I think she has good heart.

My lessons I enjoy very much. I learn many new things I didn't know before. One of the teachers is Mr Harris and he is very kind and patient and shows me many new things. Did you know in the Sistine chapel every brush stroke is the first? The reason is because the plaster absorbs the paint so fast that you cannot do it again. So you must be right the first time. If not, no chance to correct. Chinese watercolour is the same. Because I don't think I can ever be this good, when I think of this I become very sad.

Mary and I go to karate last week. It is very funny. All other people are men so everyone wants to practise with us. Actually, they all want to practise with me. I

*think the reason is because I am Chinese and they think
I know kung fu. Bruce Lee is so famous. But I don't
know any.*

*Last night we went to disco. It was so loud. I tried
some beer. I know you like very much but I don't like
the taste. The flashing lights were very colourful, made
me think of abstract expressionism.*

*I must go. Mary and me go to Henley for lunch today.
It is Sunday, so no classes,*

Best Wishes,
P.S. By the way, is Eric alright?

Once again, I brandished my pen. Yet, as I started my opus,
my conquests after the disco stood in the way – albeit
naked, so it wasn't all bad – but nevertheless between me
and my muse.

I banished the memory. Mere dalliances. Diversions.
Scratching an itch. But, as I raised the pen and the words,
'I too went to a disco' spilt onto the page, I had to stop in
mid-sentence. It was bizarre, but I felt soiled. In those
months before she'd left, Venus had become my con-
fidante, yet here was something I could not confide.

'I found it all rather common,' was the best I could
manage.

'Fit as a fiddle,' said Uncle Yan.

'You seem much improved.'

'Attitude,' he said.

He turned to Matilda – battle-cruiser boobies – who
giggled. I wondered if he'd paid someone to amputate her
brain, but remembered the 'Stanley, a lady has principles.'
No, she was playing a part, though to what end, I couldn't
imagine. She knew her stuff, though. The way she had
tickled my—

'—dildos.'

My teacup went flying.

'Stop gawking. She's spoken for,' he gave me an admonitory stare. 'I said: what's this I heard about you looking for other manufacturers?'

How could I tell him that I thought he was going to die? After he'd trusted me for so long? I felt awful about it. And it wasn't only longevity. It was him having only a single machine and the competition due to a proliferation of plastics factories in China.

There was only one way to tell him. To his face.

'Well, Stanley,' he said, 'I'm glad your business outlook has matured.'

'Goddamned best motherfucking goods you ever done.'

'Thank you, Axel.'

'I was gonna ditch you. But, Mister Stanley Fen-fucking-shaw Price, this is great stuff.'

It's hard to feel proud of a vibrator, but that brought me close.

'And the change to the variable speed control. Fuckin' mind-blowing.'

Variable speed? 'Yes, well, we um—' The line was already dead.

'Eric!'

It turned out he'd done the variable speed all by himself.

'Um, splendid.'

'And Mr Price, I have idea. . . .'

'Well Stanley as you know, the Chinese are kind of set in their ways, but what I didn't think was, it's the *gwailos* who like the junk bonds. Can't get enough.'

He put out a cigarette, lit another.

'Ain't no secret between us that I've been up and down

all my life and, when I met you – well, I was down. But I've been up, too. In the Vietnam War, I flew for Air America, which as you know was a front for the CIA. We weren't smuggling drugs – they were the cargo. No, the Vietnamese had their money, the Dong, and the GIs got paid in coupons they could only use on base, and then there were greenbacks. . . .'

The details escape me – currency smuggling was the essence – but, half a packet of cigarettes later: 'We were taking in suitcases of cash. Eight million US dollars in two years – and that was in the sixties when a million was worth a goddamn. We had more than we knew what to do with. And that was the problem.'

He effected a dramatic pause by lighting another cigarette.

'See Stanley, and I know it sounds dumb now, but back then, we thought America was winning the war. So we took the proceeds and bought ourselves a shrimp factory.' He tapped the ash into an overflowing ashtray and delivered the punch line: 'Outside of Saigon.'

'Is that what made you drink?' I asked. 'Or what made you stop?'

That brought him up short. For a moment. One blissful moment of silence. 'Well Stanley, my old man, he was a preaching man and I don't know why, but he hit the bottle pretty hard in his later years. So I stay away from religion and booze.'

He looked at me.

'The taste of pussy is better.'

'Things are looking up,' I said.

Germin agreed that they were.

'Mr Kim is happy with the new vibrators?'

He was. What had started as smuggling was now a

legitimate business.

'And no more problems with cash flux?'

'Cash flow. No.'

'See: business is much better when you're not on the piss night and day.'

Germin shrugged. 'It isn't fun any more.'

I sat behind my bureau. Once again I was the only one with nothing to do. Things happened around me without me being a part of them. Our customers specified products; my staff sent them drawings, samples and finished goods. Other staff sent invoices, chased bills and brought cheques to sign.

Socially, most other people my age were bringing up children, while the twenty-year-olds didn't want an old codger like me cramping their style. My circle, with Doc gone and Germin leading a life of abstinent virtue, was down to Legal George and Luke. They would pop into the club for a quick one or two after work, but the days of seven, eight, and a taxi to less salubrious climes had slipped into the past.

As to my plans for Venus, although money wasn't yet stacking up in the bank, when the dildos bounced back (not a good image, I grant), and the travel and smuggling had recovered from our crooked accountant, and the General's leveraged thingamajigs started selling, there would be an avalanche of cash. That would arrive about the time Venus would finish her studies. Together, she and I would start our new life, she painting as we explored the world.

Had she still been in Hong Kong and doing her lessons, I may have noticed the newspaper headlines.

Chapter 10

To the greeks, the Fates are the three daughters of Night. Clotho spins the thread, Lechesis allots to each of us our measured time on this earth and Atropos – she was all set to arrive.

I staggered from the clubhouse to my car through gusting wind and pelting rain after being trapped in the club by a typhoon. The clubhouse was safe and theft in Hong Kong is rare – or my car wasn't worth stealing – so there was no point in locking the door. So it was only after I had manoeuvred myself into position that I realised how awkward car keys can be. Taking a careful grip of the steering wheel, I leant forwards until things swam into focus. I attempted to insert the key, only to get it into the wrong one of the two keyholes I saw in front of me. I rested my head on the wheel, tried another two or three times and succeeded. The engine started and, as I lifted my head from the wheel, a loud continuous klaxon of which I'd been aware – the horn – stopped.

It must have been one in the morning as I drove out on to the road. The sky was pitch black, gusts buffeted the car, the rain hit the windscreen in gushes. I drove around a street sign that lay flat on the pavement. A fine spray from the gap between the doorframe and window caught me in one eye. White lines stretched away in front of me. Another tide of water inundated the windscreen.

I worked out the problem and switched on the wipers just in time to see a branch dive through the air towards me. A gust or an angel swept it to the side just before impact, but I had already yanked the wheel. The car swerved. The lights of an apartment block loomed. I braked, made it. Wound down the window for air. Splash, I was drenched. The window winder jammed. The handle came off when I tugged it.

I came to Island Road. Open to the sea, the storm raged with furious intensity. The ghostly glow of the sand, the white caps of breakers crashing to shore: something elemental stirred within. I came to a straight and accelerated. A bend came. I slewed around it, spray flying up. Another gust wrenched the wheel from my hands. The car skidded. I would not brake. I wrestled the steering wheel into submission. Accelerated. A wall appeared. An arc of water fountained up. The car came out of the skid.

Panting, I stopped. I leant on the wheel and gathered my breath. What had got into me? Driving drunk was normal – and legal – in Hong Kong, but even in that wobbly condition I was normally the most sane driver on the road.

My head came up. I laughed. It felt so good to have broken the routine.

Reader: should you find yourself in a rut, before you beg Night for release, listen, please, for the sound of her Daughters' laughter.

Uncle Yan must have been quick about it: he'd been released from hospital only six or seven months previously. Matilda – whose name I wasn't supposed to know – sat next to him, her tummy round and taut, her skin glowing. She smiled with the pride of a mother-to-be.

'When's she due?' I asked

'Another mouth to feed in six weeks.'

His words were gruff, but there was a smile on his face and pride in his voice. 'Congratulations,' I said.

As Uncle Yan turned his back on us to snap his fingers at a waiter, the mother of his child bestowed on me a barely perceptible lift of the eyebrows and smile of unblemished evil.

'Brandy!' I ordered.

Yan and I conversed the way old friends do, jumping backwards and forwards from topic to topic, nothing important yet all of it vital. Matilda no longer had to replenish our glasses and fawn over us because, as bearer of the next of Uncle Yan's brood, she had sufficient status not to. Instead, she played dumb, offering the occasional smile when Uncle Yan looked at her.

'How was your check up?' I asked when we were about to leave.

'All clear,' he said.

For the first time in months, his smile had no fear.

Dear Stanley,

What reminds me to write to you is that Hong Kong is in the news. Britain and China are talking that maybe China should take Hong Kong back. I hope not, because my father very distrust the communists, you know he came to Hong Kong to go to China but the Cultural Revolution made him very difficult, lost too much money.

Last week makes me to feel very embarrassed. We draw a man, but he is naked. I don't know where to look, really. I never see before. But Mary is very appreciate, says he is very beautiful. She helps me to follow his curves and explains about muscles. So I try a second

*time and it is better. I see she is right. He is very
beautiful.*

*Later she shows me another drawing. It is like your
education products, but she makes it so big and says it
is for funny. I feel very shy.*

Must go. Karate now.

Best Wishes,

I didn't know whether to slap my knees or burst into tears.
But at least I knew where things stood on the physical
front.

The racing seemed to have become a regular thing.

'Give me ten and I'll lend you a hundred at twenty per
cent,' General G. commanded. The previous time, I'd done
rather well; I obeyed.

It is only at the horse races (and stock markets) that
Hong Kong crowds become animated. Even during the
riots that were in progress when I first arrived, there was
little in the way of animation. Violence and action a plenty,
but their hearts weren't in it.

The hooves pounded the turf; the crowd took to its feet.
The shouts took on a rhythm, fists pumped in the air.
Those besides me in the box leant over the railing. 'Number two, number two!' yelled Legal George. 'Six six six!'
came from behind me. The jockeys were high in their
stirrups, the whips smacking the rumps.

Six nine two became six nine seven – where did number
seven come from? It went like the clappers. Six seven nine
it gained – the line within lengths – six seven nine, seven
six nine.

Number nine fell. The crowd roared.

Seven six two as they thundered across. Picked out by
floodlights, shredded betting slips erupted into the air,

snowflakes against the green of the track and the dark of night.

Impassive, Luke stood. He shook his head. 'Must be my lucky night,' he said. He showed me his ticket. 7-6-2. With numbers seven and two both rank outsiders, he'd made a small fortune.

Which he seemed to be doing at almost every one of the meetings I went to. I could do with some of his luck.

'You owe me a hundred and twenty,' said General G.

'But . . . but. . . .' I babbled, 'I lost.'

'Lesson number two,' General G. explained: 'You borrowed the money. You chose how to invest it. Win or lose, you still need to repay it.' He regarded me with something approaching pity. 'The down side of leverage. When you go down, you go under.'

'John?' I said.

'This Kwong Tat factory of yours,' he started. 'It's expensive.'

It wasn't the first time he'd suggested this. China had declared that Shenzhen, that cluster of pig farms over the border, was a 'special economic zone', with low or no taxes and cheap labour. Hong Kong people didn't trust China and didn't trust the communists, but in the decade and a half I'd been in Hong Kong, costs had rocketed: rentals always had been outrageous, but labour was going up too. And, unlike the halcyon days of the Factories Inspectorate, the government had begun to take its own regulations seriously, which racked up the costs even more. Although Shenzhen was cowboy territory, it was said to be cheap and the regulations poorly enforced.

'Yan has supported me since day one and he won't go near the place.'

'Dump him.'

'Relationships are more important than short-term profit.
I know Yan's factory is more expensive and maybe he
should open in China. But we make sex toys. They are
prudes up there. They won't permit us to operate.'

'I've taken care of that,' said John. 'I've found this factory
that has connections with. . . .'

Connections, connections. Who you know has always
been as important as what you know, but whenever I heard
talk of China, it seemed that whom you knew was the *only*
thing of importance. It didn't sit well.

'Have you considered the quality?' I asked.

'Quality? These are not things you give to your children
at Christmas.'

Strange way to put it. But the answer was no.

Germin, sober now for some weeks, and I regarded the
ledger. Between accounts this and accounts that, and something called depreciation, there were only two numbers
that either of us understood: the profit and the bank
balance. Both of which were heavily laden with black.
Business had been booming. Tourists and businessmen
arrived in ever-increasing numbers, Hong Kong people
were travelling in group tours and on business, also in
ever-increasing numbers. Germin could barely keep pace
with the demand for our cheap tickets.

'Peter was right,' said Germin, speaking of our crooked
Scouser accountant. 'This is too much money. It is crazy
to keep it sitting here doing nothing. We could buy a few
stocks and shares and make some money.'

I followed his logic, but. . . .

'I have thought about it,' he continued. 'With some of
the money we can buy some futures from this general of
yours. We buy also some shares, blue chips. The rest, we
keep in a fixed deposit.'

It made sense, but: 'I'm not happy about it—'

'And now I am telling you something.'

'—I mean, Peter was able to swindle us because we didn't know enough about this to stop him—'

'I have made a conscious decision to start drinking again.'

'—and we still haven't paid back Yan. He came up with the money when he was in hospital dying. I'm not sure he'd want us ploughing his money into something we know nothing about—'

'I cannot stand the tedium. There is nothing here. Nothing. I drink myself to death, so what? At least I have fun. Alcoholics Anonymous: pah. I'd rather be a well-known drunk. Months it is. I thought if I stopped drinking my life would become full. All it's done is show me how empty it is.'

'—besides which – empty? There's plenty of money here.'

'I don't care about the fucking money.'

'So we're agreed then?'

Yes, we were agreed.

Dear Stanley,

The winter term ended. It was so busy, really, but frustrating. I want to paint my own things, but still they make me to do still life and sketches. It is so boring. Mr Harris says I must learn to walk before I can run. I should not complain.

Yesterday was very sunny, so Mary and I went to Hyde Park to do watercolours. There are some women doing sunbathing topless and Mary paints them. Her painting makes the women seem different, more curvy like cats. Mary is so good at painting, I wonder why she wants to do industrial design. It seems a big waste. A

*man came over and watched us paint. He want to buy
hers and said he would pay £50 for it. Can you believe?
£50! Enough for two weeks of living. But Mary said no,
her painting was not good enough. Later she told me
maybe he is wanting more, has some bad thinking, but
I tell her why not take for £50? But her family is rich.
£50 is nothing to her.*

*Remember Tomas? I told you I think he is very dislike
me? I am so wrong! He is always looking at me and I
think he is very arrogant or maybe racist, but two weeks
ago Mary and I were in the canteen and Mary has to
go to the washroom. Tomas comes to me and stands at
the table. When I look up, I see he is very handsome but
also shy. He cannot look at me so I ask him to sit down.
Then I ask him how is he and he says very fast that he
wants to talk to me for a long time but is too frightened
because he thinks I will not like him but he wants to go
out with me as a date! I don't know what to say. I feel
very shame, but Mary comes back from the washroom
and he goes away. After that I see him looking at me,
but he never comes to speak. What shall I do? Now is
Easter holiday so is one month before next term and I
don't know what to say. But next year he will do
sculpture, so maybe it doesn't matter because I won't see
him so much.*

*Next week Mary and I are going to Florence to see
the Uffizi Gallery. I am very exciting about it.*

*Hope you are well. Is Eric alright? I never hear from
him. By the way, my painting from Hyde Park is
sending with this,*

Best Wishes,

The improvement in her craft was beginning to show. That
drawing she'd first done of Stanley in his jaunty casuals in

front of the hills of the NT had shown precise draughting skills but, in other paintings she'd shown me, her interpretation had been at best minimal and at worst confused. Now, in this painting, Hyde Park was a background of pastel blue behind a lawn of lime green with bright, clearly delineated spots for the flowers. Between the sky and the lawn was a series of exuberant blobs, some of them vertical, some triangular, others more – well – blobby. And, on the grass, were two white blobby balloons with very pink nipples.

I longed to be there with her, to see her grow as an artist – and also as an adult. For my Venus was fast losing her innocence at the hands of this Mary, and I could perhaps protect her. Yet, what did I expect? Venus was not at the College of Arts to become a technical draughtsman producing instructional manuals for sex toys, but to blossom as an artist, and an artist above all must be able to depict the human form.

So I wrote my critique and offered encouragement.

With the exception of Tomas. An earlier letter had said 'handsome . . . like Hermes'. Hermes was also the Greek god of deception: I sharpened my pen with sweet words of malice.

But other gods had plans of their own and Clotho, her thread now spun, she passed it to her sister, Lechesis, the spinner of fortunes.

'Well Stanley as you know, the markets have taken a hit. . . .'

I de-binned the paper. *Historic Moment*, read the headline. Venus had mentioned it, too, a couple of letters ago.

It wasn't ours, you see. We'd annexed Hong Kong island and the Kowloon peninsula, but my idiot ancestors had only leased, not annexed, the New Territories. The NT account for three quarters of Hong Kong's land area, nearly all of its water supply and, without them, the colony wasn't viable. China wanted them back and my government, the elected representatives of the country on whose behalf I'd spent years tramping through snake-infested, sodden grass, was accommodating that notion.

To me, it was monstrous; to the five million other people who lived here – many of whom came for the precise reason of escaping the very system to which Hong Kong was to be consigned – it was the end. And, to cap it all, Margaret Thatcher had tripped and fallen on the steps of the Great Hall of the Oppressed (alright, The Great Hall of the People), which accident, in Cantonese slang, was an omen of apocalyptic proportions. The Hong Kong people voted with their feet: the stock market plummeted and, with it, General G.'s business.

'But that's only our customers,' I protested. 'As brokers, you said we'd make money both ways.'

Well. . . . 'We got to thinking that it was dumb to be telling these people they should be buying into this market when we weren't doing it ourselves. Unethical, if you get my meaning. So we made ourselves a small investment. Well, as you know—' I tensed: every time he told me something I knew, it was something I didn't and nine times out of ten bad '—and as I showed you at the races, the way to make money is to leverage your assets meaning that with ten dollars you can borrow say, one hundred, so if the underlying stock doubles, you make eighty after paying the interest. Much more than you would if you just bought the underlying stock. Of course, lesson two: if it goes down. . . .'

'How much?'

'The market's taken quite a hit.'

'Do we have anything left? Give me a guess.'

'The underlying securities are down thirty per cent.'

'Surely that's alright? We invest a hundred, down thirty, we still have seventy?'

'Well, these contracts – let's call them by their proper name – these futures, they don't work like that. That's why we call them leveraged.'

'Meaning?'

'If the market goes down by thirty per cent, your five per cent gives you thirty divided by five.'

I found a calculator: 'A factor of six?'

'Five point four seven. Approximately.'

'We've lost six times our investment? And we have to make good the difference?'

'In a kind of—'

'We're wiped out.'

Well, he got himself to saying that if that was the technical term for it, he figured we were.

At least we still had the dildos.

'Thince Axel met with hith unfortunate accident, we've made a few changes,' his sidekick lisped down the phone. Joe and I had had little commerce over the years: Axel and I dealt with each other, Joe with my staff and, on the couple of trips to New York that I'd made after the first one, Axel and I drank bourbon and whisky while Joe barely showed up. Conversely, on Axel's single trip to Hong Kong, he'd taken a perfunctory tour of Yan's factory, nodded approval, and proceeded to empty Wanchai of hookers. Joe, on his trip, had made a detailed inspection of the factory only to hide in his hotel for the rest of his stay.

'What unfortunate accident?'

The silence that rebounded down the line was an eloquent way of saying that I would never know. Concrete footwear at the bottom of the Hudson River, I suspected.

'Anything we can do to assist?'

'That's very kind of you, Mr Prithe,' came down the line. I felt a sudden urge to be addressed as Fen-Fucking-Shaw. 'You could "assist" us by reducing your prices. We have a quotation which is fifty per cent lower.'

Picking myself up from the floor, I asked: 'Who the hell from?'

'We can't tell you, Mr Price. We're making dildos, vibrators, blow-up dolls. It's a price-sensitive market. These are not things you give your children at Christmas.'

Where had I heard that before? At least I still had the travel.

'Germin, I did not agree.'

He belched loudly. With gusto. Resonantly. Like an opera singer delivering a crescendo. An aroma of beer flooded the room.

'Whatever,' he said. 'Done it is.'

Done it is. 'You bought General G.'s futures?'

Belch.

The travel business, too, would have to pay back all losses. Times five point four seven.

All of which was but a prelude.

'Stanley, how could you? I treated you like a son.'

What on earth was Uncle Yan on about?

'He's pink, Stanley. My son – your son – is pink. Not yellow. Pink.'

I sat, open-mouthed, my lower jaw quivering. This was the eighties, before AIDS had made prophylactic-users of us all and, although it had been just that one afternoon, battle-cruiser boobies and I had gone at it full tilt. The pregnancy had gone to full term and Uncle Yan, released from hospital only seven months ago, couldn't possibly have sired the child. And that lift of her eyebrows just a few weeks ago at lunch, that smile: it hadn't been of un-blemished evil, but the love of a mother for the father of her child.

My mouth and limbs refused to obey my command. I'd spawned a child, by her? By Uncle Yan's floozy, his all-but-concubine? How could I woo Venus if I was lumbered with this . . . this creature?

'I've had the pair of them sent back to China. If it was within my power, I'd have you sent with them.'

The turn of phrase: *I've had them sent . . . you sent with them.* . . . A chill hand took hold of my viscera. The rich everywhere have a power all of their own, but the rich in Hong Kong were above the law. If Axel had been sent to the bed of the Hudson, the bed of Victoria Harbour had its own share of fish-eaten corpses.

'He has your nose,' said Uncle Yan, a choke catching his voice. 'You have forty-eight hours to return all that you owe me.'

The relief was too sudden for the emotional part of the brain to kick in. Forty-eight hours. If I moved this pot of money to here, that to there, if I could find a buyer at a discount for the shipment that a customer had cancelled (it happens), I could repay him.

I made it to the toilet just in time. I puked. And again. Repay him. Yes. Before he changed his mind.

I'd barely recovered when the damned telephone rang again.

'Uncle—'

'I'm at the airport,' said Luke. I could hear him panting. 'If they catch me, look after my wife.'

'You're married?'

I had to look for the inner pages to find Luke's photo-graph: *Race Fixing Syndicate Broken.*

I sat there, numb. Luke, that pillar of probity, that man

who had made his friendship contingent on my own honesty, had been on the take all along. It didn't make sense.

Or didn't it? I'd known him for over a decade, yet the personae we put on for each other in the club – he, I, every other member – were acts of self-defence in a city that punishes non-conformity: the only thing anyone ever talked about at the club amounted to banter, gossip and grumbles, the latter mostly about English sports teams.

Beyond a vague notion about law enforcement, I had no idea what he did, whether he even had children. Or was married. The man that I knew was not the man that I believed myself to have known. I read and re-read the article, trying to convince myself that the grainy black-and-white print (in those pre-colour newspaper days) was not the bronzed and fit man that I knew, that the article said something different, that the phone call hadn't happened.

I stared at the receiver, the dial tone buzzing, hoping against hope that some flash of trivia would come down the line.

It didn't.

'Really quite interesting,' I said to no one in particular.

A few days later, John intruded on my continuing stupor.

'I'm out of here, man,' he said. 'Opportunities. These are the eighties. Got to keep moving. Starting my own business. Toys.'

'Christmas toys?' I asked through the numbness.

And then, on a street, I turned a corner and came face to face with Louis Verner D'Arcy the Third. No more spray-on suit, he was in tattered denims and a T-shirt, with shoes that barely fitted. Mutual recognition took maybe a second; he took off and ran.

My days in the army, along with weekend cricket, left me with a vestige of fitness, though if he hadn't stumbled trying to avoid an old lady, I wouldn't have caught him.

'Why don't we go for a pint?' I asked.

It turned out that he was an actor come to Hong Kong seeking fame in the *kung fu* films that, with Bruce Lee a legend, were all the rage. As it happened, the only role he'd been offered was by one General G. Foswitz.

'I think it's because I fitted the suit.'

Fat Golden Profit had delivered – for General G. By the early eighties, expat life in Hong Kong had stratified. At the top, there were the old codgers like me, who spent their lives moving between one club and the next. At the bottom, were the types who passed through for a few months, teaching English in cram schools, doing menial jobs, or working for companies such as Fat Golden Finance.

'He never paid them on time, but they never stayed long enough for it to matter.'

In the middle were General G.'s chosen targets. They were full-time teachers, junior civil servants and others who had a modest, regular income, but who hadn't been here long enough, were not wealthy enough or in the right circles to join the clubs. So who weren't on my radar.

'Half the time he never even bought what they'd ordered. Just pocketed the money.'

The company was three months behind on the rent and an angry picket of unpaid staff and cheated customers made the papers in the next couple of days. The police came by and made enquiries, but the other victims were not alone: the sizeable amount of cash I'd invested had gone into General G's pocket. The market crash had been his excuse to empty the till of what little was left.

I let Louis V. go: he had nothing to give.

As to the plastics, Axel hadn't been the only customer driven away by the low quality and delays. What Uncle Yan had fixed, he'd fixed too little and too late. I hadn't noticed because it had taken the better part of a year for the order books to run down, but run down they had – and they'd stopped filling up. It didn't take many phone calls to work out that many customers had defected to John.

The travel business was no better: the part of the profits that Peter the Scouser hadn't embezzled and General G.'s futures hadn't eaten, Germin had drunk.

And there was a child, whom I'd never know, but who had my nose.

I went to the club, sat at the bar and ordered a whisky. Its aroma stroked my nostrils as I raised my glass in an ironic salute to the Daughters of Night. The third is Atropos, the unturnable, the one who won't allow you back. *Drink*, she caressed me, *be mine.*

The true sense of a Greek tragedy is a man who falls victim to his own character flaws. But I had no idea what mine were. I'd run an honest little trading company that delivered decent quality products at a fair price, just as Max had sold tickets and delivered our sex toys to Korea at a decent price for a decent living. The general was a character, a flim-flam merchant perhaps, but I hadn't pegged him as an out-and-out conman. As to Uncle Yan's son, Matilda had been a more than willing participant. Indeed, I'd declined further enticements of hers.

I raised the whisky to my lips. The sweet smell of the spirit lured me onwards.

My hand stopped in mid-motion, the glass half-way to my mouth. It wouldn't be only one whisky, wouldn't be a single long day at the bar. This was the drink that would propel me down the path of self-destruction, the bender that would never end.

Drink, she caressed me, Atropos, harbinger of death.

Bring it on. A well-known drunk over an anonymous alcoholic. And I thought of another pearl of Germin's: 'I have all the excuses I want. So do you. The reason. . . .' he'd paused.

The liquid fire hit the tip of my tongue. The sudden shock brought Venus to mind. I had not told her any of this and Eric wrote to her so infrequently that she was in no position to know. I had time. Price's Plastics, albeit without its sole supplier and most profitable customer, was still a going concern.

'The reason,' Max had said, 'is that I like it. I like being not in control.'

I put down the whisky, undrunk, and made for the door. I stopped. I turned my head over my shoulder, shook my head in a *sod you* and walked away from the Daughters of Night.

Chapter 11

THOSE WHO HAVEN'T HAD the rug pulled from under their feet may find it odd that I didn't wallow in a guilt-fest of self-recrimination that, had I not entrusted my destiny to the Daughters of Night, I wouldn't have found myself in these straits. I have never been one for such speculations – or speculations of any type – besides which, there was no time to reflect. Having ruled out drinking myself into the grave, there remained two other alternatives: I could do a bunk, or remain.

It would be nice to write that the army teaches survival with honour, that I stiffened my upper lip, firmed my resolve, refused the ignominy of returning to England yet another failed expat, *et cetera*; or that I drew inspiration from Venus's command of her own destiny. It even occurred to me that nothing now stood in my way: I could return to London to shower her with gifts – which I lacked the wherewithal to buy – and woo her – nothing, that is, except it would be creepy.

The reality was simpler: Venus was mine and I needed the money to keep her.

I sacked everyone bar Eric, the secretary and a couple of clerks. There was much gnashing of teeth but, beneath the histrionics, my staff realised that I paid them their due. I shut down the husks of my various businesses and, as to

Uncle Yan, the sooner I could pay him back, the less the chance he'd think to dump the child on me.

Callous? It takes more than ancestry for a child to be one's own. I hadn't sat with the mother through morning sickness, hormonal swings and cravings; hadn't spent the nights with my ears pressed to the dome of her belly hoping to hear the foetal heartbeat or feel a kick. I hadn't held her hand through the contractions, hadn't cradled the newborn, hadn't undergone the life-changing moment of that first smile. It had been a one-off on a whim and, if she'd told me she was pregnant, I'd gladly have paid for a safe abortion or found some accommodation if she'd chosen to keep it. She'd given me none of these choices.

Not to mention that having to juggle nappies, milk, and Matilda's more than adequate means of producing it, would be difficult to square with my plans for Venus.

I emptied every account but the only thing I possessed that came even close to the amount I owed Uncle Yan was a tenanted house in England, the tenant being my mother. He was a much better landlord than I and, a gentleman to the core, showed a most forgiving attitude when it came to the payment of rent.

It would also be nice to claim that what happened next was a plan.

> *Dear Stanley,*
>
> *Summer holidays were so good. I really enjoyed very much. Did I tell you my plans? Did you get my postcards? Me and Mary first go to Paris. It is an amazing city. We go to the Louvre almost every day. I think the guards at the door find us very funny, but what to do? Actually, we see very little of Paris, just spend our time in the Quartier Latin talking with other artists. I learnt some French, too.*

After Paris, we went to Barcelona. Me and Mary were talking with people in a café and they told us about a man who uses the fountain in the square for his shower because he doesn't want to pay for water, thinks the government should give water for free. So next morning we went very early to the fountain and waited and made some sketches. Then he comes out and takes his clothes off and makes a shower in the fountain, just like people say, in the square, where everyone can see. Naked. I cannot believe! Mary and I make a sketch while he showers. After he is finished, Mary goes and talks to him. His English is difficult to understand, but he tries very hard. His name is called Gabriel, and he comes to Barcelona to study sculpture. His family is very poor so he must work even though his government pay for him studying. I think this is much better than Hong Kong where government does not help people for education. In Hong Kong poor people cannot do like this.

Gabriel showed us many things in Barcelona we would never know about. In Spain, they have tapas which remind me of Chinese dim sum which I know you don't like. He knows many people and they all like him very much. After two or three days he lets us to live in his house to save the money. His house is very old with high ceilings, makes me to feel comfortable. It is nice, but sometimes makes me to feel lonely because he and Mary are always together. Not long after we move in she goes to his room for sleeping. The next morning Mary is so happy, her eyes very bright. I always think those things so disgusting, but she tells me when it is her choice and her man, it is so beautiful. That is the word she uses. I never think like this.

When we come back to England Mary misses him very much. On the train it was very funny. We met a

priest. He tells us he is going from Nice to Marseilles.
Then he says he has a wife in both towns! Really! I can't
believe.
    I hope you are well. Say hello to Eric. Is he healthy?

Best Wishes,

I couldn't help but wonder if Venus, my Venus, was not quite the innocent I wished her to be. It was possible to believe – the more so given Eric's spectacular ignorance on the subject – that those early drawings of Venus's were uninformed by a working knowledge of the use to which the toys would be put. But the nudity – twice now, and the second time without any judgement from her – and her evident though unstated knowledge of what Mary and Gabriel were up to, not mention that art schools were hotbeds of fornication, did make me wonder if she was losing that innocence all too quickly.

Yet she also said she'd never thought of sex as a beautiful thing. Nor, I realised, had I. Fun, invigorating, immensely satisfying, yes. But not beautiful.

Venus not thinking of it that way could be read in two ways: that she'd tried and hadn't enjoyed it, or that she hadn't tried it.

My fists were clenching and unclenching in front of me; my fingers waggling and stretching in angst. I reined myself in. It was her friend Mary, not Venus, who was jumping into bed with an exhibitionist; it was some dicey priest who was running two wives. And, given the wanton abandon with which Emma and I had approached things when I was that age, I was hardly one to throw stones. I deplore double-standards and so, I decided, must grant Venus the freedom of youth. Being unsullied is a state of mind, not body.

So, with time on my hands, I wrote what I wanted to

say – in French – binned it, and replied to Venus with the exact opposite.

How was I to find new customers? As I was ironing my shirt, ruing the fact that I could no longer afford help for such chores, the question preyed on me. My original customers had been referrals from Uncle Yan and I'd employed a salesman after that.

People of my class simply do not walk up to a complete stranger and say, with a smile and an outstretched hand, 'Hello, I'm Stanley and I sell dildos.'

My technique on shirts, I reflected, looking at the scorched remains in front of me, was also wanting.

'Eric,' I said, as if to reassure myself that he was man and not vacuum. 'This China thing. How does it work?'

He didn't understand.

'Let me put it a different way. If we were to move production to China, how difficult would it be?'

He thought connections were very important.

'They are everywhere. But how does one do business in China?'

'John have good connections,' he said.

I wandered over to what had been John's part of the office. His desk was a large table covered in engineering drawings – ah, the technology that goes into a simple vibrator! – but, as I stood there feeling like a peeping Tom, I noticed some papers amongst the chaos: *Dongguan People's Number 2 Work Unit Plastics Manufactory, Shuntak People's Ironworks* and the like.

Stanley's Number One Dildo Works?

'Any ideas?' I asked Eric.

'Has some names.'

'Splendid.'

I was restless and idle. I daydreamed about Venus, marriage and sprogs. Which were not going to happen without money, which I wasn't going to get without customers – and John had absconded with pretty much all of them. So I took a took the plunge and, instead of hiding in the club, where my entrance was in any case barred by the trifling matter of a gargantuan unpaid bill, I chose one of the best hotels, the swankiest bars.

The room was darkened. It was furnished with comfy chairs, facing each other across low tables. People engaged in muted conversations over piped muzac while nibbling on peanuts taken from silver bowls delivered by waitresses with their *cheong sam* split up to the hip. With a jolt, I remembered Lily in hers on the night of Ron's party and had a sudden pining. A rather physical one: Thatcher and strap-ons.

The crowd was mixed. At one table a pair of *tai-tais* sat, squirmed around in their seats, legs crossed, chatting urgently, their jewellery flashing reflections across the dark ceiling. At another, a large Indian gentleman in a suit and his wife in a *sari* sat sprawled across from each other in resolute silence; next to them, a Western man and Chinese woman were locked in a conversation of animated gestures and laughter, while next to them a pair of couples conversed man-to-man and woman-to-woman across each from other. There was no conversation I could insert myself into, no obvious takers for plastics – educational or otherwise.

'G&T,' I ordered.

A lady entered the bar. She seemed alone, wore a floppy hat and a dress of several voluminous layers. There was a hint of blond under the hat and she walked as if to music. She took a table, ordered and extracted a book. In the absence of any potential customers, and having blown my allowance on the drink, I straightened my tie—

'Watching the girls go by?'

I span.

'Ralph,' said the speaker.

Damn. But there was a reason I was paying these exorbitant prices: 'Stanley,' I introduced myself as the blonde started reading her book.

Ralph hailed from South Africa, in Hong Kong for a few days on business. A Roadie, was I? (A Roadie being a Rhodesian – his choice to use the old name). Now there was a country. Would I care for a drink?

I would.

Ralph ran his own company, dealt mostly with super-markets, supplying household goods. Nice little niche. Back then, South Africa was subject to economic sanctions from just about everywhere – bar Hong Kong. 'That Apartheid thing? The rest of the world should mind its own bloody business. . . .' he trotted out the usual apologies '. . . a whole bunch of do-gooders who know nothing about my country hear about this Nelson Mandela—'

I kept my mouth shut, not because I didn't have an opinion – having grown up as I did, I had an opinion and it wasn't Ralph's – but because I couldn't afford to argue.

'What keeps you busy?' he asked.

'Trading. Manufactured plastics.'

'From China?'

'We're just getting started.'

> *Dear Stanley,*
>
> *The new term is so busy, so I not write for so long. I'm so sorry, really. I hope your business is not have problems, like my father. And so many others. I don't know why there is such a problem.*
>
> *Class this year is much better than last year. Now I study what I want, and I learning and practising very*

carefully, all the time. But I worry you find these things boring.

Remember Tomas? I told him because of Eric, I cannot go out with him and he became very sad. I thought he would cry! But when I told him maybe we just be friends he was very happy. He is a nice person, but I think maybe a little strange. But his art is very good, you can tell when you see it. He says he is trying to represent post-industrial trauma.

Mary is very sad after we came back from holiday. She misses Gabriel so much, I cannot dare to talk with her about our holiday. They write to each other almost every day. She says she loves him very much. It makes me very sad, because Eric never writes to me very often and his letters are so short. Is he alright?

Please write soon,

Best Wishes,

I imagined her, as absorbed in her work at her easel as she had been that day in the NT, drawing the world in through herself and putting the good bits on paper. Only now, she would be improving her technique, experimenting with colours and brushes and blobs, and berating herself for any mistakes.

And I imagined myself, standing behind her as she worked her magic on the cone of Kilimanjaro, the lions at their kill.

Eric, at least, seemed to be removing himself from the picture. If he loved her, the fool hadn't a clue how to show it – a straightforward 'I love you' is far more effective than pawing in public. And she, for her part, was confiding in me more and more: my long-distance wooing seemed to be working.

As to Tomas: despite Sandhurst, the army had given me

an inkling on strategy. The game forced upon me was the long one and I needed to discredit him without being seen to do so. Tomas's surname, I remembered, was no Smith or Price but some bizarre Slavic affair, all consonants and no vowels. The chances of there being two students with that same name were remote. I had the address of the school: I faked a parcel from Eric and sent Tomas a dildo.

I wondered what post-industrial trauma is. Still do.

'Telephone very difficult,' said Eric.

'I find them rather easy. Pick up, dial, speak, that sort of thing.'

'No. No telephone in China. So I wrote to factories.'

I was stopped dead – by his use of a tense other than present. I shook my head: 'And?'

The factories had replied with alacrity. So, with more than a little trepidation – not least the risk of encountering my son and her mother – I found myself standing at the border between Hong Kong and the world's largest communist country.

It was the signage which struck me first. Not the actual words, but the lettering: all square and clunky as if, rather than mould it from plastic, which is what they'd done, they'd attempted to chisel it from stone. Right-angled letters such as L and E were easy, J not too bad, but O became a rectangle and C and W were so distorted as to carry an abstract quality, though much less pleasing than Venus's paintings. They sometimes split English words across two lines but without a hyphen, as when Eric headed to the counter for:

HONG KONG AN
D MACAO COMPAT
RIOTS

I found myself moving through the system with a group of excitable English tourists who, I noticed as I saw my pen passed from hand to hand, were ill-prepared for the stack of paperwork of which I'd been forewarned. I suppose communists had little better to do, but surely it would be self-evident if someone went through with an air-conditioner or the like? 'Elementary,' I thought to myself, 'he nearly made it but was detected by the trail of knickers dribbling from the open door of his washing machine.'

'Where are you going?' asked a lady with a blue-rinse hairdo and some awful accent from the north of England.

'Dongguan.'

'Ooo, where's that? We're going to Peking, to see the Forbidden City.'

'I'm going to see a factory that makes dildos.'

'Oh.'

I shouldn't have. But I was not in the mood.

People talk on trains the way they do on no other form of transport. One is confined yet free: if the company in one's booth becomes arduous, one can move to another or go for a walk. On an aeroplane, there is often no other seat, so the best tactic is not to engage, while a cruise liner – well, full of plebs with money, so I wouldn't know. As to buses, I took one once and vowed never to repeat the mistake. Necessary for transporting the great unwashed, I suppose.

The train passed through bucolic scenery consisting mostly of rice paddies and fish ponds, stunningly green, with the occasional cluster of shacks set to one side. Livestock roamed free and peasants toiled as they had since the dawn of history.

I found myself chatting with Eric.

'Is your family from China?' I asked.

'No. We come Hong Kong.'

I was about to correct his English, but I'd been doing so for the better part of a decade to no effect. So I held my tongue and we speculated instead on businesses and factories in China; we watched the awful poverty in the fields outside.

'Mr Price. When I go to America I see it is so rich. China has five-thousand-year history. Why so poor?'

Not a novel observation, nor one for which I had an answer.

The station at Dongguan had the feel of a disused morgue. Uniformed persons with stony eyes attended ticket counters from which no one bought tickets, uniformed charladies swept floors upon which nobody walked. A uniformed piss-master sat at the door of a toilet at which, from the smell however, pee seemed much in abundance.

As we approached the exit, a group of people approached us.

'Mr Price?' said one.

'The same. Mr So?'

The translator – for it was he who had spoken – introduced a man with a four-pocketed Mao suit and several gold teeth.

'Welcome to Dongguan. Mr So is very happy to welcome our foreign friends to the. . . .' the translator read from a sheet.

I stood, nodding my head as he parroted words he seemed to not quite understand.

From the back of the car, a massive Soviet affair with seats like armchairs, I watched the town go past. There were no other cars, but bicycles everywhere and, on them, women. A wealth of women. And not the dumpy peasants I'd once rounded up, but women with long hair and pearly smiles, shapely even beneath the shapeless and uniform clothing.

I nipped that thought in the bud: this was communist China.

The streets were lined with low-rise buildings of concrete, each much like the next, as if the town could afford but a single architect. Such shops as there were, were drab-looking affairs from which emerged customers without any goods. I dropped by a department store in a quiet moment: the shelves were stacked with goods that one would purchase only in the absence of alternatives; the pride of place was given to a television set, black and white, which nobody knew how to turn on.

They saved the best for the last. The hotel. Thank goodness I'd been trained by the best army in the world.

Mr So, spectacles gleaming in the gloom, beamed at me as an assistant, supervised and assisted by a gaggle of clucking lackeys or, I suppose in this country, proletarians, pushed a large red button on a green-enamelled machine.

Behind us, vast halls of silence lurked.

The machine produced a gurgle, a squawk, a fart, a sigh, and a then a pink tube of plastic. When it came to dildos, there was room for improvement.

'Mr So is very happy you have come,' said the interpreter.

Mr So grinned his gold-toothed smile.

'I am very happy to be here,' I said. 'Very impressed.'

The first course was roast-suckling pig, a Hong Kong staple. The second was entrails swimming in unrecognisable gloop.

'Beer?' I asked.

'*Maotai?*'

I shuddered.

It arrived. No brandy snifters or wine glasses here: the only glasses were cheap water ones. We chucked out the tea and tipped in the *maotai*. I'd heard tell of the stuff and it did not let me down: a sniff and the hairs fell from my nostrils; a sip scorched the back of my throat.

Another dish arrived and another, intestines and rodents. As honoured guest it was my privilege to be fed with the morsels; the bits they selected were always the slimiest. Having to be seen to enjoy them did not enhance the experience. The *maotai*, at least, obliterated the taste.

Eric had another *maotai* and went bright red in the face – a common reaction to alcohol amongst the Chinese. They gave him a cigarette.

'You smoke?'

'Venus not like. You not tell her.'

'Wouldn't dream of it.'

A shame there wasn't a whore I could stitch him up with.

In the army, one is trained to plan for the worst. So, when I opened the door of the toilet the next morning, I was not optimistic – and the hotel for its part did not disappoint. I played catch-the-dribble, did my best with a razor and descended for breakfast.

'Morning,' I said.

A waitress was leaning against a wall some distance away. With some effort on Eric's part, she was persuaded to serve us. I ordered a hearty eggs and ham.

We discussed the price (good) and the quality (dismal). Breakfast arrived: the tea was Chinese green tea, served with milk; the *pièce de résistance* two broken eggs fried so little as to be almost raw and two bright pink slices masquerading as meat. I attempted to marshal an egg on to my fork, but it kept slipping between the tines. Eric's technique dispensed with such frills: he leant over his plate, slurped and an egg disappeared.

I gagged.

'Cheap means more profit,' he observed, speaking with his mouth open. 'You not like?' he pointed at my plate.

'All yours,' I said.

So it was that day, the next and the one after that. A factory, a meal of slime and miscellaneous animal parts washed down with *maotai*, Eric sucking down half-fried eggs for breakfast. For the first time since I'd left the army, my weight went down; I survived on beer and *maotai*.

We met Mr So's competitors: smiling men with little conception of markets, customer satisfaction or dildos. They had funny ideas about the West in general and Hong Kong in particular. 'You force girls into slavery,' I was told by a manager as I stared out over rows of girls with dull eyes who repeated mechanical tasks designed for machines. 'We want to export to America, one thousand pieces per month,' as if the entire continent, from New York to LA, from El Paso to Chicago were some minor city in China. 'We want to learn,' they would proclaim, but no one was allowed out of China to do so. Their management was a bureaucracy, their production lines a cottage industry, their ambitions as broad as their horizons were narrow. But they were cheap. Damn, were they cheap.

'Back to civilisation,' I said as Eric gobbled rice, his mouth open as usual.

'Urmph blah.'

'I think you're right. This is the way to go.'

He smiled: 'Yes,' he said.

Dear Stanley,

I feel lonely, so I write. The reason is because Mary left last week. She missed Gabriel so much, I think she must be very in love with him. So she has gone to Barcelona. I feel very happy for her, but also very sad. Really, we did everything together. Like you told me about you and your friend Forsythe.

I see Tomas sometimes, but he is become very shy of me. Now he has a girlfriend and I think she is jealous because she won't let him go out with me like before. She is called Alice. I think she is at LSE, but I'm not very clear.

At least I have more time for art. I painted this yesterday and thought of you,

Venus

The painting, a testament to her blossoming craft, was a new departure. Her previous works had been watercolour landscapes, in bright colours and blobs, with humanity limited to one or two figures off to one side – Stanley in his jaunty casuals or a well-endowed sunbather. This was acrylic with accurate lines depicting two faces only, one looking into the eyes of the other. The woman was sharp-nosed, with thick eyebrows over deep-set brooding eyes which stared down at him; the man looked up to her, his eyes slightly dilated and creased at the edges in alarm. But it was the colours that drew my attention: almost the whole painting was in shades of grey, the only colour their crimson scowling lips, their amber irises and their burnished blue eyebrows.

Tomas at the mercy of his new dominatrix, perhaps? I hoped his girlfriend had applied my little gift. Without lubrication.

Hardly the words of comfort Venus needed. She'd

remembered Forsythe: what started out as a paragraph became an essay. I'd known Forsythe for barely five years and yet, as I wrote, I realised it was he whom I met at the officers' mess, to whom I turned when pining for Lily and he alone who stayed in touch when I was in civvies. Albeit sanitised of Wanchai, Lily and the huts near the base, that little essay became an unburdening of the heart.

'You can supply at these prices?' said Ralph, my South African bigot, through the crackles of international telephony.

'You got the samples?'

'Yes—' a burst of static intruded. '—good enough for the kaffirs.'

'Can't hear a word.'

'I'll send you a telex.'

I allowed myself an inwards smile. A new customer and a supplier, all of my own. Another dozen and I'd be cashed up for Venus on her return.

Chapter 12

As a man who made most of his money selling artificial genitalia of the non-instructional kind, there are few professions I can look down on.

'For goodness' sakes,' I blustered down the phone to my landlord's lawyer, my office landlord having had the impertinence to demand his rent. 'My company's finally over its troubles, we have a good order and now you're going to put me out of business.'

'Mr Price, we have already granted you considerable indulgence—'

'Grant me more.'

'If it were me, but my client—'

'Do as you will. I don't have the money.'

I do not know whether, though I doubt very much that, the importation of plastic penises into South Africa was legal. The kinds of plastic parts that Ralph ordered were not, however, fake human ones but toilet brushes. The moulds for these were a great deal simpler than those for our usual lines – I'll spare you the engineering – but the assembly more complex.

'Can do?' I asked.

'Yes,' said Eric.

Cum laude from one of the world's top universities and

here he was making toilet brushes and sex toys.

Then again, he had Venus.

Winter was unusual. Normally cool, that year it alternated blasts of Siberian chill with dampness and drizzle. For days, clouds obscured the sun and then, in the space of an hour or two, the sky would clear and a wind would arise that struck like a dominatrix's bullwhip and left me shivering in my boots.

Swimming seemed the logical thing to do. It was early morning and the breakers rolled ashore as troops to the mess hall. The beach was deserted. I stripped to my trunks and, in the wan light of the breaking day, dipped a toe in the water. Nothing for it, no timid immersion, no gradual testicular retraction. A deep breath, a dash through the breakers and I was in.

The shock of the cold was nullified by the exertion of one brisk stroke after another into the bay. By the time I was out of the shallows I had warmed up. I stopped for a moment and trod water. I glanced back at the apartment blocks lining the bay and, above them, houses on the Peak.

The Peak. It was on the Peak, at Ron's, that Lily met the man who stole her away.

Teeth gritted against a surge of sudden anger, I kicked harder out, into the bay. Never again, I vowed, would I allow myself to be robbed. But the thought made me angrier still. Germin had drunk our travel business into the ground and General G. turned out to be charlatan of the first order. And now, it was happening again under my nose: John had stolen most of my business outright and what remained, my landlord's lawyer stood ready to erase.

And then there was Venus, who seemed to end every letter with an entreaty to tell Eric to write. I had everything that I needed to torpedo her regard for him but, without

Eric, what little livelihood I had, I would lose. I wouldn't have the means to woo her, let alone to support us as we explored the world, she painting, I exploring.

I stopped, trod water and turned: the tide had taken me farther than I'd realised. Much farther. I turned again. To my right were cliffs which, even if I wasn't dashed against them by the waves, offered no purchase. To my left was an island from which squads of rowers would paddle in their fours over the weekend, but none at this hour. Boats were moored towards its shore.

My arms were cold, my legs blocks of ice. I took one stroke, another. God, it was lonely – as life itself. Futile humbug, yet the instinct was strong. I tried different strokes to rest one set of muscles while straining some other. The shore got no closer and nor did the boats. I wrenched myself through the rising swell. My arms were like jelly, my legs pathetic. Where had my strength, my vigour gone?

A boat. I bobbed over another wave. I hadn't imagined it. I reached with feeble arms for the platform at the back. Pulled.

I could pull no longer. My fingers were numb. I felt myself slip back into the water, the cold water. I heard myself splutter. There wasn't a thing I could do.

'Need a hand?' came a voice.

I didn't believe a man could shiver so much. I sat on a plastic chair, swathed in towels and blue of skin, the shivers so violent they sent the chair bouncing around the after-deck of their boat. They offered me a polo shirt: the years had exacted their toll, I reflected as I squeezed into it. He and I looked to be the same height, but his shirt was a very tight fit.

He was tall, leather-skinned, with sun-bleached flaxen hair, deep wrinkles and light blue eyes. She was blonde and lithe, with the stoop of tall women.

'Dumb thing to do,' he said without reprimand.

Taking the tea she offered, I nodded my thanks.

'Give him a whisky,' he said. 'He's over the worst of it now.'

'Breakfast?' she asked.

'I've no idea what possessed me,' I said, through chattering teeth.

We ate pancakes, syrup and bacon in silence as the sun rose over the bay and the traffic that snaked along Island Road flowed and ebbed with the coming and going of rush hour. I had things to do, but felt no urgency. They didn't ask me about myself, nor did they volunteer information. We sat in a comfortable silence, sipping tea, listening to the waves lap at the hull.

He took me ashore in their inflatable. I was about to return the polo shirt but he stopped me:

'It's yours.'

I looked again into his eyes. They had the faraway look of a mariner's, but more complex. Gentle, tired, a little hurt.

'Would you like to come over for dinner?' I blurted out. 'I live just up there and you'd be most welcome. Really, I live alone and don't cook very often but—'

He looked at me.

'If you'd like an evening on dry land,' I curtailed my gibbering.

'Sure.'

The writ for my rent arrived that morning at almost the same time I did. I chucked it on the stack of other unopened demand letters. There was nothing to be done.

Or was there?

I went to Eric's corner. It was part of the office but was almost not of the office. Other desks were littered with paper. There were mounds of the stuff. Hills of it. Sarcophagi of ancient Chinese emperors, for all I knew, lay buried beneath it (interred with our toys for a happy next life). Mine was a *Marie Celeste* of an office, its deserted grey-painted desks and towering stacks of yellowing paper-work adrift at sea.

Then there was Eric's corner. Fastidious. Neat. Self-contained. His diagrams hung from racks, labelled. His correspondence was in files, cross-referenced and clear. He himself was perched in that aberrant island in front of a drafting table absorbed in the creation of an intricate series of lines that one day, I supposed, would be translated into a mould for toilet brushes. I stood there watching the design take shape beneath his pen. Venus at her painting came to mind: the absorption, the blocking out of the world.

An absorption that was not mine to have.

His hair was combed and shorn, his shirt was ironed and, beneath it, I saw the outline of a vest that I suppose was ironed too. He had that cared-for look of medium-ranking civil servants and poodles. What did he do at nights? Dream? Aspire? Masturbate in silent confusion?

Yet there was also the brandy-guzzling cigarette-smoking Eric of China.

'Eric,' I said.

His pen slipped. He emitted the local vernacular for *fuck*, and asked what I wanted.

'John's number,' I answered.

'George,' I said. 'Thank you.'

Alone of my Chinese friends, George still returned my calls. 'Better to have tried and gone broke than not to have tried,' he'd shrugged off my situation. But this time, tonight, horn-rimmed glasses somehow dulled in the light, he hesitated before shaking my hand and taking his seat.

I was *persona non grata* at my club – where George was now the first ever Chinese committee member – so we were at another of his: also a former bastion of colonial hubris that would, in its day, have had purple-faced elder members suffering nuclear neurological bombs on seeing a Chinese other than staff on the premises. And those purple-faced members would have congratulated themselves on their foresight: let one in and the lot will follow. But now, in the eighties, although the gap was still there, it was diminishing fast. This was a sports club and, although the Chinese – now referred to as *locals* rather than *chinks* (though we were still *gwailos*) – are too clever to stand in front of a man about to speed-bowl a fast, hard ball at one's groin, they constituted the body of Hong Kong's best racquet-sports players. As to taking a Chinese wife, although a few people – mostly jilted expat wives – did bat an eyelid, and a few companies batted rather more, it wasn't the thing it used to be. True, the poor Eurasians were still stuck in the middle, and a Western woman taking a Chinese husband had social mountain to move, but the balance was shifting.

'I suppose you can guess what this is all about?' I asked.

'I don't know what you expect me to do,' he said, almost a whisper.

'How friendly are you with the fellow?'

He shrugged. 'I didn't realise how strongly you felt—'

'Of course I do. He's about to wreck everything. Just when I thought—'

Our eyes met.

'Live with it, Stanley. She's already set the date.'

Date? 'No they haven't. I have two weeks to reply.'

'Jo asked you?'

'Jo?'

There was a pause. 'You mean,' he said, 'this isn't about her and Benjamin?'

'Who?'

'She's to be married. Jo.'

'It's about your friend Timothy Grant,' I said. 'My landlord's lawyer.'

'Timothy?'

'He's suing me.'

'Is that all?' he said. We burst out laughing.

'Nitric?'

'Flurmp,' I replied. Eloquent given that I'd been woken at four in the morning, half-way through sleeping off my share of the five bottles of claret Legal and I had demolished.

'Nitric, you there?'

Not at my best. 'Germin?'

'I need your help bad,' he said.

> *Dear Stanley,*
>
> *Thank you for your letter. Your trip to China sounds very interesting. I think you and Eric are very brave to go, I would never dare.*
>
> *Winter is very cold this year and it makes me feel very sad. Also with Mary. She writes to me from Barcelona, she is so happy. Also I like your story of Forsythe, makes me not miss Mary so much. Gabriel pays her very much attention and she is learning Catalan. I really admire her. I speak such bad English and now my Chinese is no good too. The reason is because my mother scolded me in her last letter because I wrote the characters wrong, but I never use them any more. I feel very ashamed. Hong Kong is like this. We are taught in English, but we speak Chinese, so the result is nothing.*
>
> *Did I tell you Alice and Tomas broke up? It is very funny. She told me Tomas had some bad thinking, wanted to use a bad toy. I do not understand. After all, I find out she is very nice.*
>
> *Tomas asked me to come to a CND meeting. Because*

*I am so lonely after Mary left, I feel interested to go. I
found out many things I never knew about how dangerous
nuclear weapons are and how much money they spend
on weapons when many people starving. When I was
there I saw a poster. It said that for $17 billion all
poverty could stop, and this is how much the world
spends on weapons every day. Next month there is a
protest march so I will join.*

   *So late already! Tomorrow I must get up early. How
is Eric? Ask him to write,*

Best Wishes,

I've never been one for politics. To the extent that I'd ever
bothered at all, I'd ticked the box for the Tories but, after
leaving the army, registering was too much of a palaver and
I'd lost interest. But the Campaign for Nuclear Disarmament
spread a dangerous lie, and Venus was at an impressionable
age. And this Tomas seemed to inserting himself into the
picture again. There was no time to lose.

But I couldn't afford to hop onto a plane – barely even
a bus for that matter – and nor did I have a spy on the
inside. All I could do was write. To protect her.

I selected neutral territory for my armistice negotiation.
Jimmy's Kitchen was a place of cheerful fare such as Beef
Wellington, Roast Lamb or Liver with Chopped Onions.
John showed up half an hour late in tattered denims –
before the days such things came into fashion – and mouldy
sports shoes. I was glad I hadn't chosen anywhere posh.

'Eric?' he asked.

'Couldn't make it.' Because I hadn't invited him.

He flopped down and inserted the statutory digit into
a nostril. He nodded in my direction in a manner that
acknowledged my presence without being a greeting.

'How's tricks?' I tried.

He extracted the digit, inspected its yield and shrugged.

This didn't have to be awkward. His attempt to steal my business, I knew from the grapevine, hadn't come to much. He hadn't my eye for quality and his customers were deserting him. 'I want to make peace,' I said.

'You started it,' he said, a child robbed of its sweets.

'You—' started it, I was about to say. But I took a deep breath and swallowed my words. 'We are where we are. I want you back, John. I need your flair, your imagination.'

He shrugged. But he was listening.

'Let bygones be bygones. With my contacts and your—' His what? I realised I was leaning forwards, my elbows on my knees. I leant back. 'I mean together we could—' Could what?

He was looking at me now, not through me.

'Say something,' I said.

He shrugged. 'You don't get it, do you, man? You talk about flair. Have you seen yourself in the mirror?'

'You can just abuse me.'

'I don't know why you're here. You don't even deserve your own business. Just ride on the backs of others.'

He stood, turned and walked out.

I'd been about to order lunch, but noticed the prices. It wasn't expensive, but it wasn't cheap either. I paid for my coffee and wandered back to the office.

'How much are those lunchboxes of yours?' I asked Sara, my secretary, *lunchbox* being the vernacular for the styrofoam cartons in which fried rice, noodles, or whatever are served. By the time the order arrived – at a fraction of the price I habitually paid for lunch – I was famished.

I'd been aware that the remaining employees of my business empire took their lunch in the conference room. In the military tradition, I had always maintained a proper separation – may need to send my troops off to fall on their dildos sort of thing – so had never joined them. But with four troops, the situation was absurd.

They had their ritual. Sara cleared an area on the conference table. Eric extracted sheets from yesterday's newspaper and spread them out. The lunchboxes, along with builder's tea in paper cups, were unpacked. They ate in silence – well, given Eric's technique, silence isn't the word, but the absence of chitchat.

As I juggled chunks of barbecued pork from box to mouth with chopsticks, I looked over the newspaper. It was all in Chinese. Hoping that conversation may drown out Eric's mastication, I asked 'What's this?' of a picture of a long line of people snaking around a building.

'Bank big problem,' said Eric, a gentle mist of food particles spraying from his mouth. 'No have any money.'

'Which bank?' I asked, hopeful it was one with which I had an overdraft.

'Overseas Trust Bank,' he sprayed.

Where had I heard that name?

I was shocked when I saw Germin. His skin hung in loose folds. His teeth had rotted, his hair had lost its lustre, his eyes had no shine. His clothes were crumpled and grey, his collar was frayed, there was blood on his neck where he'd cut himself shaving. He smelt of armpits, genitals and rotten vegetables.

I had no idea if he was drunk or sober and doubt he himself knew.

'We go tonight?' he asked, but hesitantly, the breezy confidence of the old Germin gone.

'It's not for another two days,' I said. 'Stay at mine. A couple are coming for dinner.'

Men who live alone can be classified any number of ways: those like Doc who chose solitude and those like me on whom it is thrust; those who withdraw by small increments from the world and those who, like me, make a conscious effort to engage. Those who can cook and those who cannot.

'You cannot serve this slop,' Germin said, having cleaned and shaved, with four hours to go before my rescuers were due.

'What do you—' I started.

He was already dashing down the stairs. He flagged a taxi and instructed the driver in—

'You speak Cantonese?'

Although showered, his odour as we approached the city was back on the rise. I wound down a window; the smell became overpowering. It came from without.

'You can't be serious?' I said.

'The food is always fresh. Not like that shit you buy from supermarkets.'

'Half of it isn't yet dead.'

He plunged into a crowded, pungent and noisy Hong Kong street market. When I'd explored them with Forsythe, it had been as voyeurs, not as buyers. Germin marched in undaunted and, as I struggled in patent leather shoes not to slip on the offal underfoot, I remembered the scroll of love poetry Forsythe had bought from the professional letter-writer. To this day, I haven't an inkling what it said.

Germin zoned in on a woman who was perhaps a quarter of his size. She had grey hair, wore loose-fitting pyjamas and sported a toothy grin.

'My grandmother,' said Germin. 'She works here since she was eight, saved every penny and invested it all in taxi licences. Worth millions. But she likes it here; it is where her friends are.'

I thought of the newsstand at the entrance to the office

next door, and the owner's son dropping her lunchbox off from a Rolls-Royce. All her years of hard graft to be rich, yet she appeared to be living in poverty – while I was living in poverty yet appeared well-off.

'What do you cook?' he broke into my thoughts.

'Hotpot.'

'Are these people important?'

'Friends.'

'They won't be after one of your hotpots.'

By seven thirty, the apartment was smelling of Germin's cooking, not him. I had to concede, he'd done me proud. In almost no time, he'd whipped up a vegetable broth; pork chops and garlic mashed potatoes with sauerkraut for the main course, topped off by a Black Forest cake he'd expropriated – at my expense – from Hong Kong's sole German restaurant.

Delicacy being first amongst Teutonic virtues, 'You rescued this asshole?' was his opening gambit when I opened the door to Henry and Diane.

Henry nodded a wary smile.

My saviours were sailing their sixty-foot ketch around the world with no fixed itinerary. They'd been on the move for five years and had travelled the entire Pacific Rim. They were now heading to the Western Hemisphere via the Indian Ocean. I find sailing a bore, but the explorer within listened with rapt attention as we ate.

'My sailing days are over,' Max said. 'Got scared of the water.'

'Where did you get the recipe?' Diane asked me.

'Max cooked it,' I confessed.

'I was the chef in my ship,' he said.

'The sailors must have been the best fed in the business.' She savoured the pork.

'They liked only potatoes and bratwürst,' he said. 'When I made this stuff, they threw it over the side.'

He was next on the menu if her eyes were anything to go by.

Henry and I sat on the balcony sipping port while – over my strident objections – Diane and Germin washed the dishes. Henry's gaze swept the bay. It was dark, but there was a smile on his face.

'Far call from Wall Street,' he said.

'Banking?' I asked.

'The creative side of the business.'

The moon rose over the hills, a clear, bright moon. With a sudden rush of desire, I recalled the huge moon in the high parts of Nepal and experienced a sudden vision of being there with Venus, she at her easel as I pottered around, the crisp white of the peaks towering above us.

'Asset stripping,' his voice broke the spell. 'I looked for companies with strong assets and weak cash flows, bought them, shut them down and sold off the assets. I was good at it, damned good. And I loved it.'

'You retired?'

'If you'd asked me ten years ago where I'd be today, I'd have told you Wall Street, where else? But one morning, I'm on my way to the office, nothing unusual, another day. I buy my paper, wait for the elevator. One comes, I'm not in it. Another comes, I'm not in that one. Two full hours and I'm not at my desk. The day comes and goes and I haven't gone up. Don't know why to this day. Burn out, I guess.

'But we had some great times,' he said, and told me about them.

My turn came. Looking at the moon over the bay, as I told him about my time with the Gurkhas, the urge strengthened: to be back amongst those mighty mountains, the deep blue sky above me, with those brave, honest people. 'Sort of fell into plastics by mischance . . .' How had I come to this? '. . . diversified . . . financial investments . . .' How had those dreams of exploration become so remote? '. . . and then there's our expansion into China which—' which what? 'Which, um—' How long before I was exchanging red packets with Chinese inspectors of factories? How many more bigots like my new client, Ralph, would I have to endure? 'I'm sure you don't want to hear about it,' I said.

He looked at me, silent, for what felt like minutes. 'You get sucked in,' he said. 'When you do, you don't know when to stop. You may think you do, but you don't.'

There was a murmur in the Night: her Daughters again.

I drifted awake the next morning. Unusual for me: I normally pop the eyes open, and am up and running.

As I lay in bed, I thought of Henry's words, of Max, of the titanic battle ahead of me to get plastics from China to South Africa and money from South Africa to Hong Kong. I thought of Venus, life, aims, of all that had landed on my plate; of how little I'd ventured.

Of the Daughters of Night.

I knew what I wanted. It was a matter of getting there. Plastics but were a means to an end.

Germin had had a bad day. Shakes, shivers, cramps.

'Are you up to it?'

'I have to be,' he said. His face was contorted by pain: inner, spiritual and deep.

I bundled him up, got him into the car and drove him through the evening traffic. Commuters rushed home, neon lights flickered on in the dusk. People queued up at bus stops in drab lines. We stopped at a traffic light.

'Look at them,' said Germin, nodding at the crowds rushing past. 'Look at their eyes. They see nothing. Like machines. How can I handle it, Stanley?'

I looked at him. It was the first time in years he'd addressed me by name.

'Like fucking machines. . . .'

He asked me not to come in with him but, as the door swung shut behind him, instinct took over.

Inside, they sat in rows, on plastic chairs. Young, old, fat, thin, all men.

Germin lurched to his feet. 'My name is Max,' he said. There was a catch in his voice. He lurched around, his head twitching, his mouth opening with no sound coming out. His eyes landed on mine; the sight seemed to calm him. He blinked, took a deep breath. He pursed his lips, bit his bottom lip. His gaze went to the floor. 'Maximilian.' He looked up: 'I am an alcoholic.'

Chapter 13

'MR PRICE,' SAID ERIC. 'I sorry John and you cannot solve this problem.'

'I'm not.' I assumed Eric was still in touch with John: how far could I trust him? Time to find out. 'Sit down. How long have you been here? Pretty much from day one. Your Uncle George is very proud of you.' I was rambling. 'There are going to be some changes around here and I thought you should know.'

Somewhere over the third bottle of claret with George, he'd come up with a gem. My company was something called a limited liability company and it was my company rather than I that owed the money. Specifically, it was the company rather than I that signed the lease for my office. Thus, it was my company and not me that was being sued. I stood to lose the company, but 'How much is it worth?' George had asked. The order books were all but empty, it was three months behind on the rent and the furniture was worth maybe a few thousand: it was worth, in short, nothing.

'Your Uncle George has suggested that I shut this company down and make a clean start. Now,' I held up my hand like a traffic policeman, 'I want you to understand that this is paperwork. It'll clear out the dead wood and let us move onwards—' I was rambling again.

'What about landlord?'

'We'll find a new office. Smaller. I hope you and Sara will stay with me.'

'You don't pay landlord?'

'He'll have to take his chances with the liquidator – along with everyone else.'

Eric smiled: 'This clever thinking,' he said.

Dear Stanley,

Really, so busy! I must prepare for my final project and there is so much to do. Thank you for your letter. I'm sorry business is quiet, but I'm sure it will get better soon. I am happy that Eric comes with you to your new business. How is he? I think he must be very busy with your work. The reason is because he never writes.

I hope you won't be angry, will still be my friend. I went to the CND march. You said in your letter that nuclear missiles keep the world safe, but I cannot agree. I wish you would see it. Really. War is very wrong, and nuclear is very dirty, very dangerous. Do you know in the last two years there are red alerts two times already? The waste from nuclear power stations can never be disposed. I'm sorry, I know you don't like it, but I really must tell you. And the people on the march were friendly, not drug dealers and hippies like you said, although it was very cold and raining all day. But I think it is important.

Tomas and me have become good friends. He is very interested in Chinese culture and is always asking me about porcelain which makes me very embarrassed because really I know so little. He knows all the techniques and how the glazes are made and fire at different temperatures. I don't know why he studies sculpture because he knows so much about this. It makes me feel so sad. Maybe I know too little about Chinese culture, should try to learn, so I think to myself maybe in my art I should try to use Chinese techniques. But here, nobody knows to teach me. Just say to use watercolour. But it is different.

Tomorrow Tomas wants me to go to a Communist Party meeting. I already told him I am not interested, but he wants very much so maybe I go anyway. He is very handsome and when I with him, others don't disturb me. I hope you won't be jealous,

Best Wishes,

When a woman says not to be jealous, she means exactly the opposite – which put a smile on my face. And when she hopes I'll still be her friend. . . .

But Tomas, a pinko as well as a rival. I shouldn't have been surprised: communism and CND exploit the same naïve utopian yearnings. But my little stunt with the dildo had back-fired. Far from detaching this limpet from Venus, it had detached Tomas's girlfriend from him, and sling-shotted him back to my Venus.

It was a call to arms. Daddy Venus, though he hadn't fled communism as such, had settled here to avoid it. Perhaps a reminder was in order.

I hit Hollywood Road – where Lily's shop once was. Pushing aside the memories, I wandered down what was now a long, winding street, where most shops were in the same line. It took some time but, amongst Ming-dynasty vases made three weeks ago and Tang-dynasty scrolls painted in the back room, I found what I sought.

I had been the recipient of a well-disguised blessing. Although General G. had cleaned me out, he had instructed me in the delicate art of introductions: 'Hello, I'm Stanley and I make dildos,' was no longer a problem.

'Don't know what you mean about tho-ose,' said an Australian I'd met in a hotel bar, making two syllables of one word as they will, 'but do you do brooms?'

A limited market for strap-ons down under, it seemed, but if brooms it had to be, brooms it would be. Customer number two was on board.

Germin would have made a wonderful wife. My apartment, where he was staying while he sorted himself out, had lost its aura of dignified decay. Since the beginning of my troubles I hadn't had the money to employ help and, although far from being a slob, my attempts with bucket and broom lacked a certain panache.

'And you complain about the backpackers?' he said.

No longer was there the accumulated dust in the corners, the Petri dish in the fridge. And boy, could he cook. No mean talent myself – my stew surprise was spoken of from Sheung Wan to, ahem, Stanley Fort – I was shamed by the variety and quality Germin produced. It was like returning to a five-star hotel every evening, but without the expense.

Another thing I came to appreciate was that he kept me sober. With him recovering from alcoholism, I kept the house dry. He didn't ask me to; to the contrary: 'It is a disease. Not everyone suffers. You drink, sometimes you get drunk, but after the hangover you get on with life. It is different for me. If I cannot trust myself in your house, how can I trust myself outside?'

Yet I resented his self-control. I resented the limits a teetotal house put on my movements.

Then, one night as we sat on the balcony sipping tea and looking out over the bay, he said: 'I'm going to write a book.'

I surmised Eric's mother ironed him whole.

'Broom is no problem,' he told me. 'Handles not so easy.'

'Don't they have wood in China?'

'Better price from Indonesia.'

That was new.

'I have good connection with Indonesia,' he continued. 'My fiancée's father from Java. I think he can do handles very cheap.'

'That's right,' I said. And with studied nonchalance: 'Venus, wasn't it? Yes, I remembered she mentioned her father came from those parts.'

'So okay?'

'Yes, quite.'

The persistence of a vacuum indicated he wasn't yet ready to leave.

'Anything else?'

'I found these,' he said. He handed over some pamphlets for trade shows in places that were then still exotic: Singapore, Thailand, Malaysia. 'Maybe you should go.'

'Maybe we should.'

George's legal manoeuvres meant that I'd be thrown out of my Repulse Bay apartment.

'I need somewhere smaller, Germin.'

'I understand.'

'Nearer the new office. Cheap.'

He nodded.

'You see, this place is much larger than I need and it's a long way to the office in the morning, especially now that I've sold the car, and it's the most terrible nuisance getting to Kowloon and so much easier if I could just walk to the office. I can't think of a good reason to hang on even if I could afford to.'

Apart, that is, from Venus dropping by for a swim. It

broke my heart, but there was aught I could do.

'I'll find somewhere,' he said.

'I mean if I had the cash I'd look— You've found a place?'

'No. But to write, I need solitude.'

I purchased, by raiding petty cash in the office, a new shirt. First impressions and all that.

Venus's father insisted on booking and paying for the meal. All I had to do was show up and be fed. He'd chosen an Indonesian restaurant in Causeway Bay and had arranged for the table to be partitioned off from the other diners by screens. The eatery was a spit and sawdust place, but I'd long since learnt not to be fooled by appearances. The food, not the decor, was what mattered in this part of the world.

'My Western friends call me Bob,' he introduced himself. 'Eric and Venus have told me so much about you.'

He was pudgy, his skin was covered in freckles and his thinning hair was too black for a man his age. He had a round face, unlike Venus's. When he spoke, it was quickly, the words distinct like bullets from a gun, the r's cracked off, neither rolled like a Scot's nor softened like an Englishman's.

He started with family. His was enormous and, as to mine: 'A man of your age should be married. With children. Who will take care of you?' He remembered our Gurkhas in Indonesia, the riots in Hong Kong, and we worked out that we'd arrived within months of each other. We glanced off politics which, as the talks dragged on between Britain and China about returning Hong Kong to Chinese sovereignty – and condemning its people to communism – had people so absorbed in the newspapers that they bounced off each other as they walked down the streets. We talked of business, swapped anecdotes and, as the coffee turned up, landed on broom handles.

'A little whisky?' he asked.

He kept a bottle at the restaurant – Glen McTodger or something – but it was no gutrot.

'I'll pass on the ice,' I said. 'Ruins the flavour.'

'All these years I've been drinking with ice and none of my Western friends told me,' he tut-tutted. 'And you, Eric?'

'Coca Cola.'

'No, you must have a glass with us.'

'I mean with Coca Cola.'

I shuddered but Bob rattled off the commands and he was obeyed. Eric drowned his whisky in coke, drank the abomination and went red in the face.

Eric and I stood outside, watching the rear lights of Bob's car disappear. Eric swayed, a bamboo pole in the breeze, his face lit up like a traffic light.

'Yak for the doe?' I asked, this being the Hong Kong equivalent of one for the road ('doe' being the Cantonese for a road and 'yak' sounding a bit like their word for 'one').

'Already late.'

'Tell your mother it was my fault.'

He looked at me. His brow creased. 'Mum and dad live in Boston.'

I was on the verge of asking him if he would drop by to iron my shirts as his technique was clearly superior, but decided against it. He may acquiesce.

We found a pub. I sipped beer; Eric, whisky and Coke.

'I got an idea,' he said.

On the opposite side of the bar was a tall blonde with juicy red lips and cleavage like Emma's.

'The stuff we make is too complicated,' Eric told me. 'Brooms. Toilet brushes. Toys. Make more money on cheap things. Plastic bags. Styrofoam cartons. Easy to make, big margin.'

In spite of the blonde, I found myself tuning in. It was as though he'd been rehearsing this for a long time and, although I first had to suppress the urge to tell him why he was wrong, I started to wonder if perhaps he was right. 'To whom do we sell?'

'Europe and America no good,' he said. 'Competition too much. But these ten years Malaysia, Thailand, so called develop countries will be big success. Bob says Indonesia come up very fast. Now poor but after ten years rich.'

'And you have the connections?'

He didn't, but he'd thought about how to get them – hence the pamphlets for trade shows that he'd dumped on my desk.

Something changed that night. No longer was I sitting next to Brahma's unfinished piece of the cosmos. The ideas spouting out of Eric created an enthusiasm that was almost infectious. It wasn't just the ideas; it was that they cohered into something bigger: a strategy. The drinks went almost untouched. Eric saw business – any business – as something to create, not something to fill the time before I went off exploring.

Almost infectious.

When they tossed us out into the crisp dawn, I asked him: 'Why haven't you raised this before?'

He shrugged: 'You never asked.'

After he'd gone, I found a whore. It had been a while.

One could swing perhaps a small kitten, but by no means a tomcat in the new office. It was partitioned into four cubicles, with a common area at the door. I needed to purchase a new desk as my room was too small for the old one. Besides which, George had told me to make a clean break.

My external window overlooked Nathan Road, the main thoroughfare of Kowloon – rents were cheaper than on Hong Kong island where the old office had been, besides which, the area was crawling with buyers from all over the world.

The lady from the newsstand downstairs at the old office had been a comforting presence – and her discreet supply of hard porn had kept me abreast of the market. When she got wind I was doing a bunk, she had her son ferry me and my box of personal possessions from the old office to the new in back of her Roller. The besuited man in the front seat, it transpired, was a uniformed chauffeur; the man in the back in a T-shirt and shorts who I took for a coolie to help me carry my stuff turned out to be a brain surgeon (a real one – only in Hong Kong), her son, an affable fellow who knew his mum would rather die at her post than retire.

I'd been in the new place three days when I received my first call from my landlord's lawyer. 'Stanley—' he purred, oozing saccharine friendship '—the hearing is imminent and we are offering you the chance to settle your debts honourably.'

'What debt?' I asked.

A loud silence came down the line.

'If you mean the money due from my former employer, I'm afraid you'll have to join the queue. I resigned as director some time ago. I'd be delighted to help where I can, but I washed my hands of the matter. . . .'

The sound of apoplectic breathing came down the line.

'Do let me know,' I said and hung up.

With a grin on my face.

The brooms were despatched; the money from South Africa came through. It would take my landlord in Repulse Bay another six months to evict me, so I used the money to settle my bill at the club, with enough left over to for a small commission for Eric. Not much of a transaction, but I was solvent again.

Chapter 14

Dear Stanley,

I know you said not to write because I should concentrate on my final project but I am so tired and anyway, I miss you.

It is all studying, very busy, in the last ten weeks, so I have not done very much to write about. I got a letter from Mary, she is so happy with Gabriel, I feel jealous sometimes. I wonder why Eric never writes.

I have been out with Tomas a few times. He knows I am coming home soon and says he will come out to visit me when he has saved enough money, but he never has any and his family is very poor, so I think he is pretending. Maybe when I sell my first painting I can bring him out as a present. I know he is very interested in China and he also wants to learn about Mao. Did I tell you I went with him to the Communist Party meeting? They are very kind people, but I think they believe things too easily.

I must get on with my revision. See you in July,

Venus

She missed me – I sat for sweet minutes with a smile on my face. Though no mention of my gift, dammit.

I looked out over the bay. Tanning bodies lay sprawled

upon the sand. They were nearly all Westerners as the Chinese associate tans with being a peasant, thus poor, and who would want to be poor and even worse, advertise it? I wondered if Venus had thought of that after her shock at the flesh on display in Hyde Park.

The time was drawing close when she would return: would she sprawl with them? Would her innocence still be intact? Would this empty flat echo to the sound of her laughter?

Would she marry Eric?

Me?

Eric deposited a tome in front of me, a trade directory for Thailand. Names littered the pages, Scratchipopcorn, Pratsaregoodphun, that sort of thing. Where did one start?

I picked up my pen:

> *Dear Mr ——,*
> *We are a Hong Kong company specialising in the provision of high-quality, inexpensive, plastic manufactured products. . . .*

'Sara,' I commanded. I gave her the letter and trade directory. 'Send this to everyone I've marked.'

Eric and I took the train to China.

'Do you need me?' I'd asked.

'Very important. You give them big face.'

'All I did last time was drink.'

That ceremonial function, it seemed, was vital.

Fields rolled by the train window. Lush green blanketed the earth, crops ripened in a profusion of fertility. No wonder they called it the Middle Kingdom: 'Look at the character,' Uncle Yan had once told me, and drawn it, a vertical line intersecting a horizontal oblong. 'Half-way between heaven and earth.'

Yet that bucolic idyll was deceptive: the wide, empty streets, the bicycles and empty-eyed people, the awful drabness. I hear it's changed for the better; I hope so.

'Venus will be back soon,' the words tumbled out of my mouth.

Eric looked at me, his brow wrinkled.

I hadn't intended to speak of her, but: 'She writes to me. I correct her English and return the letters. She's improved so much that it's hardly necessary.'

'Thank you.'

'How did you meet her?'

He looked at me.

A direct question is impolite in Chinese, especially an intimate one. 'Sorry,' I said.

'Do you think she still likes me?' He was looking intently out of the window. I couldn't see his expression, but the stress in his voice relayed the pain. 'When she left to England she was so young. I am older than her.'

'Age doesn't count for a lot in these things.' I spoke more in desperation than hope, as I was yet older than him.

'She was nine when I met her. One week before I had a dream. When I met her, I couldn't believe it—' And, in a rush, it all spilt out: how he'd waited for her coming of age, had taken her to school in the morning and collected her in the afternoons, how he'd endured four awful years – in those days of expensive and difficult communications – at school and MIT, fearing without being able to find out if her heart had been stolen. How he had watched her blossom from child to young lady.

'Will you marry her?' I asked.

'My family don't like. My father says Bob is only a trader and not even one hundred per cent Chinese.'

'It matters? In this day and age?'

'Can you help me?'

Intercede? I'd be only too pleased.

'I know you are a good friend with my Uncle George.'

Which pulled me up short. It was George who'd introduced me to Eric – the same George who'd defended my living in sin with Jo, the same George who'd answered the phone when I was down and flat broke, who'd charted a course out of my debts. George, the most thoroughly decent person I knew, who kept up with everyone because everyone wanted to keep up with him. And here was I, scheming to backstab his nephew.

His nephew, the biggest fluke of them all, was in front of me now. His face was drawn in distress and hope, imploring my help. And this was no longer the sucking-himself-out-of-existence Eric. There was the 'fuck' that escaped his lips when I had once disturbed him, the red-faced boozer waving a cigarette in the air, the man in the pub, full of ideas. He was now the best in the business; the variable-speed control on the vibrators and many other minor innovations were his; he'd turned down better offers when times were good, including I suspected, from John, and now that times were bad, he was still by my side.

He was also the man who'd been with Venus for over a decade, and yet had let her take her own time. Maybe that was his mistake. But there was also her subtle pull away from his arm round her waist when we visited Repulse Bay to look for my flat, the way she always stood slightly apart from him.

Perhaps she didn't like intimacy in public.

To the extent I'd thought about it at all, I'd thought of leaving Venus to him as a kind of abandonment, that she'd be sucked into that Eric-shaped void in the cosmos. But, without me noticing, that void had been filled by a man.

Intercede? No. I would not. I'd leave Venus to make up her own mind.

Believe that, reader, and I have a bridge to sell you.

I went to Thailand before Venus returned. One of my exploratory letters had borne fruit and I hadn't been there since the Jo days.

It was the month before the monsoon and the country baked. On the streets during the day, people dashed from one island of shadow to another to avoid the unrelenting blast of the sun; in temples and *wats*, saffron-robed monks chanted mantras in front of gold Buddha statues that themselves seemed to sweat. In the few oases of air-conditioning, shoppers shivered in air so over-conditioned that the spicy-hot food was cold on arrival.

My contact was a colonel. He had spent a couple of years on the border with what was then Kampuchea, dealing as best he could with the tide of refugees escaping Pol Pot's genocide, just as I had held back those escaping Mao's madness.

It turned out his interest was to sell, not to buy; we parted friends. Fuelled by beer and bonhomie, I went to a restaurant, ordered a curry and a bottle of the local Mekhong whisky. It did the job. Three hours later I was on a dance floor on which twenty women shared as attire forty stiletto heels, perhaps three ankle chains, and not a stitch else. I took half-a-dozen, assorted shapes and sizes, back to my hotel. A world-weary and wry-smiling man at the embassy took four days to replace the passport they stole. The money was never recovered.

Back at the club:

'Maximilian is writing a fucking book?' said the man with the highball.

Our subject up to that point had been cricket – this was the era of Ian Botham and Geoffrey Boycott and the English side was almost invincible. I had done nothing more than slip in a jocular aside.

'He moved to his own place to concentrate on it,' I elaborated.

'About us?' The bar had gone silent.

'About himself, I think. His problem—'

'But what if we're in it? My wife—'

The thought hadn't occurred to me. Now it hit me with the force of a googly.

A council of war was convened. I was appointed ambassador.

Sara smiled at me. She was a nice lady, but in need of orthodontal work.

The letter she handed me was from my friend the Thai colonel. Goodness only knows what I'd told him: he was after a quote for what seemed to be enough ordnance to equip a small army. Then I remembered he'd mentioned something about rebels in Burma.

I'd never taken much interest in weaponry. Yes, I could strip a gun and reassemble it, and hit a man-sized target from a credible distance, but I was no sharpshooter. But the list of things he was after was well beyond my range. Black Stars. Kalishnikovs.

'Eric!'

But Eric couldn't help. We needed someone in the Chinese army, and Eric's family were native Hongkongers living in Boston.

'Doesn't Bob have family in China?' I asked.

Ellen hit. She wasn't just a typhoon; she was the mother of typhoons. At two in the morning I was still awake. Gusts slammed into the windows, hurling rain with the impact of pebbles. Trees on the hillside danced in the fury, branches whipped in the air.

So I went for a walk.

In the dark, battered by squalls, I groped my way to the beach. The wind howled over the crashing breakers. I heard but could barely see, the sea. Rain hit me like pins. For the protection my coat gave me, I may as well have been naked.

I remembered a night in Nepal in a hut on a mountainside, more a shed than a hut. We'd been eating dal and rice by the light of a wan paraffin lamp. Typhoons, like East Asians, drop by with polite notice; storms in the Himalaya just hit.

One of my men had been out collecting firewood. We stepped out into a blistering maelstrom of hurled ice and darkness. Keeping voice contact was impossible above the screech of the wind. Roped together, we stumbled forwards. Within ten minutes my feet and fingers were numb. We were no closer to finding him and the men were in danger. I flashed the torch on and off twice to abort the search.

No one responded. I flashed again; they didn't see. In the end, we didn't find him, but he us.

'Didn't you see my signal?' I asked, once back in the hut.

They wouldn't lie. So they remained silent, eating their dal.

All of a sudden, there on the beach, Ellen seemed trivial. A drop of rain and a bit of wind, nothing more. I shook my head, smiled and set off back home.

Apostasise the Daughters of Night at one's peril. Half way home, they revenged my disdain. A sudden gust brought down a tree. I jumped, but not fast enough. The bone in my shin shattered so quickly I didn't realise until I tried to stand up.

It was as I lay in hospital for the next two days that it occurred to me how few friends I had left.

Germin came.

'How's the book?' I asked.

He held his thumb and index finger a certain distance apart.

'When will you finish it?'

'It will be some time. There is so much to write.'

His enthusiasm made me wonder if, after all of these years of dicey businesses, of trying to make it big when business bored him to the core, he'd finally found his vocation. Yet I had to give him fair warning: 'They don't like it, you know, at the club. They're all frightened you'll drop them in it. Puncture their respectability.'

He looked at the ground, nodded and pursed his lips. 'I should have known.'

George came. 'They should be looking at your head, not your leg,' he said. 'Going out in the middle of a typhoon. Have you seen the papers? They're still cleaning up.'

I perused the scenes of chaos in the newspaper he'd brought: a narrow, steep street in the old part of Hong Kong with a pile of cars washed down, higgledy-piggledy on top each other at the bottom; a freighter washed ashore, listing to one side, a mounting death toll.

'Jo sends her regards.'

I sent mine.

Eric brought flowers. Sara brought cheques to be signed.

Then I was out and it was time to meet Bob. We talked about a lot of stuff that was neither here nor there before we got to the nub of the matter. When I told him what I was after, he took a long sip of whisky (no ice) and said,

'What you ask is something I think I can arrange. I have a cousin who is senior in the People's Liberation Army in China.'

He sipped again.

'But it is something I would be very hesitant about becoming involved in. Gun-running. It's not a question of morality, though my daughter would have my head on a plate if she found out. No, it's a question of becoming involved in a business I know nothing about. I sell timber. You look at a piece of wood and you see what? Colour? Maybe grain? Hardness, perhaps? I see value. I see the type of tree, its probable origin, the price per tonne for raw timber, the price for the finished product. I see shipping charges and whether it will be cheaper to ship by weight or by volume. All this I see. But, if I look at a gun, I know which end the bullet comes out of, that is all.'

It was a moment of epiphany – belated, I grant you. The only business of mine that had survived was the one I knew something about. Albeit learnt on the job, I could spot a dud dildo quicker than a whore says 'erectile dysfunction'. As to the backpacker's travel, General G's leveraged thingamajigs and what-not, I hadn't a clue.

'My daughter telephoned last night,' he interrupted my rapture. 'She asked me to tell you her arrival time. We shall be going to the airport to greet her, of course. If you are available, please come along. I realise it must be difficult for you to walk—'

'I'll be there.'

'You care for her?'

He could be very direct.

'I must ask for your help,' he said, 'with Eric.'

He refreshed our whiskies and sipped.

'People of my generation, Stanley, have different expectations from people of hers. When I married her mother, we both knew this. I was to provide a home and she was to keep it. There was no talk of love. My parents gave me a choice of brides and I chose her. She has been a good mother to my children, she has kept the house well and I have been fortunate – but I am sure it is she who has brought that good fortune. This is the way things are.

'But this business of love. . . .' He sipped his whisky. 'Love is such a rare thing in this world, Stanley.'

He sipped again as I ground my teeth with effort not to blurt something out.

'In Chinese we call our daughters *chin gum*, a thousand gold. You Westerners think we treat them like chattel, buying and selling them for marriage. But in the traditional sense, when they are married, they become part of the groom's family; we never see them again. If the bride is unhappy, her family can claim back the dowry. A form of insurance, if you like.'

He sipped.

'This Eric. I do not know if he can provide for my daughter. It is all very well talking of love, but even I do not know what love is. I, a sixty-year-old man. Do you?'

That was rhetorical, thank goodness.

'So I want you to talk her out of it. She will not listen to me.'

A gurgling noise came from somewhere. Me.

'She needs someone older. Reliable.' He looked me in the eye. 'Someone who can take care of her when I am gone.'

I didn't need a car that night. I floated home on air.

The very next morning, I'd got around to unpacking boxes from the old office, when I happened upon a dust-covered bundle of papers. Share certificates. In the Overseas Trust Bank.

My shoulders slumped. The newspaper story on the day when I'd first joined Eric and Sara for lunchboxes came to mind: the run on OTB.

'Eric!'

But Eric was already hovering. 'You very lucky,' he said. The unkind thought that he was being sarcastic flickered across my mind. But he could barely do sentences, let alone sarcasm: 'Government rescue.'

'You mean. . . .'

But I was already dashing out of the door, to find a stockbroker.

'Who on earth are these people?' I asked Eric.

'For toilet brush.'

'I thought they were being made by the People's Number Four Toilet Brush Factory, not this Wang Kah Trading?'

He gave me a look of the type that I suppose rocket scientists reserve for students of – well, for Wangkahs such as me – and explained. The chief brush-maker of the People's Number Four had a monthly salary the equivalent of a half-decent meal at the club – about thirty renminbi or, say, a couple of pounds sterling. A man of vision and acumen, he considered this generous remuneration beneath him. Eric had thereby come to an arrangement whereby Wang Kah Trading Co. Ltd accepted our order, skimmed off some money for the chief brush-maker, and passed the rest on to the People's Number Four.

'How on earth does the factory turn a profit?'

'Doesn't matter. China government pay all loses.'

'Splendid,' I replied. But I groaned inwardly. Barely off the starting blocks in China and it was already back to the bribes.

Eric must have read my mind: 'No problem,' he said. The brush-maker's commission was a legitimate business expense, and Wang Kah would make money.

My broker had already sold those ancient shares in the bank. 'When's the payment from Australia due?'

'Day after tomorrow.'

Venus, the money. In only another two days, both would be in my hands.

A cheerful taxi driver delivered me to the airport. As we zoomed through the tunnel under the harbour, I recalled the days when the only ways across were the ferry and, during the wee hours when the ferries didn't run, *sampans*. Germin, in one of his more exotic binges, had turned one such crossing into an orgy. The precise details varied with each retelling, but always contained a pair of tourists who had been less than enthusiastic spectators.

'Prudes,' he said. 'It was only a blow job.'

Now, I was driven through the Cross-Harbour Tunnel in air-conditioned comfort to the improbable airport of Kai Tak. There's a famous photo of one of Kowloon's canyon-like streets with a plane caught in mid-flight between the buildings lining those streets, the final approach so low it was as if the plane was suspended between the very rooftops: the sharp turn before landing that saw most arriving passengers terrified – which better prepared them for what was to follow.

I was thinking about anything but the business to hand. I, like those passengers, was terrified. Two years had passed. I had changed: had she?

The Arrivals section had a double-glass door and a ramp, tiles of white linoleum and slightly greying paint. We stood there, Bob, I and her family, making small talk as we eyed the steady procession of passengers. The business-class drunks lurched off to the taxi rank outside the door, others were greeted with smiles and hugs, a few with haversacks scurried through, I assumed for Sonny's hostel or the like.

We all spotted her at the same time – as did a few other onlookers. She stood for just a moment, at the top of the ramp, scanning the faces. Her hips and breasts had filled out; she was no longer skinny but slender. A woman's figure. Her face was unlined but her expression – quizzical, expectant – was ever so slightly more guarded.

Her eyes landed on mine and widened in surprise; a smile exploded, a frank, unconcealed joy. Those other spectators followed her, lust written large over their faces as she bounced down the ramp. She arrived, greeted her parents in Chinese – no hugs or embraces, just a nod and how are you – and turned to me.

'Stanley.'

Her voice was deeper, more resonant. She offered her hand to take. As I felt its warmth on my palm and heard myself squawk a reply, her eyes went over and beyond my shoulder.

They returned to mine. A fleeting shadow of disappointment crossed her face. The smile returned.

'Thank you for coming,' she said.

I left her with her family and returned to the office.

'Why weren't you there?' I asked Eric.

'Traffic jam.' But the roads had been clear and we both knew he was lying. 'Did she ask for me?'

'No,' I said. I alone knew I was lying.

'Where's Eric?' I asked Venus.

She stood at the door of my flat, dressed in a T-shirt and miniskirt. She was wearing the Red Guard's cap I had searched Hollywood Road for: it had arrived in London, but the subtext – that communism was not to be trusted –

didn't seem to have registered.

Her eyes locked on mine: 'I thought you would invite him.'

'I thought you would.'

The direction of her gaze flicked from one eye of mine to the other, almost as if probing for a sign of complicity. The faintest shadow of a smile caught her lips.

'Come on in,' I said. 'There'll be more food for us.'

Her smile broadened; my stomach churned.

'What can I get you to drink?' As I uttered the banality, it came to me that I had little idea what her tastes were. In one of her letters, she'd mentioned not liking beer, but she hadn't said anything more on the subject. I could hardly credit that she'd be guzzling vodka by the bottle, but wine, soda water, cocktails?

'Hot water,' she said. Her accent was no longer Hong Kong but a mixture of cockney and stockbroker. 'The English found it so funny. Really. They drink water out of the tap, or tea, but not hot water.'

'I think I can arrange for some,' I said and, the plaster cast gone but still limping, made for the kitchen.

She followed, close behind me. I bumbled around with the kettle and tap. 'Water shortage in my early days here,' I said. Damn. The old codger in me had taken hold of my mouth.

'My father told.'

'Told me,' I corrected her. Damn it again. I was no longer her tutor.

She led the way back to the living room and scanned the available items of furniture. In a flash it struck me how similar my flat was to Doc's. Not the specific decoration, but the functional feel of the place. The settee and coffee table, but no framed photographs on display; the dining-room table with no condiments, a couple of Jo's dancing

Shivas that had moved with me to this flat, but no paintings on the walls or potted plants on the balcony.

A slight smile, as if at some inner joke, graced her lips. She went to the balcony window and stood in silhouette before it as she fiddled with the handle. Her shoulders were sloped, her upper torso slimmed at her waist and broadened again. Her hair reached most of the way to her hips. I went over and showed her how the locking mechanism worked. I elbowed her in the stomach by mistake – a gentle nudge. She looked at me, smiled, and elbowed me back.

She slid the door open and a distant rumble of traffic entered, along with a slight waft of heat. She entered the balcony and leant over the rail.

My lower lip, I realised, was in pain from my teeth biting down on it. Venus was not, a mental scream pierced my head, like those others I'd seduced in that very spot.

She turned, crossed her arms under her bosom, and said: 'I should have brought my swimming costume.'

'Not much swimming in London,' I stuttered.

I brought my own glass of water to the balcony, took a seat, and gestured to her.

'I don't know how to swim,' she replied as she sat. 'Perhaps you can teach me.'

I remembered my own near drowning in the bay: 'I don't think I should,' I said. That story emerged and the conversation blossomed. We each knew the broad outline of those past two years, but she hadn't had the writing skills to convey her amazement on her arrival in London, the sense of history and power that had engulfed her, the energy of the city as it buzzed with the boom of those early eighties.

'Mary preferred classical music and took me to the Proms,' she said. 'I find it so funny. I thought classical music was boring, but everyone clapped along. When they sing *Rule Britannia,* everyone was so proud.'

And, at some point, with a grimace: '. . . makes me to try hashish, but it makes me cough very much and I feel sick so I don't like.'

With a frown of confusion: '. . . bad toy coming from Hong Kong but don't know who sent it.'

I stared hard into the bay, glad the dusk obscured my features.

We returned to the sitting room and the empty table, set for two. I'd agonised over the setting – me at the head and her at the other end? opposite sides? – and settled for me at the head and her to my left. Max had given me a recipe that 'even you won't fuck up' and I wheeled out beef stroganoff. 'Sorry, I don't know any Chinese dishes.'

'I had plenty in Soho,' she said.

I pushed the memory of those Covent Garden days and Sharon to one side.

She misread my expression, reached out and touched my forearm as she had so many times in my office. An innocent gesture that had set me on fire. Her touch lingered as she said: 'My father said times have been difficult.'

And so I recounted the two disastrous years that had just passed. I'd concealed them in my letters, but to watch her as the minutes flew by and the shadows lengthened; to see her react, to see again how her nose crinkled when she laughed and how she tossed her hair, that lustrous hair; to feel her presence, made me realise that I could confide in her without fear. And the repeated touch of her fingers on my forearm as she made a point, sometimes lingering, more of a stroke than a touch. In our classes, I had never reciprocated. This time, I did; she looked at me and smiled.

Then Eric turned up. Only in the conversation, to be sure – but of all people, I was the one who inserted him into it. I'd been talking of our first trip to China and '. . . Eric was splendid,' slipped out.

Her eyes changed. 'He never told me about it.'

'Probably thought it mundane. Maybe he—'

'He never tells me anything, Stanley—'

She took my forearm with both of her hands. When news had come through of her acceptance at the Royal Academy, her touch had been light, a child full of glee. This time, it was the touch of an adult clinging to a life raft.

'—what's happened to him? He wrote less and less in the last year. I've been away two years and he didn't even come to the airport.'

I could scarcely believe her words my ears. The blade was honed; Eric stood without so much as a sliver of armour.

'People change,' I said, oozing compassion. I kept the gloat off my features: 'Feelings change.'

'Oh Stanley—' She collapsed into my arms, her body racked by sobs.

Her whole warm body.

I couldn't help it. What started out as an comforting nuzzle became, as she looked up, a long stare into each other's eyes. There was a moment's hesitation, an unspoken negotiation. Our lips touched. Her arms tightened around my neck; her tongue flicked around the edges of my lips, sweet, tickling.

My tongue responded. Then we were clenched, our lips locked on each other's, tongues no longer flicking but probing deep inside each other's mouths. My hand was on her cheek, smooth and warm beneath my touch, her breasts pushed into my chest. I didn't want to go further; I had planned to wait, to bide my time. But I wanted her with every ounce of my being. My hand slipped down.

She broke. Ran to the toilet.

I sat, panting. Too far, too quick. I shook my head. Looked at my feet. What was I to say; how was I to apologise, to set things right?

   'Stanley?'

   She'd come out of the bathroom.

   Naked.

   Save for the cap.

Chapter 15

ND, THIRTY YEARS LATER, I sit at the bar, waiting for them. Had she ever told Eric what happened that night? Would it matter? Would he care?

The two women on high stools pay up and leave, the young professionals are at the stage of backgammon where the beer has befuddled the bets, and Eric and Venus are late. What could I hope to achieve, after that night so long ago?

They are successful now, she in her art and he in his business. He made much of Price's Plastics. The profits pay for her studio, materials and all the rest. But, more important, he holds back the world, creates a space in which she herself can create.

I pay up and leave.

What she gave me that night, I could never repay.

She walked towards me, step by hesitant step, her breasts rising and falling in short breaths.

All those times when she and I had been alone in my office and I had held back, failing to return her gestures, failing to reciprocate her smiles, came back to me. Being a gentleman hadn't come easy. And now I was paralysed. Stunned, muted, I averted my gaze to her face.

She looked at me. Her brow wrinkled. Doubt flickered

in her eyes.

An invisible hand pulled me to my feet.

'Where you been?' Eric had shouted. 'Three days we need your signature. Money coming already. Must pay Wang Kah. Why not you answer phone?'

'I don't know where I've been,' I said. Had I walked through the streets of this great city engrossed in confusion? Had I sat at home in disarray? Had I thought or just acted? Was it drink? Sobriety? I don't know to this day.

'Eric, I need you to sign some documents.'

'What you talking?'

'Sit down and calm down. I need. . . .' I started, but my voice trailed off as he scanned the documents Legal George had prepared. 'The company's yours, Eric, lock, stock and barrel. If you don't want it, it's no one's.'

'I need you.'

I shook my head: 'You never did.'

Her body, perfect, covered with a fine skein of sweat, the swelling of her aureole, the fine down of hair, were everything I'd ever imagined. A smile broke across my face as I drank her in.

There was an almost imperceptible slump of her shoulders: relief that I was not disappointed? How could I be?

As she covered the next few paces, the lines on her brow, the crinkle at the bridge of her nose, the droop at the corners of her eyes, were replaced with a radiant smile.

A radiant, innocent smile.

She came to a halt before me. I stooped to embrace her and, when she looked up, there was a gentle stroke of her hand in my palm as her breath tickled my ear.

Germin's autobiography – much atrophied by threats of libel – was published about a year later and well-received. He recounted his own ups and downs, his highs and lows, the long nights he remembered and days he forgot, the girls and the boys – yes, he'd experimented – and, by writing it down, had made sense of it all.

In the bar, waiting for Venus and Eric thirty years on, the trajectory of my life in this city had passed before me: the girls, the conmen, the friends; those honoured and those betrayed. I'd had a ripping good laugh at the time, but beneath the laughter there had also been the boredom and pain, the long empty nights and the times when the Fates played me ill. The first red packet from Uncle Yan was innocent, but I'd taken the second in the full knowledge that it was a bribe; the way in which sex had gone from joy to distraction to compulsion. As Max had once said, the excuses were plentiful; the reason was that I liked it. Irrespective of the damage it did.

I thought of Max's book that night, as I waited for Venus and Eric, and decided to write this one of my own. To make sense of it all.

The scent of her hair filled my nose, the aroma of her musk lay thick around. When she guided my hand upwards to her breast, her nipple hard under my palm, I almost wept.

I never did see Uncle Yan again, though I made it a habit to send a card and some cash every year to my son, care of him.

They were a generation apart, Uncle Yan and his peers. They came from China to Hong Kong despite and because of us Brits, and turned a backwater into a powerhouse. They built buildings that scratched the stars and created business empires that covered the globe. It was a certain time and a certain place, but it was also industry, acumen and innovation; integrity, opportunism and the single-minded pursuit of their dreams.

Lily tracked me down on the Internet. 'Stanley,' she sung, over Internet phone, 'your Lily still a-misses you.'

Was it she that I wanted? A virginal, sensuous Lily? Or was it a second chance at my youth? Squandered – as Venus's could have been that night.

Her eyes looked into mine: eyes full of hope, aspiration. Alive and hungry for life.

Eyes full of pain.

The pain and confusion of love.

'Nepal, eh?' said Legal George. 'Not my cup of tea.'

I've lived here, in Pokhara, since handing over the business to Eric that morning. I take tourists trekking in the Himalaya. It won't make me rich, but I make ends meet and it's a healthy life. Gone is the beer gut that self-deception hid from my gaze. I read a lot. I enjoy my work and, when it's the monsoon and tourists don't come, I explore: I've revisited Kilimanjaro and seen sunset over the Serengeti, heard the rumble of the Victoria Falls and witnessed the lions at their kill. But I've ventured also to the icecaps of the north and the vast sweeping dunes of the equator; I've stood on the ancient rocks of Machu Picchu and traversed Siberia on the express.

The money? Those backpackers I'd ridiculed, do what I'd always wanted to do, but on a shoestring, and are none the worse for it.

And, as to those most handsome of women? Woman in the singular now. I met her on a trip. She's of my own age, background and interests, and mother of our two priceless Pricelets. And, yes, I helped her through hormonal wild swings, lay with my head on the dome of her swelling belly, and had my entire life turned upside-down in an instant with those two first smiles. And, although we don't have a word of language in common, I tracked down their step-brother, my first son: patching things up is still work in progress.

Would the Greeks call me fortunate, though I not be dead? What a load of old bunkum I'd talked myself into believing: Sod 'em. I would.

'He loves you, Venus,' I said. 'Eric doesn't wear his heart on his cuff, but he loves you.'

She looked at me, standing there perfect, naked, vul-nerable. Her irises flickered as her eyes searched mine.

'He's terrified that you've stopped loving him.'

She was mine for the taking.

'Go to him,' I said.

I draped a towel over her. And, as I rose, I felt my shoulders square and my chest thrust out, an honest man.

Author's Note

Love, like or hate this book, I'd be delighted to hear from you. If you bought it online, please leave a review with the retailer. If you are a member of Goodreads, you can review it here: *https://www.goodreads.com/book/show/58292291,* or follow the QR code below.

Acknowledgements

John Lanchester said in a book talk that his novel, *The Wall*, came to him almost for free. It fell off the pen, with almost no need for correction or revision. In much the same way, *Price's Price* rushed off the pen in an intense part of my life. My usual target for a first draft is a thousand words per day, but I was working seventy-hour weeks on projects with serious deadlines, preparing to get married, and this novel was scribbled sometimes a couple of hundred words, and sometimes a burst of a couple of thousand, between doing this, that, and the inevitable other.

The first draft was typed with almost no revision, and received early encouragement from the late Andrew J.T. Colin, the not unrelated Andrew Colin and, although Veronica Colin despised it, a reaction is better than a shrug of the shoulders. Thanks to all of you, for this and much else.

Rejected by a now-dead agent, however, the novel languished in a drawer for the better part of two decades. Part of me sensed that, although it had come out easily, it wasn't quite ready; it needed a reader who was both sympathetic and critical. Through *The Literary Consultancy*, I found Craig Leyenaar, whose perceptive insights and patience brought the novel into its current form. Thank you, Craig.

I also thank my friends Cameron Dueck and Dominic

Sargent, both of whom found Stanley repugnant, yet were kind enough to offer constructive and helpful feedback, and to Douglas Bulloch and Karl Hurst, who likewise helped me hew some rough corners off the ashlar. Thank you also to Joe and Aki at TLC, for running such a super enterprise.

About the Author

Chris Maden stumbled into Hong Kong ten years to the day before its reversion to China, and fell in love with the city. He has spent his adult life in the town, contributes to the Hong Kong Free Press and Hong Kong Review of Books, and was chair of the local writers' circle as this, his first novel, went to press. When not writing, he mentors start-ups (which is a polite way of saying that he tries to stop them making the many mistakes he made), or hikes, sails or goes on long lunches. He is happily married to a woman he loves, and who puts up with his nonsense – which is never in short supply.

You can follow Chris on *www.chrismaden.com* or:
Facebook: *www.facebook.com/chrismadenauthor*
Instagram: *chrismadenauthor*
Twitter: *@chrismadenauth1*